AND US SERIES BOOK 2

PASSIONS, HOPES & Us

by

WILLA DREW

Moving Words Publishing

One heavy strand to anchor Substance onto Time
Many round and round to infuse into everything
Woven all together to spin the Garden of Infinities
Wait now wait as the Knowledge grows and blossoms

- The Diviner, On the Orbweaver

CHAPTER I

Tight fit

The morning's grey light slips through cracks in the broken stone and spills over the pages of Hadamard's book, scattered over a slab table. Overhead, twisted roots dangle from the rock ceiling, dripping water onto the surface of a quiet pool nearby. Thin streamlets trickle down the craggy walls that shut me in. The tang of minerals saturates the heavy air. Outside, the winds howl, whipping rain against the trees.

Apart from the hilltop grove, the grotto is the next-best place to write for a lumbering beast such as I. Cramped? – yes. And close quarters for one of my bulk, with limbs bowed and bent. But I am comfortable nonetheless, tucked into this cave beyond the entrance overgrown with vines and mosses, beyond the hardy greenery that grows in patches where the light gets thin, and beyond the leaf-litter that mats the floor. Pockets of dark shadow lurk about me, but I do not fear them. Darkness I befriended long ago.

Alone in the gloom, I once strode for days with little more

than a flickering light to guide my way and a flickering hope to cling to. The reality that my friends were likely dead burdened my soul and weighed heavy on every step, and all the while I struggled with the knowledge that I might be next. Starvation or cloakers would get me, I was sure. Little did I know there were worse things to contend with in the dark reaches of Theia. Far worse, as it turned out. A short list is in order: unimaginable beasts, brutal slavers, a former king more dead than alive, and shadows that serve only evil, to name a few.

But still, not all hope was lost. Not yet. And there were far greater experiences to be had…

CHAPTER II

Retreat

Nud Lenokin jolted awake, sweating after another bad dream. He lay on the hard stone floor, cocooned in his cloak. Every muscle ached.

Dark thoughts lingered in the back of his mind; dark thoughts for dark places. The Pip rubbed the sleep from his eyes and slipped the bog stone out of his pocket. It sparked red immediately and he scanned his stony surroundings, eyeing every cleft and fissure suspiciously in the flickering light.

No face-sucking cloakers. No hags. I'm good.

Nud pushed himself to his feet, feeling drawn and thin and lacking in color or substance, like the leached blade of a fallen leaf. He cupped water from a small pool and swished the refreshment around in his mouth. The liquid wasn't quite enough to wash away the bitter taste of last night's supper, slow to fade. The smaller bits resurfaced regularly in his mouth, those hard pieces of exoskeleton that'd broken off the main bodies of his creepy-crawly meal so easily, only to get caught between his teeth. Nud launched them into the air from the tip of his tongue. *What I have to do to survive around here,* he thought.

The anticipation of getting back to the world above outweighed the hollow pang in Nud's gut. *Get moving,* he urged himself. He was more than ready to take his chances swimming to the surface. Bog queens or not, the original entry cave was the only sure way out.

Nud raised his stone in front of him and started through the rubble-laden passages, lighting the way in pale red pulses. Guided by his keen memory and without Kabor to slow him down, the next leg of the journey went by faster than anticipated. The Pip's mind was preoccupied, at first. Something about the architecture in the man-made section of tunnels kept nagging at him. They looked like ruins to him – Akedan ruins. But what really whacked Nud clean across the face was that everything would actually look better upside down.

Once that idea wormed its way into his skull, Nud saw the evidence everywhere: Archways should close in at the top, not the bottom, to better support their load. He found inverted signage and even stumbled across what appeared to be upturned stairs. And it was no wonder that the passages were littered with cave-ins if the ceiling was meant to be the floor. How the place got that way, he could only begin to imagine.

Nud crossed the main chasm from the man-made part into the natural caves with little difficulty. And while striding through the water-formed passages that followed, he began to whistle a tune he'd heard at the Flipside. The tune brought him back to the bog and the Mire Trail, to Holly, and to his meeting with Mer. Then he hummed another song that made him think of Oda and dancing, Paplov, and even clouds drifting high in the sky of the world above. Light thoughts for dark places. That was enough to keep one foot swinging out in front of the other.

And as Nud hiked on, he began to run his fingers along the smooth walls of the limestone tunnels he strode through, appreciating the texture of their elongated forms. They were like natural works of art, sculpted by time, water and gravity. At one point, he noticed the ceiling held a rat's jaw of cave icicles, dripping wet with the cement of their spiky, ground dwelling counterparts. "Ah, yes," he said to no one, eyes scanning. He'd first beheld the scene but from the opposite direction shortly after leaving the entry cave on that ill-fated night. "I'm getting close."

A short walk after, Nud's stomach began to flutter as he came to the next cave along his path, littered with what he assumed to be bat dung. *I'm almost there,* he thought. His pulse quickened. The Pip knew that it connected to the final tunnel, the one he'd have to crawl through to get to the water. Despite everything bad that'd happened, a sliver of optimism shone through to his bleak, desperate soul. Anticipation gripped him. *Finally, I'm going to get out.* Nothing could hold him back now from diving into the pool, powering through the tangled mess of weeds and popping up at the surface of a pond like Everdeep, just off the Mire Trail. *Nothing.*

Until he looked up.

Nud stopped humming and froze. His thoughts swirled. His body tensed.

Like sheets of flattened bodies, they hung from the ceiling and they clung to the walls. Some dangled by a ropey tail jammed into a crevice, while others lay flat against the rock surface. The vile, face-sucking "cloakers" were everywhere – an entire nest of them.

Nud took a step back. Gravel crunched underfoot. A stir

spread amongst the hive. Walls and ceiling suddenly came to life. One after another, cloakers let themselves drop. They dropped and twisted into arcing glides and bore straight towards Nud.

Charged with sudden energy, the Pip turned and bolted down the tunnel. A hundred shrill calls shrieked behind him to the flurry of flapping wings.

As he sped away, a fast cloud of face-suckers shot past Nud, spun in mid-air and dive-bombed him, head-on. He veered into an unexplored side tunnel before they could get him. Some of the hot pursuers missed the turn, but others banked and swooped in to follow. They screeched and flapped as they gained on him. Nud ran along a downslope. It was steep. Dashing faster than his legs could carry him, he lost his balance. He stumbled.

Another angry mass zipped past him. Again, they spun about in a coordinated manner. This time, the cloakers spread themselves wide, hovering at face height. Nud ducked and dodged, batting them aside as he charged through their ranks. The largest latched onto Nud's arm. The Pip tried to shake it off in stride. A few crazed moments later, he tore it loose. But he'd taken his eyes off the uncertain path ahead.

The drop was as sudden as it was unexpected.

The ground beneath Nud's feet simply disappeared. Had he known the pit was there, he easily could've cleared it. Instead, he toppled in and whacked the far side. Waves of pain reverberated through his body. He knocked, tumbled, and skidded down the pit, stirring up dust and rocks in his wake. Then, suddenly, he broke free.

In a split moment of suspended time, Nud floated – unconfined and in perfect free fall. The sensation was strangely familiar ... like a dream from long ago. He was flying once again, open air gushing up around him. The whole of his body tingled as he floated, euphoric and helpless, eyes fixed on the receding hole in the ceiling above. The cool air prickled the back of his neck and rushed past his ears. Nud breathed in its freshness through his nostrils. He felt a surreal smile form on his lips.

Thud.

Roll.

Splash.

The world went fuzzy and then black.

*

When Nud came to, everything felt wrong – his limbs, his back, his head. They all felt terribly wrong. And wet ... partially submerged. A current of shallow water gurgled past him.

The Pip slowly opened his eyes. It was dark ... no ... a muted spark ... flashing. Red.

CHAPTER iii

Water dancing

The air about Nud hissed with the rush of water, flowting past him. He lay sprawled on his back, half-submerged. Lightheaded and dazed, the Pip's senses slowly came into focus. A blur of fractured light informed him that his bog stone was near. When it flashed red, the mist around him ignited like tiny dots of iridescent flame. Truly, the hollow belly of the cavern he'd fallen into possessed an otherworldly quality. He felt his bruised forehead – sticky. The inflated wound there was tender and his touch made it sting like mad.

Nud stared at the vacant eye socket in the broken ceiling above him. His heart thudded dully at the sight. *So much for that idea,* he thought. Getting back to the entry cave and swimming out of that place simply wasn't going to happen. Not without wings.

The Pip rolled over to his side and curled into a drenched ball. He squeezed his eyes shut for a long moment, until the shooting pain subsided. Water slopped off him as he propped himself up on one elbow. Numbness shivered through his limbs. Nud ran his fingers through his hair, then rubbed the goose egg on the back of his head. Fresh blood trickled down his neck and plopped into the stream before being whisked away.

The events of the epic chase replayed in his mind: the cloud of face-sucking cloakers, the side tunnel, blindly plunging into a pit…

What if they followed me?

Panic gripped his chest. *Not again,* he told himself. His arm was torn up and the flesh on his face still felt raw where the first one had scraped him. Nud paused to listen in the dark for the shwishing sounds cloakers make or their beating wings.

Nope.

The bog stone flickered on. His eyes darted about the cavern, but he saw no cloakers lurking about.

Hopefully they don't come down here.

Nud drew a deep breath through his nostrils. The air smelled like the sea. He licked his lips and tasted the salt. In all ways, the winding stream he lay in appeared to be seawater, or near to it. The Pip gathered his strength and sat all the way up. Dizzy, he felt his lower back beneath the cold water – bruised and cut. He could see where he'd impacted the mound of cave fill under the hole and how it'd redirected his fall. The terrain around him was jagged and rocky everywhere, except where the slope of the fill met the stream … except exactly where he'd rolled. *Damn, a few feet left or right and those rocks would've split me in two.* With a slight shake of his head, Nud thanked Ekkon the Wanderer for small favors.

The bog stone flashed away like usual, underwater. The Pip fished it out and placed it on a flat rock beside him. In fixed images, it revealed a chamber wide beyond the measure of the light's reach. He shrugged off his pack and slowly pushed himself to his feet, but shooting pain shot up one leg as it buckled under him and he toppled back. Determined, he tried again and clambered to a staggered stance, balancing his weight on the surrounding rocks. Both legs quivered under the load.

The Pip slowly got to work. First, he tended to his wounds, taking careful notice not to touch the scratches and bruises that scattered his body. He doused them in the salt water and bandaged up what he could with strips of cloth torn from his already-frayed clothing. He wringed out what was left of his tattered cloak. Next, he pulled his waterlogged backpack out of the stream and emptied its contents onto the shore.

Straightaway, Nud set his bow against a nearby rock, then pulled three arrows out of the pack and jabbed them into the fill, just in case more cloakers showed up. He looked over his gear. *I can't keep lugging all this stuff around,* he decided. So, one-by-one he chucked the less-than-impressive pieces of deepwood into the stream. The current swept them away into deeper darkness. Next, he rummaged through the rest of his stock, setting aside to dry the remaining arrows, the two special pieces of deepwood pointed out by Fyorn, a few extras that looked good, plus a small woodcarving of a crow that must've have been jammed into the corner of his pack for ages.

Then he heard a familiar sound.

Chk-chk-fwip … chk-chk-fwip.

Damn.

Nud reached for his bow.

I guess cloakers do come down here.

At the next pulse of light, Nud quickly scanned the cavern to locate the creature. He spotted it on the ceiling … alone.

The face-sucker dropped down and fluttered to a nearby rock.

Clear shot.

Nud yanked an arrow out of the ground, notched the shaft, and gave it some draw weight. The cavern went dark.

While he waited for the light flash on, the Pip trained his bow where he thought the creature would be. *I can't let that thing get away*, he told himself, *it'll only bring more.* He set his stance, drew a breath and held it in.

A screech sounded. The light flickered on. In a flurry of flapping wings, the cloaker shot up and bee-lined for the hole. The Pip tracked its course, canted the bow slightly, and aimed a smidgen ahead of its course. The light flickered off.

Nud let the arrow fly.

Thwunk!

Seconds later, a thud sounded. On the next flash, Nud saw that his arrow had found its mark. The creature lay motionless, on the ground. The Pip limped over to the bat-like creature and wrenched his arrow out of its flesh. He wondered about the meat, but quickly dismissed the idea of consuming it. *Not without fire to cook that vile thing – could be full of worms, or worse.* Just in case he became desperate though, Nud buried the carcass in a shallow section of the saltwater stream.

When he finished piling on the stones, Nud rinsed off his hands and the arrow. *Now what?* He gazed downstream to the edge of illumination, and then upstream.

"Which way leads out?" he called to the salty watercourse. Only the echoes of his voice responded.

Nud rubbed his chin as he gazed at the rushing water. "It seems in a hurry to flow down and deeper," he reasoned aloud, "my least favorite direction." He swung his gaze upstream again. "That way then, to the source." The Pip only knew of one brackish body of water – Dim Lake. The stream had to be part of that same system.

Without warning, a snap like thunder shook the cavern. Loose rocks showered down from the edge of the pit. Nud scrambled out of the way, tripping over the uneven terrain. From far off, a cascade of splitting and crackling followed. Then a loud crack sounded from above. Nud ducked between two big rocks in the water, burying his head in his hands. The slab in the ceiling shifted, broke off, and came crashing down next to him.

Ekkon's Wheel, Nud thought, staring at the broken chunks. The Pip tilted his gaze to the tons of rock still vibrating over his head. *I can't stay here.* Small bits rained everywhere.

Then the rumbling stopped. The crackling and splitting sounds gave way to echoes in the distance. The dust thrown up soon cleared. Only the burbling of running water broke the silence.

Nud rose to his feet, dripping wet, and rushed over to his belongings. As he stuffed them into his pack, an odd-shaped hunk of deepwood caught his eye. The piece broadened at one end into a heavy burl, while the other end tapered to a natural, curved handle – a perfect club grown in the wild. Solemnly, he weighed the burl-wood in his hands – solemnly because it reminded him of Paplov's woodcarving. Nud missed the old gaffer, but now wasn't the time to reminisce.

He practiced a precision swing, then another. *This could come in handy if another cloaker shows up,* he thought.

"Shatters," he declared, calling it by its new name. He loosened his belt-rope a stretch and hung the club at his side. It hooked in rather naturally.

Dirt fell from the ceiling and small stones rattled when they hit the ground.

I need to get out of here. The Pip slung his backpack onto his shoulders and gathered the archery gear. He picked up the last piece of deepwood too – a long shaft with good grain – and started on his way. In step, he nearly flung the piece into the stream, but stopped himself. At the last second, he decided instead to use it as a walking stick to help him along. Besides the burlwood, that was the only other piece Fyorn had labelled "special."

One more thing. Mouth feeling dry and salty, Nud surveyed the chamber for a pool of fresh water before setting out, however small.

Shroud's Well, water all around but nothing to drink. He bit his parched lower lip and shook his head. *Such a cruel curse.*

*

An ominous feeling came over Nud as he plodded on for nearly a day. He followed the stream's winding path as it cut through the rock. *Did I make the right choice?* Evidence of roof collapse was everywhere and once in a while, a loud crash sounded from ahead. As bad or worse, the lightless and barren landscape had nothing to offer. The going was rough with all the loose cave fill, no fresh water, and no signs whatsoever that the living had ever visited the cavern. Nothing scurried in the dark, nothing fluttered above, and nothing cried out from the shadows.

Determined, Nud kept to his pace, stopping only to sleep, salt his wounds, and make a few modifications to his gear. The first modification was to use a thin strip of leather that he peeled from his pack to fasten a perfectly sharp rock he'd found to one end of the deepwood shaft. He made a decent short spear of it. "Sliver" is what he named it.

For the second modification, Nud undid a leather tie from his backpack and worked it into a crude cord and setting. He used it to hang the stone around his neck, and imagined he could even wear it like a headband if he wanted to. Nud added a flap to block the light in case he needed to hide in the dark.

Eventually, changes to the scenery became evident. The ceiling heightened until its bland features disappeared beyond the reach of his light. Soon after, the debris piles grew enormous and their composition altered from the regular jagged rocks of roof collapse to something else altogether. Signs that old-worlders had once been in the area began to show through the rubble. Among the scattered rocks, bricks began to appear, and twisted metal, and broken glass mixed with manufactured bits and pieces. Nud stopped to examine a few odd, glassy tablets that littered the cave floor, unlike anything he'd ever seen before. He slipped the most intact ones into his pack.

The ruins he clambered through differed greatly from what he remembered of old Akeda. There were no outlines of buildings to poke through, no partial structures to enter, and no deep wells to rappel down and explore.

No, these ruins were the crumbled mess of a city obliterated.

*

Time went by in the cavern. Days, maybe, virtually unnoticed. He'd survived on nothing but drops of water until then, lapped up from a handful of sweating rocks along the way. The weary Pip had found his stride and had shut down as many mental and physical facilities as possible: minimize navigation; minimize ups and downs; minimize exertion; look only where needed; and minimize thought. Nud likened his state of mind to conserving energy during a long, deep dive.

While half in a daze a distant glimmer caught Nud's eye, flirting with his vision on the edge of darkness. He was tempted to ignore it. *Stick to the plan,* he told himself, *keep to the stream, the path.*

But the dryness in his throat urged him otherwise. *A glimmer like that could be water. Fresh water.*

Never mind, came the counter-voice inside, *a waste of energy.* Nud's aching legs were reluctant to shift his momentum. *Keep on; stay focused.*

Nud let out a heavy sigh. *No.* He stopped, swung around and staggered over the debris-laden ground towards the sighting. On approach, the reflected pulses of light appeared to waver. His breath bottled up in his chest. *Is it just my eyes?*

Closer still, in disjoint flashes the glow began to broaden. Slowly, surely, it spread wide and tall into a shimmering veil of light, pulsing in the stone's radiance. The hope became real, tangible. Tiny, stretched droplets of water rained down from unseen heights. Nud watched as they pattered the surface of a freestanding pool with soft, tingly splashes. A floating sensation welled up from deep inside. *Water ... fresh water.*

Nud jabbed *Sliver* into the ground and rushed towards the shallow depression in the rock. He clambered up the rimstone and cupped the precious liquid in his hands. It was cool and clear. He let it run through his fingers, then cupped some more and splashed it over his face. A trickle ran down his cheek to the corner of his mouth – no salt. Slurping up a long draught, smooth and golden, the liquid slid down his throat and bled into his chest. He felt the coolness pool in the bottom of his stomach. Nud shut his eyes and focused on that feeling for a long moment. A sense of acceleration came over him. Dizzying. When he opened his eyes again, something extraordinary happened – something to compound the good feelings sweeping over him.

The stone around Nud's neck began to flicker wildly. At

the same time, he felt a warmth within him begin to grow, and as the bog stone grew brighter, his consciousness seemed to inflate along with it. The sensation stacked mental rush upon mental rush, a high upon a high. The Pip rose to his feet in utter astonishment. The light brightened and then steadied into a single beam. Then the sensation changed, like falling. A gentle fall though, with a wide, slow sway to it. Nud floated into fond memories: good times and laughter kidding around with friends, family, blue skies … easy times. A sudden, peaceful feeling flared up inside, comforting and reassuring. A sense of calm washed over him. *I did my best.* In all directions, the darkness crept away, it crept into the dark places where shadows go to hide.

Fuzzy at first, Nud's eyes soon adjusted to the dazzling brilliance. The layout of the great vault that he stood in revealed itself fully for the first time. Nud tilted his gaze upwards in awe. The high rock ceiling was most bizarre. Like giant, broken spikes, the vestiges of a once great city hung from the sloped roof of the cavern – a wedge of land violently cut out, overturned, and set to lean on its side.

Remnants of buildings, roads, tall towers and the skeletons of long dead trees dangled precariously. Nud could see how debris on the cavern floor lined up with barren spots on the overturned landscape that had given way. Together, top and bottom could be pieced together to make an entire city, a city of the kind only old-worlders might have endeavored to build, long ago.

Farther out, the tallest buildings of the Hanging City spanned from ceiling to floor like pillars of ruin, windows smashed and large sections missing.

As far as the eye could see, there were only ruins in every direction – no cave walls, no end to the stream or to the piles of debris. Out of the corner of his eye, he chanced to witness a large section of building material snap and release from the ceiling. It struck the ground with a resounding thunderclap and sent a bulging cloud of dust billowing up.

Abruptly, as quickly as it had come, the world shrank to nothingness. The light vanquished. Nud waited patiently in the dark, anticipating the usual pause before start-up. However, the darkness persisted. A deep chill sank into him as he waited longer … and longer. The chill soaked into his bones.

Is that it?

Nud shook the bog stone – it didn't help. He knocked it with his knuckles and lightly tapped it on the rock floor – nothing. He immersed the stone in water and swooshed it around – still nothing. No matter what he tried, nothing worked. So, he put his makeshift necklace back around his neck. *Has doom finally arrived?* It had been lingering there from the start.

The Pip's dark thoughts began to work their way inward; dark thoughts for dark places. *I'm never getting out.* He broke into a cold sweat and collapsed onto the rimstone. *It's my fault my friends are dead.* His emotions didn't stop there. They kept spiraling downwards. *Paplov is sick because I didn't do enough.* Nud's heart began to race. His chest felt tight and his head throbbed. *What's happening? I can't stop. Make it stop.*

Nud's worries multiplied and they, in turn, fed on one another to multiply some more. A wave of anxiety rushed over the Pip and held him fast in its grip. Unable to take it any longer, Nud rose to his knees. Hands trembling, he ran his tingling fingers through the pool of water and tried to distract himself from despair. The water felt cool to the touch, but it wasn't enough. He traced small concentric circles, then larger ones, faster and faster.

His mind flooded with despair. *My parents. Why didn't I try harder to find them?* Nud thrashed at the water violently, sending handfuls soaring into the air. A part of him wished that the old gods of his father would just be done with him. If they still had power anywhere it would be down there; down in the deep recesses of the world, lost but not completely forgotten. *Like me.* He let out a scream.

Then, out of nowhere, water noises sounded from the pool.

Nud's body tensed. He gulped air, afraid to breathe. With slow steps and trying not to make a sound, the Pip backed away from the pool. Gently, he clambered down from the platform. He bumped into *Sliver* in the process, yanked it from the ground, and held it defensively in front of him. But rather than run off, despite his fears Nud felt drawn to the noises. He waited in the dark, still and quiet. Yet curious. Anticipating.

Without warning, the bog stone flared up. A blinding flash of light re-lit the cavern. But the light was not alone in its coming. Nud watched the water in the pool with grim fascination, for it began to ripple as though *he* were tracing *his* circles in the pool again, yet without his hand to guide the motion. His heartbeat erupted as thrashing waves once made were made anew – every motion duplicated like an echo, not of sound but of deeds done. Nud stumbled back. His mind scrambled to understand. At once, the animation halted.

Have I finally gone mad?

Within moments, the bog stone resumed its normal pattern of flicker, as though nothing had happened.

"What are you?!" Nud demanded of the dancing pool. He tilted his gaze upward and yelled to the rock ceiling. "Are the old gods really down here?" The chamber echoed his words.

Nud motioned to the pool, still gazing up. "Are these the ghosts of your dead city?"

A chill ran through his spine at the thought.

Without further delay, Nud retraced his steps to the stream and, at a hurried pace, resumed his long walk.

Less than an hour into the hike, Nud's ears homed in on the faintest hiss. The sound grew louder as he approached, filling the cavern over the random gurgles of the stream. His spirits rose again. The roar of rapids intensified. Finally, at long last, Nud came to an end of the great black cavern that'd held him captive for so long. A roaring torrent poured out of an intricately carved opening in the rock wall – the source of the stream. With the frothing water, a steady breeze of salty air blew out. The gaping cave mouth was set between two massive columns – manmade – built solidly into the rock.

The columns were styled in the likeness of two giant mermaids with sultry expressions, and with hair that flowed above and around the arched cave opening. The mermaids' tails curled towards the stream and flattened beneath the tumbling water, dolphin-like. They caught the outflow and flipped it on its way.

Something peculiar struck Nud about the inner depths of that watery cave. The Pip sheathed his bog stone and peered inside. In the distance, ever so rarely, a misty glint of blue-green light fluctuated. Literally, at long last, he beheld the light at the end of the tunnel.

The way out?

CHAPTER IV

The Dim Sea

Many Stouts mistook a form of rare, light-giving cave moss as signs that gnomes lived in the deep places of the earth, taunting and luring goodly passersby with glittering gems and gold they could never possess. Any beguiled person who reached for the treasures found only dust, and if particularly unlucky or offensive to the gnomes, a knife in the back. It'd been Kabor who had told the story of the moss, only observed to grow in the mouths of a precious few caves and the entrances to old mines. He'd heard more whispers than a rover and seemed to know a great many things about secret places. But even he never mentioned *this* secret place.

Nud strolled casually past the stream head to the rocky shore beyond. A great body of water stretched out before him. He stood in a grand cavern aglow with faerie illumination. The Pip looked about in wonder. Like the stars of a hazy twilight, colored dots of light beamed down from above and reflected off the water's glassy surface. Across the wide expanse, colossal spires rose out of the liquid glass like island pyramids, while columns of rock braced the netherworld sky.

Nud breathed deep, filling his lungs with the sea air. In it, he tasted a hint of freshness that could've only come from the world above. *There must be multiple openings to the surface here*, he surmised. There was no question in Nud's mind – he'd found the way out. And as much as he wanted to feel good about his discovery, somehow, he felt empty inside. *Kabor should be here,* he told himself over and over again. Nud would've given anything to share this sight with him. *Yes, he should be here.*

All at once, a sudden pain swelled up in the Pip's head, dull and throbbing. Nud raised a hand to massage his temples. *What's happening?*

The pulsing intensified. Ripping. Undulating. Like pieces of his brain were being torn out of his head. Nud dropped his spear. Gritting his teeth, he grunted at the pain, building as he stood. He buried his head in both hands, but he couldn't stop the flood that followed, as though some dam holding the anguish back just let loose in his mind. Nud fell to his knees, reeling. Eyes wide, he gasped as the final wave shot through. Intense. Biting.

A long moment later, the sensation damped out. Nud stole a breath, relieved.

Slowly, the Pip lifted his head, eyes searching for some kind of explanation. As he swept his gaze over the calm waters, an uncomfortable clicking noise welled up in his head. The disturbance rose in volume. *Not again.* Nud moaned and shook his head violently, as though the sensation were something he could fling off. But the pressure only mounted. He cupped his hands over his ears. But the clicking only became louder; piercing. At all angles, it wormed its way through his cranium and it tunneled into the hidden depths of his mind. He fell onto his side and clamped into a ball.

Without warning, the noise ceased. Nud braced himself for the next onslaught of mental anguish, rocking himself slowly and whimpering "no, no, no…". But nothing came. Cautiously, he lifted his hands from his ears. A muffled silence filled the audible void, like being underwater. It lasted but a moment. A long moment.

Out of the prolonged hush arose a deep and cavernous voice. It called out to Nud like an old friend. The voice seemed to come from all around, nowhere and everywhere all at once, near and far, here and there, permeating like resonance.

"HUUM haa," boomed the cavernous voice. The words rolled in, paced and rhythmic, like waves crashing onto shore. "I have been waiting a long time for one like you to arrive." The voice seemed strangely disconnected and hollow. "You are Nud Lenokin, if I am not mistaken."

The Pip didn't answer.

"Nud, is that you?" said the voice, seeking confirmation. The tone was suddenly different, almost too familiar. *Father? … No.* He couldn't quite place it.

A long sigh followed, and then it started again. "HUUM haa. Tell me, have you come to me for something? What is it you want most?"

What do I want most? Nud thought. *A way out … my friends… my parents … I'm hungry.*

Nud gathered his composure, straightened out and rose to his feet. In his most practiced diplomatic tone, the Pip answered: "Yes … my name is Nud." His eyes darted about the cavern. "Nud Lenokin of Webfoot, and I just want out." Nothing in plain sight hinted at the source of the voice. "I don't want any trouble – food if you have any to spare." Nud looked up, behind. Nothing. Then he focused his eyes out to sea, on the shafts of sunlight that beamed down through breaks in the rock ceiling. "But mostly I just want out through the cave roof … Sir."

"Sir" seemed like an awkward way to address the voice. Nud normally reserved "Sir" for councilors and diplomats. This voice seemed larger, more voluminous, more deserving. Pressing on, the Pip tilted his gaze to the ceiling and pointed to what must have been a sizable clump of glowing moss on the roof of the cavern, one that might be accessible from a nearby column, impossible to climb.

"Out through one of those daylight holes, Your Highness Sir," Nud continued, knowing the moss needed at least some access to natural light. "Do you know the way? … How do you know my name?"

The voice resounded back in reassuring tones. "I know *all* the children of the dark. And I know *the Way*. I can get you *what you Want*." A long pause ensued, followed by a watery sigh.

"HUUM haa," the voice went on. "I know *all* the ways and all the names of all the ways and all the names of all the things you are apt to meet along all the ways."

Nud fidgeted with his hands and shifted his feet while quietly waiting for the voice to continue, to explain further, but nothing more was forthcoming. Nothing more was offered by the hollow voice that only seemed to exist inside his own head.

A breeze blew up in the moments that passed, and the lightest of wavelets caressed the twilit shore. Nud hollered out. "Hello? Are you still there?"

Were you ever there?

Time passed and normal sounds crept back into the Pip's ears, mostly wind sighing in the cavern heights and small waves lapping against the rocks. Nud turned his attention back to the "starry" sky and the daylight holes, searching for a way up. Then he peered out across the waterscape and noted a subtle patch of paleness.

What he gleaned wasn't a protruding rock, but something was definitely out there. It seemed to flutter. Nud shook his head, blinked, and peered again into the dimness. The second look told a different story: there were two shapes, long and curved, like a pair of giant bull horns. Nud unsheathed the bog stone for a better view. The light flashed on, yielding a long and steady pulse.

Yes, horns. And they were moving … gliding his way, each with its own thin wake trailing behind it. Nud sheathed the gem and backed away from the water. The horns were deathly white and as tall as a man. Fleshy and flexible, they swayed this way and that way with the grace of charmed snakes.

With an abrupt gushing sound, the "horns" flapped open and fanned out wide, like a lizard's frills. A flush of adrenaline tingled through Nud's body. He crouched to a low stance, ready to spring back. He kept his eyes on the flaps as their orientation adjusted, homing in it seemed, like an animal's perked ears. His heart froze in his chest when they angled his way. A part of him wanted to bolt and hide. But something inside urged him to stay put.

Once again, the sounds of the world grew muted. Every muscle tensed as Nud Lenokin waited.

Lulled by a slow and steady rise, the Pip gazed in wonder as a massive, writhing form broke the water's surface, fully the size of a whale. The fans appeared little more than fixtures on the colossal forehead of the great beast, dwarfed by the creature's sheer bulk and ample length – a true leviathan out of stories of old. The form rose and rose until it towered high above the water's surface, glistening white. Sheets of water drained down its imposing frame and crashed alongside it.

The body of the beast was long and thick, and Nud glimpsed a whale's flat tail. Spiny ridges covered the head and back. The forebody propped up in an odd manner – too high, it seemed, as if supported by a ledge just beneath the surface.

A sudden movement followed – the leviathan twitched and curled. Nud hopped back and nearly ran. But there wasn't much to run to other than loneliness, starvation and the prospect of being suffocated in his sleep, so he stayed put.

The thing may have laughed at that point, or scoffed, or maybe it just blew something out of its blowhole that needed blowing out. After the spray was lost to the breeze, the leviathan raised its bulk even higher out of the water and skittered landward. Nud thought the beast might crawl up onto shore. Three great, red eyes faced the Pip: the eyes of an albino, fixed to one side of its huge whale-head. He'd glimpsed three more on the other side as well.

What Nud did next was out of character and stupid. Feeling compelled, the small Pip approached the creature. He made his approach in sure knowledge that he'd be perfectly safe. Nud stepped forward to meet the abomination and find out what it would have of him. He halted at the water's edge and gazed into that triplet of eyes, searching for something friendly; searching for something familiar he'd heard in that voice. Nud saw only his smaller self, set against the deepest red and encircled by tiny specs of light that shone like knowledge. Nothing more. Slowly, persistently, the Pip's senses recovered from a certain numbness and complacency that is difficult to describe. A cautious step back seemed in order.

The leviathan spoke at last, with a low and devouring growl in its voice. Yet its jaw did not move. "HUUM haa …

daylight holes … not the way 'Little Newt' … this side a fall, the other side, savage creatures will tear you to shreds."

The fanned-out horns rippled in slow vibrations; the words echoed in Nud's head. *'Little Newt' – my father used to call me that.*

"HUUM," the beast bellowed, "HAA … there is another way. I know the Way; I can get you what you Want. First, tell me 'everything.' What brings you here, little one?"

"Where is here?" Nud asked.

The leviathan's voice rolled in response. The rumbling sound that rolled along with it was not quite a laugh, *per se*, but the embedded inflection could have passed for amusement.

"HUUM haa," he boomed, airily, "You have come to my shores, tiny Outlander. Leggy beasts call this place the 'Dim Sea.'"

"A Dim Sea indeed," Nud said, eyes sweeping about the massive cavern. Obviously, this creature, whatever it was, didn't know a lot about surface people. Nud didn't think he looked anything like an Outlander. The Pip mulled over what to say next. He couldn't get his thoughts out straight.

"I'd like to find my friend Kabor, if he's alive, and I want for us – me and him – to return to the surface … the bog, that is. The bog is where I live. I'm from Webfoot, you see."

A long, awkward silence followed, during which the eyes of the leviathan seemed to stare straight through Nud. The only sounds were the roar of the rapids and the winds whis-tling through breaches in the stone. At one point, the Pip thought to speak, but the moment he opened his mouth a low and subdued thrumming noise arose in his head, cutting-off at just the right level to scramble his thoughts. Nud's words scrambled along with them before he could get them out.

The voice returned, at normal volume. "HUUM haa," it

said, "I can help you. Let us talk first though … It is lonely down here. Let us roll along the shore as we become … better acquainted, HUUM? I dislike sitting still. I must say that I feel I know you quite well already. HUUM haa … Walk alongside as I sail the shores of this great and cavernous sea."

Nud felt pity for the leviathan. The Pip had never been so utterly alone as during his time underground. Perhaps this one had spent its entire life that way. And this magnificent creature was not only sentient, it seemed inviting enough, in its own way. Nud's single, greatest fear evaporated – that this was the end. *No,* he decided, *this is a beginning,* and the fear condensed into a triad of hope, admiration, and awe.

A new source of energy overtook Nud. He spritely hopped from stone to stone to keep pace with the drifting leviathan. They exchanged news and facts about a great many things. Ecstatic to have someone to talk to, Nud opened up completely to the beast. He told it *everything*: his life from early on, all about Paplov – whom the leviathan seemed already to know a great deal about and wanted to meet – as well as his parents, the bog, and Webfoot. Nud went into detail about the Flipside, the menu at the Flipside (indeed, Nud was incredibly hungry), Turnsby, the Bearded Hills, the Akedan ruins, and Deepweald. The leviathan seemed to be quite familiar with those topics as well. But then Nud revealed things the beast knew little or nothing about: the Hurlorns, the giant black spider he discovered in a box, deepwood (at which time Nud promptly revealed *Shatters*), his friends, the bog queens (which caused a grumble), and even the discovery of the bog stone. These last few, above all else, clearly sparked the creature's interest, and he prodded Nud to tell all and leave nothing out. For the most part, Nud obliged, but he specifically avoided talk of Fyorn. The woodsman preferred to keep to himself, being a Kith ranger and all.

Unannounced, the *White Whale* whipped around and slid away from the shore. It furled its two fans into horns and made a shallow dive. Nud watched as the beast propelled itself to open water and then slowly looped back in a wide circuit. After a rolling dive, the leviathan surfaced not far from where it'd started, but oriented the opposite way – back the way they'd come.

"HUUM haa," he started. "You must be starving."

The leviathan unfurled its horns. Moments later, a scattering of small white fish began to appear – dead cavefish, drifting sideways. They were blind and looked a lot like catfish, but longer and slenderer than their darker cousins in the upper world. Within a minute, more than a dozen had appeared.

"Please, help yourself," offered the beast. "They are perfectly edible to leggy ones like you."

And so, Nud did just that. In the star-shadow of the beast, he scooped up a handful of the small morsels. The leviathan's casual thoughtfulness had put it into the Pip's good books. The raw fish felt soft and slimy in his mouth, but the flesh was strangely sweet. His stomach couldn't take so much at once though. He stashed some away in his backpack, wrapped in yet another strip of cloth torn from his cloak and soaked in saltwater.

Once finished, the White Whale addressed Nud. "HUUM haa," he said, "may I see this sparkling stone of yours?"

Something in Nud's gut didn't feel quite right just then. He thought it might be the small, white fish, but it could've been the bigger one in his midst. Reluctantly, he unsheathed the bog stone and held it out from his neck for the White Whale to see, in all its glory. Pulsing red, the light saturated the glistening surfaces of those many eyes. At first, the creature just stared at the gem without so much as a flinch – no motion, no words, nothing. All the while, his eyes sparkled in the flicker of the bog stone. Nud grew to anticipate such long pauses, having come to the conclusion that the leviathan liked to take his time examining things, or thinking them through first before speaking on them. Or maybe he just had slow ways.

"Do you know what this is?" Nud asked, breaking the silence between them.

The leviathan didn't answer. Much time went by again and the beast became … fidgety, if ever a whale could be fidgety – rolling and displaying subtle shivers. Something was wrong. Nud covered the stone. Soon after, the creature regained its composure.

"Huum. Huum. Where did you find such a wonder?"

Nud told the leviathan the bog body story straight out. He certainly didn't want to raise the ire of this one. There was a long pause after he finished.

"Exotic," was all he said. All three eyes on the one side of its face fixated on the stone, dangling in its sheath around Nud's neck. After a good long look, the leviathan began to speak once again. He seemed to believe that his turn at telling had come. In low and soothing tones, the creature recited many old stories and some recent ones about the lightless caves, which he called *Everdark*, and the Dim Sea caverns, which he called *Everdim*. Most of what he told Nud, the Pip understood plainly, but some of the events he spoke of were beyond Nud's comprehension, for the Pip didn't recognize all of the terms or places referred to just yet, and explaining them all at once would've proven far too laborious. The leviathan's bass voice was calm, slow between words, and most steady. There was power to it. In true Pip form, Nud committed all the leviathan told him to memory, if not understanding, for later pondering.

As he listened, Nud looked to the fans and then to the eyes for some inkling of emotion or bodily response, but nothing of the sort was forthcoming. The beast's exterior was a cold shell. All of the White Whale's life resided in its voice. Conversing with such a creature differed greatly from conversations with people – the looks, the body language, the intonations – all different or absent. Nud just got used to not seeing any lips move, or smiles, or frowns, or eyebrows rising, or any intense wrinkling of the brow or shrugging of shoulders.

However, over time Nud also began to see that the fans actually gave the beast away ever so subtly, in small wavers or ripples, and they seemed to vibrate or curl up slightly at times in response to stress or excitement, or upon making certain intellectual points.

Nud didn't question the topics of conversation he didn't understand as much as he should've – a poor performance on his part given the once-in-a-lifetime opportunity to have any and all questions answered. This creature seemed to know nearly everything about everything. He spoke of the First Men on Fortune Bay – now Abandon Bay, the native Abindohns, the Elderkin, and the plight of Harrow. He spoke of the coming of new plants, animals, and peoples, and of Outlanders, the origins of the Treaty of Nature, and the decline of mechanization.

The White Whale said friends of his lived on the shores of the Dim Sea. When Nud asked if he could meet them, the beast simply replied: "HUUM haa, you will in good time."

Many hours passed before the conversation began to wane. The Pip could only absorb so much information at once. It seemed to Nud that he'd told the leviathan everything there was to tell, and that he'd heard from the beast all there was to hear which he could handle right then and there. Drowsy from concentration, Nud lay down between the rocks and just listened for a time as the beast's voice rolled on. He rested his eyes and soaked his barely conscious soul in the leviathan's poetry of knowledge.

There was a long silence at one point, that or Nud dozed off. When he opened his eyes again, the leviathan was still at Nud's side, as close as he could be while in water deep enough to support his bulk.

The creature spoke to begin the end of their chance encounter. "HUUM haa. I will help you, but I must ask a small favor in return."

Nud tensed slightly at the words. "What would you have me do?"

"When one comes to you in my name, you must help him or her."

"Just one?" Nud said.

"Any one," he replied. "But only ever one at once."

The offer seemed agreeable, under the circumstances. Quite open ended, really. How much help Nud needed to provide was not specified, and timelines were only implicit. The White Whale may have known many things, but he wasn't so well versed in diplomacy, conditions, or the finer points of contractual arrangements. *Too easy.*

"Agreed," Nud said.

"HUUM … now you are one of the smaller ones, aren't you? HAA … 'Pip' you called yourself? You seem to have a good memory. That will serve me – I mean you – very well indeed. HUUM … you must listen carefully to every detail. I will tell you the precise way to follow. HAA … follow my words and they will lead you to what you seek."

Nud's colossal friend detailed exactly where the Pip should

go and exactly what Nud should do when he arrived there, to reach the surface. When the beast finished, Nud was pleased, and he believed the creature was pleased as well, somehow, and they parted on those terms. Well, almost. The creature swam out to sea.

The White Whale luminesced as it propelled itself through the open water, glowing from deep within and along its spiny ridges. The leviathan was not alone. Just beyond the breaking water, five long, slender figures appeared from the watery depths on all sides. Nud's jaw dropped. Emotions suddenly numb, he blinked slowly in the face of what he beheld. The slender figures were all female and the size of old-worlders.

Bog queens? Maybe. Could it be?

One of the trailing figures shot back a blank, lifeless stare to the shore. Nud recognized the look. Undoubtedly, she was one of their ilk – bog queen or something related. But where the hags were disheveled and crude, she was fresh looking and elegant, with long golden hair flowing through the water behind her. Her lean body undulated with the energetic grace of a porpoise.

With heavy eyes, Nud watched the sea creatures glide out of sight. Every so often, he observed the leviathan expelling a great cloud of vapor from its blowhole. With a content stomach and a mind full of wonder, Nud wrapped himself in his cloak and slept a deep and dreamful sleep.

When he awoke again, many hours had passed. How many exactly, he couldn't know. Nud should've asked the White Whale what day it was, assuming days were counted in such dark places. Strangely, the green stars in the domed sky had disappeared. The water was placid again; the air, still. The persistent drone of rushing water filled the emptiness.

Nud reached for his faithful bog stone and peeled off its

sheath. The sea reposed under the broken glow of its gentle light. *Was it all just a dream?* The events of the day seemed too impossible to be true. *I just had polite conversation with a creature out of legend.* It couldn't have been a dream though – Nud recalled the stories told to him and he recalled the plan laid out. A Pip remembers many things perfectly, but recalls dreams as poorly as other-worlders. Dreams are not memories; they are a sorting out of the day's happenings.

The plan of the leviathan included essentials such as where to find food, where to find Kabor (more like how to find him) and, of course, how to get out. That last part was vague though, as it relied on someone else finding Nud, in *his* name. But Nud trusted that it would all work out, somehow. He trusted the White Whale. Nud called him "friend."

The Pip gathered more catfish that he'd somehow missed, and recovered his short spear that he'd dropped at the stream head. Nud said his goodbyes to the Dim Sea, and set forth on the path laid out for him. And as he passed into the tunnel's misty veil, back towards the Hanging City cavern, Nud realized that he hadn't thought to ask for the leviathan's actual name. The Pip shrugged his shoulders and leapt to the next boulder alongside the rapids. He continued to leap from stone to stone all the way through to the mermaid columns on the other side.

I will know the name when I hear it, Nud reassured himself.

CHAPTER V

Interlude – Intricacies

On the edge of Deepweald, the storm builds and the rain pours down in sheets. Troops gather on the east line of Harrow. Already, the lightning strikes. I must hurry or lose my opportunity. Sheltered in this grotto, my limbs are whipping through pages like you wouldn't believe. Terrifying giants, I am told, are near ready to march. They are bred of the wild fiends that thrive and multiply in the Western Tor. I can hear their drums beating in the distance, loud enough to drown the very thunder rumbling in. Amot is certain they will lead a foray outside the city walls. Such beasts are not permitted within the city proper, and yet they are permitted to serve the Iron Tower with their lives. Outnumbered many times over, the Queen's Guardsmen have only their skill at arms and a handful of unproven strikers to defend themselves in a confrontation. If the giants reach the forest and break the Elderkin lines, all could be lost.

Time is wasting. We must get back to the story before the storm front rolls in.

As you must have gathered, the White Whale was none other than *the* White Whale from the tale of the First Men's flight from Fortune Bay, while pursued by the brutal Jhinyari. And as you may recall, according to Kabor's account of the legend, the White Whale made a deal with the desperate old-worders to save them, an arrangement that no one ever spoke of. Let me tell you, the leviathan is not as poor a dealmaker as I initially made him out to be. You shall see before the end. But before I divulge any more details, there are a few more items of interest that must be brought to light.

So, in order to provide you with a full appreciation of the intricacies of the powers at work, what was at stake, and what *is* at stake, I must now turn your attention to the events that transpired on the surface during the time that I wandered through lightless limbo under the Hanging City. As previously, I draw upon pristine Pip memories to fill this void, some within our very consciousness, and so the reconstruction is as complete as possible.

CHAPTER VI

Breakfast at the Flipside

On the third night of the search, Mr. Numbit bragged to his patrons that his only son would find his way home. A crowd had gathered there in vigil. Bystanders, freeloaders and the genuinely concerned alike all drowned their shared sorrows in spirits and ale, responding with little more than a few cautious words and a sympathetic hush. The very next morning, to the town's delight and surprise, Mr. Numbit showed them all.

It rained the morning Bobbin showed up at the inn.

"I told you so," the innkeep said with a grin to just about everyone that came by that day. "Free barkwood ale, on the house! Tonight, we celebrate!"

Some celebrated, others still mourned; one confirmed dead, two remained lost.

Holly returned to the Flipside that morning as well, to work her shift and gather news from the breakfast regulars. She didn't have to work right then – the hostess had free reign to come and go as she pleased, ever since showing up at the inn with no place to stay and nothing but the clothes on her back. "I need a job. Any job. Anywhere that is not Turnsby," she'd told the bartender. The soft-hearted Mr. and Mrs. Numbit took her in, no questions asked. Holly overheard Mrs. Numbit pressing her husband to find out what was wrong. The woman wanted to help just a little too much. "Sometimes," Mr. Numbit had replied, while polishing up a stein behind the bar, "it's better not to ever know the answers, or to ever have to tell them." Holly was grateful for that. Although eternally indebted to the Numbits, she lived under her own rules: never theirs … never anyone's but her own.

Holly hung her dripping wet cloak on one of the many pegs in the foyer. The typical crew of early risers had populated the great room, spread out and largely separated by empty tables. She looked in and there he was, just like that, sitting at the long table in front of the hearth, stuffing his face with cheese and bread. A fresh fire crackled behind him. Holly hurried over and embraced Bobbin immediately. She smoothed his thick, curly hair with her practiced fingers. She squished his rolls and gave them a scolding shake.

"You stupid fool. You could've been killed!"

Bobbin continued to chew on his bread as he hugged her, smiling bits of cheese.

"How did you get here?" she asked.

"I shwam," was the muffled response.

"For three days? Nobody swims for three days." Holly crouched beside the young Pip, resting her elbows on the table. She gazed directly into his lively brown eyes.

"I got lost, <gulp> I got bug-bitten, I even <swallow> ate bugs – unspiced and unsteamed! How's that for a story?" Bobbin sipped from a tankard of barkwood ale. "<belch> Want some?"

Holly turned her head away to avoid the worst of the bad air. She could smell the beer. Then she turned back to face him. "Do the searchers know? We looked for you. After you dove in you … you never came back up."

"I didn't need to. It took a while to shake that dirty old hag though. When I finally did, I tried coming back. It was dark … I got lost."

"Three days?"

"Three days. One underwater."

"You're lying."

"Belch!" Bobbin shook his head while pounding on his chest, drawing looks from some of the customers.

Holly ignored them. "Who knows that you're here?"

He took another sip from his tankard. "Half the town. Any sign of Nud or Kabor?"

"No. Jory was horribly…"

Bobbin lowered his eyes and shook his head. "I know. I heard it all." He faced Holly and swallowed the lump in his throat. "What do we do now?"

Holly felt the water building behind her eyes. The rain outside shifted from heavy to a steady patter. She pushed herself up from the table, reached into her pocket, and pulled out a pendant on a corroded chain. "Oh," she said, surprised when she saw it. She'd squirreled it away with barely a look after finding it in the bog.

Bobbin wiped his lips with his sleeve. "Where did you get that?"

"On the Mire Trail. I think one of the bog queens lost it."

Bobbin's eyes lit up when the stone on Holly's pendant flickered, just barely, almost hidden. Then he coughed when a piece of ham caught in his throat.

"Ahem," he began, slapping his chest and more

bleary-eyed for it than Holly. Bobbin cleared his throat. "So, there are more!"

"At least one more," Holly replied.

Bobbin's eyes darted about the breakfast crowd around them. He leaned over and whispered, "Isn't that evidence?"

Holly shrugged, then flashed a polite grin to a patron eyeing her. The woman was either nosy or expecting service. Holly ignored her too.

The young Pip drank deep, eyeing Holly's jewelry as he did so. After swallowing again, he said: "That's a lot different from the bit of quartz I was teasing the bog queen with."

"Different than Leno's stone too," Holly replied. "It's green instead of red, and not as bright. But they both flash about the same … I think. That hag was as dumb as a post."

A familiar voice interjected. "She's efficient."

It was Fyorn, leaning against the doorframe between the foyer and the great room. A small puddle had formed at his boots. "She only knows what she needs to know. If a hag has too much on her mind, she starts to get confused."

Holly lit up. "What are you doing here?" She rushed over to give him a hug.

"I'm soaking wet," Fyorn cautioned, raising his palms to her.

Holly hugged him anyway. "I don't care," she said, getting her shirt wet in the process. When she was done, she backed away to allow him some space. The woodsman grinned at her. His hair was windswept, his skin well-tanned for so early in the season, and he hadn't shaved in days.

Fyorn stepped into the eating area. "I was just about to head for the trail when I heard about Bobbin." The woodsman's eyes seemed to smile as he looked over the young Numbit. "I came to see if it was true." He paused, and then commented to Bobbin. "You look thinner."

Holly smirked. "Not for long."

Fyorn strode over and messed up the Pip's hair as though he were a toddler. "Bobbin, glad to see you're safe."

"Not as glad as I am," Bobbin said, just before stuffing in the last of the cheese. A sizable chunk of ham dangled on the end of the fork in his other hand.

Fyorn made a passing glance at the morsel, but seemed to have other concerns on his mind. "I just spoke with Nud's papa," he said, then he bit his upper lip. He shook his head slightly. "He isn't doing very well and he can't leave home. I fear the boy's disappearance is worsening his health … out of pure worry."

"Who's taking care of Paplov?" Bobbin said.

"I asked a neighbor to keep a close eye on him. I'll drop by when I can." Fyorn opened his hand and extended it to Holly: "May I?" He motioned to her newfound pendant.

"I'll bring some food over in a jiffy," Bobbin said.

Fyorn protested, "No, sit—"

"I insist," Bobbin cut in. He got up off his chair.

Fyorn smiled and shot him a nod of appreciation.

Holly tilted her head and gazed at Bobbin. "You're so thoughtful," she told him, and messed up his hair again.

"Why do people keep doing that?" he complained.

After Bobbin went on his way, the Flipside hostess plopped her find in the woodsman's broad hand. Fyorn took it by the chain and dangled the pendant in front of his eyes. He examined it closely.

There was no denying its likeness to Nud's bog stone, but a skilled jeweler had cut the stone and cast it in a metallic blue setting, worn and smoothed over time. The setting resembled a large coin, except with a hole in the middle to fit the stone and a wave motif impressed along its edge. Fyorn lowered Holly's stone into one hand and ran his thumb over the design. As he did so, his nostrils flared and his lips pursed. The woodsman tightened his grip on the stone's setting, to the point Holly feared he might crush it.

"What's wrong?" she said.

Fyorn didn't respond.

Holly sighed, thinking she'd read his expression. "I know," she said. "We have to get back out there and find Leno and Kabor."

Fyorn shook his head. "They're not in the bog. We looked everywhere twice." He loosened his grip on the stone.

"Then, where are they?" Holly said. "Do you think they're still alive?"

Fyorn met her gaze. "Of course I do."

Holly could see in his eyes that the answer he gave was not fully genuine. The woodsman held Holly's stone up in front of her.

"Do you see the warrior in the waves?" he asked.

She took the pendant, examined the setting briefly and gave him a quick nod.

Fyorn continued, "The frothing wave is the sigil of Harrow, dating back to the days of old Akeda."

He paused and waited, giving Holly the chance to respond. She didn't know what to say.

"Those hags answer to the Iron Tower," he stated flatly. Fyorn casually made his way to the picture window, took a deep breath and exhaled as he peered out onto the veranda. Heavy waterdrops fell from the leaky eaves. "We won't find any more answers here," he added.

Holly shifted her stance, bracing herself with one hand on the back of the nearest chair. "Are you going to search Harrow?"

Just then, Bobbin glided in carrying a platter that held a basket of fresh buns, three bowls of hot soup, and a cloth bag. "Search Harrow?" He brushed aside the crumbs on the table-top, placed the platter in the middle, and then reclaimed his seat. "Dig in," he said, as he plopped a bowl in front of himself. Holly swiped a bun and bit into it.

Bobbin regarded Fyorn. "The bag is for Nud's grandfather."

Fyorn nodded his thanks, then casually strolled away from the window. He returned to the table and took a seat beside Bobbin. The woodsman leaned back on his chair, legs sprawled and arms folded, tired eyes fixated on the basket of buns. He appeared drawn and thin, having kept on with the grueling search at the expense of his own nourishment. Yet he refrained from taking Bobbin's offering.

"Perhaps," he started. "But first I'd like to conduct a quick search along the edge of Deepweald to see what turns up. Then, maybe, gather information along the docks on Dim Lake. Problem is …" Fyorn paused and shifted his gaze to Bobbin – in the midst of a slurp – and then to Holly's expecting eyes.

"Have either of you been to Harrow, or has Gariff?"

Bobbin replied, "My parents go there to buy kitchen implements every few years."

Holly put her half-eaten bun down on the edge of the plat-ter. "I have never been," she said, passing Fyorn a bowl. She took another bowl for herself and Fyorn beckoned her to place it beside him so all three could sit together, facing the window.

The Flipside hostess obliged. "But I'd love to visit the mar-ket," she went on. "As for Gariff, his whole family used to work summers in Harrow, before they started in Webfoot. Kabor says Pops likes the atmosphere here a lot better and that the work is … easier."

Fyorn shuffled his chair over when Holly moved in to take her seat next to him. "I don't doubt that," he said. "Harrowians are generally good, hard-working folks. But the way they are oppressed … they don't enjoy the same freedoms as you and I. In some ways, it brings them together – they tend to form a variety of close-knit communities. But there are always informants among them that they have to guard against – moles, you might say, planted to keep them in line and make sure loyalties aren't being betrayed."

For a long minute, the three of them sat with their backs to the warm hearth, staring out the window amidst the murmur of patrons and the clinking of eating utensils. Holly started on her soup.

The woodsman patted the two Pips on their backs and then rested his arms on their shoulders. "The answer to your question, Holly, is this…"

Holly let her spoon sit idle in her soup as she turned her full attention to the woodsman's next words. Fyorn looked from one Pip to the other, then pulled the pair towards him in a near huddle. Holly could smell the outdoors on him. The outdoors mixed with old leather, newly crushed grass and something wet. It wasn't a bad smell; it was natural.

"No, I'm not going to Harrow," he said, "you are." Fyorn smirked. "You and Bobbin and Gariff, if you will."

"Wha—" In the midst of licking his bowl clean, Bobbin shifted his wide-eyed gaze to the woodsman. When he saw Fyorn was serious, he wiped his face with his forearm. "I'll start packing the food." In the blink of an eye, Bobbin was up and en route to the kitchen … again.

"Wait," Holly called after, "he doesn't mean *right now.*"

"If that's where they are, we have to find them." Bobbin ignored her pleas and continued on his way.

Heat washed over Holly's forehead. She threw her hands up and guffawed as she watched him leave. "I haven't been able to sit with him for more than a minute without him chewing on something or running off."

"Let him go," Fyorn said, adjusting his seating position. He rested his hands on the tabletop and folded them together. "You can't bottle up that kind of energy."

Holly swung her gaze to the woodsman. "Why us?"

Fyorn sighed. "I can't be seen anywhere near Dim Lake. Don't ask – it's a long story. No ranger can, not without serious retaliation on the Line of Control. They'd sniff me out and call me a spy, and with good reason. And Harrow is not kind to spies. You and your friends, however, would all be seen as quite innocently going about legitimate business there. None of you are a cause for concern to Harrow."

Holly nodded slowly. She liked the sound of the woodsman's plan. Like him, she didn't believe that her lost friends were still in the bog either. And it was so weird how Leno's parents had disappeared so many years ago with all the ties to Harrow – the parallels made her shiver. "Do you remember I told you how good I am at getting people to tell me things?"

"I do remember, Holly," Fyorn said. "Bobbin's a good talker too. With Grand Rejuvenation in full swing, the streets will be crowded with people excited to share gossip. By the looks of you two Pips, they'll know you're from the Tri-town area. If any rumors have been circulating about the search someone will strike up a conversation, guaranteed. News travels fast in Harrow, especially during a festival. And if you did happen to need a quick escape for any reason, it's easy to disappear into the crowd…"

"Why bring Gariff though?"

Fyorn stroked his chin and gazed back at Holly. His hazel eyes met hers. "Gariff is a damn handy person to have around," he said, finally. "I'd feel better knowing he was with you."

Holly looked down at the table, gripped a fistful of hair close to her scalp and tugged at it gently. She let out a sigh. "What am I going to tell Mr. and Mrs. Numbit? They just got their son back."

"Bobbin wants to help find his friends," Fyorn responded. "They'll understand that. I want to keep the plan between us though. It's safer that way. And I wouldn't tell the search party about this excursion either. I have ways to keep tabs on them, though, in case they turn up something useful for our own search. I'll also contact the mayor about sending diplomats to Harrow as soon as possible, but we can't hang our hats on Webfoot's expediency or Harrow's cooperation. We should leave by mid-morning the day after tomorrow – that should give Bobbin a chance to get plenty of rest and me enough time to make the necessary arrangements."

"So, we're going to Harrow," Holly stated.

Fyorn grinned. "We have to. The food's already on order. Besides, I know the perfect place to make camp. I'll send word for help to meet us there."

Fyorn reached into his belt pouch, pulled out a handful of coins and counted out one hundred griffs worth. He stacked them neatly on the table. "In the meantime, best to exchange these griffs for skulls – it'll attract less attention."

"Easy," Holly said. "We get Harrowians in here all the time."

The woodsman raised an eyebrow. "Really," he said. Then he reached for a bun, dipped it in his soup, and got started on his breakfast.

CHAPTER VII

Interlude – Best laid plans...

They were right to go to Harrow. But the reasons were all wrong.

Hurlorns are now forming a line in front of the Elderkin queensmen. They will be the first to clash against the giants. If anyone is watching, they will see that the forest is slowly expanding towards the lake. I should be with them.

No, my place is here. There is more yet to tell ... so much more ... and I have already done my part for the coming battle. On top of everything, someone must prepare for the unthinkable, the inevitable. Someone must keep the records straight.

Back to the search now: Over the next day, Fyorn devised a plan for Holly, Bobbin and Gariff – a safe plan, he felt, and one that could benefit all. He would guide them to Harrow and set them loose to gather valuable information, all under the watchful eyes of the Hurlorns.

Kith rangers are a resourceful lot and highly connected, but no plan is perfect...

CHAPTER VIII

The trapper's cabin

"So, tell me about this festival?" Holly had heard patrons talk about Grand Rejuvenation, but she never really understood what it was about.

Fyorn led the way along the forest path, refreshing blazes with his hand axe as he went. They'd taken a seldom-used route out of town: north-east through the upland hills before cutting across the plains beyond, to the edge of Deepweald. From there, the woodsman led them along a game trail. The trampled grass beneath their feet was still slick from the morning rain. He glanced back over his shoulder at Holly.

"The festival is many things," Fyorn replied. "Costumes, events, parades – a week of festivities to honor Karna, the Mother of Rejuvenation."

Gariff interjected, "My favorite part is the March of the Giants. They march all the way from the Western Tor to the docks and back."

"What kinds of costumes?" Holly asked.

"Giant costumes for one," Fyorn said. "Right Gariff?"

"Giants, bookworms, and half-dead corpses mostly," the Stout replied. He was behind Holly. "Sea monsters too."

Fyorn glanced back again. "By bookworms, you mean intellects and philosophers, don't you?"

Gariff grunted. "That's what I said, bookworms."

Fyorn added, "Those 'half-dead corpses' represent the original members of Akeda's Rejuvenation League – the First King and his top advisors."

Bobbin piped in, hiking beside Holly. "Who's Karna?" A second later, his foot caught on an exposed root and he nearly tripped.

"It would be easier if you could see the ground," Holly told him. She smirked, then proceeded to grab Bobbin's flabby waist. She gave the handful a teasing tug. Bobbin jerked away and pushed her hand gently.

"Karna," Fyorn repeated. "Yes, of course." This time when he glanced back, he too stumbled on a root. The woodsman braced his fall with the axe.

"What's your excuse?" Holly said. She reached to grab Fyorn's stomach. He deftly out-maneuvered her, and then grimaced.

"It's a dark day," he retorted. If the afternoon sun came out at all, it went unseen from beneath the dense crown cover of the mixed woods. Fyorn resumed his steady pace and talked on. "Karna, the Mother of Rejuvenation, is Harrow's version of the 'One Outside All Things' – who goes by many names: most notably the Orbweaver, along with some names I can't pronounce and others I don't know. Harrow's connection to 'the Mother' is through Karna's Vessel – what they believe is a physical embodiment of their deity. That belief is ... severely misguided."

"How do you know it's false?" Gariff said. "That's what

you mean, right, that it's a false belief." The Stout looked to
the woodsman for an answer.

Fyorn sighed and started over again. "This takes some
explaining," he said. "The First King's so-called Karna, the
Mother of Rejuvenation, is the reason we're all here."

"She's not my mother," Bobbin said.

"Are you 'Rejuvenation'?" Holly quipped. Gariff laughed,
at least.

The woodsman fumbled for the right words. "What I
mean is … we weren't supposed to be here. You all must've
heard the tale of the First King. Well, it's more than just some
legend. He led the First Men out of Karna's all-consuming,
destructive path, on a far journey that ended on the shores of
Fortune Bay long ago."

"Yes," Bobbin said, who proceeded to recite the meat of
the story. "The Orbweaver was consuming the Universe, and
by doing so gained more and more knowledge. She wanted to
know *everything*, but she could only know the nature of things
by eating them. So, she consumed nearly everything, but when
she arrived one day at the hall of the First King, he cheated the
Orbweaver out of her prize in a game of dice. He rigged the
game so that no matter what the roll, the Orbweaver could
devour everything *except* the First King and his followers,
and yet believe that she had actually eaten them a thousand
times over."

"In a sense," Fyorn said. He let out a soft chuckle. "That's
an interesting twist on it." The woodsman stopped for a
moment to clear the way, chopping at branches with his axe
where the trail had become overgrown.

Gariff added the next part. "Yep. But the Orbweaver eventually became aware of the ruse, and now relentlessly searches
for the First Men and their descendants to—"

Bobbin and Holly chimed in together, "… consume them all and claim that final grain of knowledge, hers at last."

The two Pips laughed. There were many variants of the story, but they all ended with that familiar phrase.

The woodsman chuckled once again, nodding his head in acknowledgement of a tale well told. "Very interesting … and highly symbolic, but it captures the essence nonetheless."

"So," Gariff clarified, "you're saying that Karna's Vessel is the Orbweaver's … err Karna's … representative on Theia?"

Fyorn nodded. "Everything we know about Karna suggests she is the *consumer* and *destroyer* of all material things. She bleeds knowledge and delivers death to humankind. She is a mechanical thing, a self-replicating doomsday construct – not something to be worshipped."

The woodsman paused, and then continued. "Karna's Vessel, on the other hand, is simply a leviathan with several traits eerily similar to Karna and who claims to be a direct conduit to her, but we have reason to believe such is not the case. In essence, not only is Karna false – Karna's Vessel is a false connection to a false deity."

"That doesn't make sense," Gariff said. "How could the First King get things so opposite? And how could she be the Mother of Rejuvenation if she destroys everything?"

Holly had an answer. "The circle of life," she said. "Death feeds new life. Life leads to death. It's everywhere in nature. Maybe after dying and being rejuvenated, the First King came to the conclusion that Karna – the Orbweaver, or whatever, would somehow renew all life and make it better."

Fyorn gazed at Holly, shaking his head. "No," the woodsman stated flatly. "He went mad." Fyorn swiped an overhanging branch aside, and then another. "Damn it," he said. "I missed the mark." He backtracked a ways and cursed when he couldn't find the trail. After walking in circles for a minute, he cut away a larger branch with his axe, and then followed up with a blaze on the same tree. "This way," he beckoned, with a sideways nod. "I haven't been on this trail for a dog's age."

The woodsman picked up the conversation where he'd left off. "But I believe you are right in your way of thinking," he went on. "The First King believed – believes – that his people were spared by Karna because they showed great promise at creating new knowledge, needed to solve the Final Puzzle. That is why Harrowians sacrifice their leading intellects to Karna's Vessel. They believe it feeds Karna's hunger and keeps her at bay, until the time comes for complete rejuvenation and unification – the day when all that can be known is known, and all is brought together as one to begin anew, in perfect balance."

"They sacrifice people?" Gariff asked.

"Don't worry," Bobbin said, "You heard him – only the smart ones." That won him a solid punch in the arm. Fyorn ignored the antics.

"Harrow holds the ceremony in a sacred cavern to close off the festival," Fyorn said.

Holly looked to the woodsman; her skepticism obvious. "The story of the First King is just a myth ... something grown-ups tell their kids as a fun scare."

Bobbin nodded. Gariff shook his head.

"Indeed," the woodsman admitted, "but all legends and myths come from somewhere, and some hold more truths than others."

Holly noted that he avoided mentioning how their current mission was all because they'd become entangled in part of another legend – the bog queens – that'd panned out. *I'm sure he knows,* she thought. *Maybe he doesn't want to bring it up just yet.*

After a steady climb up a long hill, the forest thinned. The sky began to clear as well, and whenever the clouds gave way rays of sunlight streamed through the overhanging branches. The game trail they were following ended at an old road overgrown with weeds, wildflowers, and small shrubs. Boulders lined the roadside, coated in lichens dominated by whites and rusty reds. Pine warblers sent their penetrating trills and slurred chirps through the treetops, and a raven couldn't help but to caw back. Pine scent was heavy in the air. After a quick drink from his waterskin, Fyorn resealed the container and pointed down the road, north-east.

"The cabin's just ahead," he said.

Twinkling sunlight on water flashed through the tall pines as they approached. A short, brisk walk later, the hikers broke through the tree line. Fresh winds whipped off the sparkling blue narrows of a small lake – their destination. The trail ended abruptly at a pebble beach that stretched to the mouth of a quiet brook. Nestled among tall pines sat the trapper's cabin.

It was a humble and submissive structure with a low roof, covered porch, and walls made of greyed over logs once kin to the surrounding trees. The windows were shuttered and the only door was barred shut. Firewood had been stacked in a neat pile under the porch.

"Last one in the water is bog bait!" Bobbin piped. The rollicking Pip dropped his pack and cloak, flung off his shoes and the remainder of his clothes. Off he dashed, leafless as they say, giggling and jiggling ridiculously in all directions as his little legs sped him towards the lake.

"He has no shame," Gariff said, shaking his head.

Holly cried after him, one hand shrouding her eyes. "That's not funny!"

Nonetheless, unable to resist the lure of the lake, Holly shrugged her shoulders and sprinted to the water after him, shedding clothes and gear behind her as she ran. At least she kept her underclothes on; conveniently adapted for water sports.

Holly glanced back as she ran, laughing. "Come on, Gariff." He respectfully declined.

She heard the Stout mutter to Fyorn, "Froglings."

Holly gained on Bobbin easily and the two frolicking Pips crossed over the beach laughing and screaming. Each claimed victory over the other when they finally hit the water, erupting into a frenzy of splashing and falling over themselves. Bobbin dove to deeper water and then popped his head out.

"Come on," he urged Holly. "It's warmer once you're all in."

Somewhat reluctant, she followed.

"Hey Bobbin," the woodsman hollered soon after, interrupting the Pips chatter. The two of them were half way out to the opposing shoreline, a ridge of folding rock. "Boat's upstream in the brush."

The young Numbit scrunched his brow.

"Boat," Fyorn repeated, then spelled it out letter by letter, "B-O-A-T. Fish'n hole too."

Bobbin's blank look froze onto his face.

"Specks," the woodsman added. "Hooks and line are in the cabin,"

"Oh." The bobbing Pip's eyes went wide at the suggestion. He pivoted his body in the water to face Holly. "Sorry," he told her, "but I have a job to do." With unseemly grace, Bobbin dipped underwater and propelled himself back towards the beach, like a pike on a minnow. The markings on his back and neck shone orange and red through the sunlit water.

Holly changed her position from treading water to a peaceful back float, gazing up at the clouds above. And as she drifted towards the shore with the waves, she heard Fyorn open the night's lodgings and rummage around for items to outfit Bobbin – a proper knife from a drawer of utensils, a clinking can for bait worms, and some odds and ends. Then he mentioned something about an old rowboat. Soon after, she heard the swish of a pile of cut branches being pushed aside, the plunk of the boat being rolled over, and finally the scrape of the hull as it was pulled into the water.

While Bobbin was gone fishing, Gariff built a fire in front of the porch and Fyorn tinkered away inside the cabin. Holly came to shore, explored the grounds briefly, and then took a seat on a stump to warm herself beside the leaping flames. By the time Bobbin rowed in with his catch, a moderate wind had blown up, sending flames reaching out of the firepit towards the porch steps.

"That boat has a leak," Bobbin shouted to the cabin as he dragged the contraption ashore.

"Really?" Fyorn called back, stepping out of the cabin and onto the porch. He raised an eyebrow to Gariff, tending to the fire. Gariff smirked.

Chest out and puffed, the proud Pip approached with three dangling trout on strings.

"Wow, Bobbin," Holly said, as innkeep's son held them up for her. All three fish were a good size, with the largest maybe a three-pounder. They spun slowly in the sunlight.

Bobbin grinned back. "I finally caught those sparkly fish."

Gariff rolled his eyes.

Holly immediately thought of Jory. A deep pang of sorrow hit her as she drudged up the memory of that conversation at the Handler's Post, but she said nothing of it. Gariff might have noticed, but Bobbin seemed oblivious. Rather than dwell on the feeling, she smiled at the round Numbit and offered up high praise for his accomplishment. Then she attested to his greatness in all things culinary. Bobbin promptly went to work boning and filleting the catch of the day, whistling and spouting lyrical nonsense as he did so.

Even Gariff had to admit that the meal Bobbin concocted was the best fish fry ever.

Later that evening, as the firelight dimmed to the glow of burning embers, fueled by a skin of wine Bobbin had thought to bring, Fyorn spun a night-shimmering web of war stories. Strand after strand of tall tales he wove: Narrow escapes, lucky shots, lucky misses, good and bad instincts, and superstitions. Those who didn't make it, but should have. Those who made it, but shouldn't have.

When he was done, Holly called him on the sum of it all. "These stories," she began, "are not believable. I enjoyed them greatly – don't get me wrong – but you'll have to come up with something better than that."

Fyorn stared at the burning embers of Gariff's fire for a long moment, a thousand miles away. He shifted his gaze to her, grimly.

"Death was ever present. Life a gift or a curse, depending." Fyorn paused, and then looked to each in turn.

"Those I fought beside who survived only did so by outside chances – a day too sick to fight, a moment's privacy to relieve oneself, a well-timed stumble to dodge the arrow that kills the man beside them, or a blow to the head that knocks one out of a losing battle. It was that bad."

He grimaced slightly, shaking his head. "And so many of them – the Outlanders – so many of them were exactly like us – not beasts like you might've heard told. They could've been us. They could've passed as Elderkin or Fort Abandoners. All lost. We won the war, but we all lost. We were disciplined. They were learning. We stopped them in time – just in time – before they gained too much."

Holly, for once, curbed her curiosity at that juncture. *It's the wine talking,* she thought. Fyorn soon became drowsy and they decided to call it a night. Tomorrow, with a clear mind, the woodsman – as Kith ranger – would assign tasks. Tomorrow, they would begin a real mission. A mission to Harrow. Butterflies formed in Holly's stomach as she pondered the excitement of the day to come, just before she drifted off to sleep.

*

The next morning, Holly woke to clinking and clanking. She set her eyes on Bobbin stirring a pot on the woodstove. A smile crept across her face as her eyes widened. She tilted her head up from the pack that pillowed her head.

"Bobbin … is that for me?" she said in a playful tone, rolling her blanket around her body like a personal cocoon.

"But of course, who else? You're the one I'm trying to impress." Bobbin gestured to the bundled-up lump of Stout flesh on the bunk across from hers. "That oaf doesn't deserve any." Fyorn was nowhere to be seen.

Holly laughed. "Fine by me. And I expect service with a smile, if you're hoping for a gratuity."

"What sort of gratuity did you have in mind, fair lady?" Bobbin said, winking.

"My secret," Holly replied, eyes smiling.

Holly's delighted state and Bobbin's banter soon stirred a grumpy Gariff. He rubbed his eyes and aimed to sample Bobbin's cooking as well. Bobbin had made the time to gather slate tablets from a rocky outcrop not far from the cabin, which he rinsed in the stream and warmed on the woodstove. They served well as platters. Before long, Fyorn returned and all enjoyed fair portions, together with a swig of leftover wine and a roll of thin bread that Bobbin had packed. Sweetened sausage, taken from the Flipside stores, made for a flavorful main course.

After breakfast, Fyorn revealed his plan. Simply put, Fyorn and Holly would search the outlying areas while Gariff and Bobbin would make their way to Harrow to gather information. This would allow the woodsman to finish his search lines twice as fast, he explained, while leveraging Gariff's knowledge of the layout of Harrow and Bobbin's fast-talk, not to mention the Pip's perfect memory. Regarding the fast talk, Fyorn likened it to the natural rhythm of speech for many of the mariner-types he'd encounter at the festival. Anyway, if Bobbin came up empty or if some nugget of information needed refinement, then later on he'd send Holly in with Gariff to tease out additional details in a more targeted way.

Holly readily agreed to Fyorn's plan, her mind swirling with all the Elderkin legends she'd read about. She wondered what other stories the woodsman must have locked up in his brain. With all the extra time alone with him, she could probe him for details on just about anything.

Fyorn turned to address the young Numbit. "Bobbin—" The Pip nodded at the sound of his name. "You and Gariff are going to take the old loggers' road north and then cut west to the edge of town when you see Dim Lake."

"Okay," Bobbin said.

"I need you to find out what you can about talk on the street. Stimulate conversations with the locals, starting at the docks. Stick to the markets, the wharf, the restaurants – public areas."

Bobbin nodded. "I can do that."

"Find out what people are saying about the recent disappearances, the attacks near Turnsby, and general sentiments about the leadership in Harrow. Be sure to swing by the tower as well – I need to know the security posture of the guards there. Report anything unusual or that might be important."

Bobbin nodded again. He was easy going and a skilled conversationalist. Fyorn's assignment was perfect for him.

"I'll report everything to you when I get back," Bobbin said.

Fyorn grinned. "Better yet, I'll send Janhurl – a 'listener' to shadow your movements. You won't even know she's there. Just whisper the message while outdoors, and she'll pass it on to me. I don't have time to explain. With luck, she'll meet you on the road in. She's expecting you. Don't be afraid."

Fyorn turned to the Stout. "Gariff, like I said, I need you to accompany Bobbin. Don't say much, just keep watch and be there for him. Be the eyes on the back of his head. Keep him out of trouble."

Gariff grimaced. "Easy. But … are you sure you want Bobbin to do all the talking?" He passed the young Pip a sidelong glance.

Fyorn flinched slightly, gathering his brow. "Why not?"

Gariff huffed. Rather than answer Fyorn, he grumbled something to Bobbin about "no double talk" and proceeded to gather what they'd need for the trip. Once their gear had been collected and packed away tight, Bobbin said his goodbyes with big, long hugs. Gariff held back a moment longer. He appeared somewhat drained, disheartened.

"Good luck," said the woodsman. He put his hand on

Gariff's shoulder. "We'll find your cousin, one way or another, and your best friend too."

With a solemn nod, the burly Stout shook the woodsman's hand. Then he gave Holly an awkward goodbye hug. Eyes down-looking, he backed up a few steps before turning around to follow Bobbin.

Later that morning, Fyorn set out with Holly to search the edge of the forest on the off chance Nud and Kabor had entered Deepweald at night and become lost. The woodsman taught Holly how to distance-pace and direction-find, and what signs to look for. The two kept about a hundred feet apart and walked traverses bearing north-south for the better part of the day, calling out as they went. Late in the afternoon, they stopped by the lake for a quick drink and a bite to eat. Holly kept a lively conversation going the whole time.

By evening, while still searching for signs and calling out names, a breeze had blown up. It was mild at first, but quickly grew strong and gusty. Hidden in the rush of the wind and the rustling of leaves was a *whisper*, according to Fyorn, quiet but clear to the woodsman's trained ear. The message came from Bobbin, compliments of Janhurl, of course. Fyorn repeated the words aloud for Holly's benefit.

"Mineral rights: Harrow has the right to exercise mineral claims in the bog and provide any security deemed necessary to protect the claim area – a technicality. It's in the treaty."

"That's from Bobbin?" Holly said.

Fyorn nodded.

"What does it mean?"

The woodsman shrugged. "I'm not sure. But it was important enough to whisper." He contemplated his thoughts for a long moment. "Could be related to a loophole in the Non-aggression Treaty."

"What about Leno and Kabor?" Holly said, her frustration building. "Isn't she supposed to send us information about Leno and Kabor? Who cares about a stupid treaty?"

"No, nothing yet," Fyorn said. "The Hurlorns have their ways about them."

"Hurlorns?"

Fyorn delicately explained to her that Janhurl, for all intents and purposes, was a creature of the forest. Holly wondered a great many things, as can be expected, including where exactly Janhurl, Bobbin and Gariff had gotten too.

CHAPTER IX

Dromeron Odoon

The leviathan's long, drawn out syllables still reverberated in Nud's mind. The White Whale had brought up three critically important matters in the twilit cavern, and a fourth implied. For starters, there's a settlement nearby. Second, on a string of chances, Kabor could be there. And, third, it might be possible to control the light of the bog stone. The creature's casual and indirect reference to the settlement implied *people* currently inhabited that site, to which Nud now had a mental map and compass. He could only imagine what they must look like – pale, hairless albinos perhaps, with large, bulbous eyes and skittish demeanors, scrambling bat-like out of holes to peer at strangers, or retreating into shadows cast by imported light.

The leviathan had been especially vague about the settlement and its inhabitants, yet quite specific about the location. Nud paced his steps accordingly, mentally following every instruction to line and letter – another advantage of

Pip memory. He never thought to question how the leviathan knew the cavern paths so well, being a marine mammal.

Kabor's last known position had been crucial to the leviathan's careful reasoning. "Chimneying up a narrow shaft" was the way Nud had put it. More so, he'd described how the shaft dropped down from the bog into a network of tunnels that lay *above* the Hanging City. The dark waters around the leviathan had churned in response to those words. In addition, the Pip had depicted Kabor as a hardy Stout, about Nud's own size and age, with experience in mines and a knack for spelunking. By the glint in his many eyes, the great beast had seemed most interested in those traits, but none so much as the last bit of news Nud'd offered, the part he'd kept in reserve. The last bit changed everything, according to the leviathan. The beast nearly rolled over when Nud explained that Kabor was half-blind.

The leviathan had taken over from there, pointing out just where such an individual might've ended up on a string of chance events: given that he survived the cave-in; given that he didn't reach the surface; given that he wasn't trapped; given that he'd followed all of the obvious signs and that he knew where to search for fresh water; and so on, and so forth. On those assumptions, the oversized lore master had reasoned that Kabor would've made his way to Dromeron Odoon, if anywhere. "He should be there by now, or soon, Huum haa," was how he put it, "… if all went well, as it should."

"As it should" had been comforting to hear – words to cling to, if not to fully believe.

Of course, the leviathan's assumptions hadn't gone unchallenged. The great beast grumbled unintelligibly and rolled to and fro in the water when obligated to explain itself. From the waves it'd made, Nud surmised the leviathan was not fond of being questioned, or didn't like to bother with explanations, or didn't take kindly to the urgency of being put on the spot. The Pip didn't ask so many questions or press for details after that, fearing what might become of him if he raised the ire of the beast, weighing several tons.

Once settled again, the White Whale had gathered its composure. "HUUM haa ... all roads in Everdark lead to Dromeron Odoon, eventually," he'd boomed, "and if anyone found your friend, or if he had followed any one of the many paths available, he would have ended up either there or here. Do you see him here? – No. Neither do I. Since he is not and never was here – for I would know if he were ever here – he can only be there, in transit, or nowhere accessible to you without further aid."

The Pip used *Sliver* to steady himself over yet another debris pile as he hiked on towards his destination. And while he balanced himself on the loose rocks, he wondered how a conversation between the leviathan, with his slow and careful ways, and Bobbin, with his fast and looping double-talk, might've gone. He laughed in spite of himself.

Nud's newfound knowledge of the terrain made travel through the dark zone relatively smooth. The fledgling diplomat had become less the prisoner and more the explorer. And he now held onto a new hope that his endless hours of fumbling through the dark and navigating by quick flashes soon would be over. It wasn't that he expected torches to suddenly spring out of the walls or that daylight holes would illuminate the way. No, it was the bog stone. Something was about to change, he was sure, something important. And it was the leviathan who'd tipped Nud off about how to bring about that change.

After describing the strange behavior of the stone at the

dancing pool, the leviathan suspected a connection between something Nud did and how the stone reacted. The Pip knew it had to be true, based on all the strange things that'd happened since finding the gem in the bog.

"Huum haa," the leviathan had said, thoughtfully. "The bare facts suggest you experienced the following sequence: thirst-hope-fulfillment-brightness. Try recreating that experience." The whale's glossy skin had shimmered in the grey-green light, as its bulk swayed gently in the water. "If you have to, go back to the pool and step through every motion again."

Nud shook his head to himself at the suggestion: a return to the pool was unthinkable. So, he spent the first leg of the journey pondering the circumstances that brought about the stone's bright and steady glow: how thirsty he'd been when he arrived at the pool, how much he'd hoped the water was drinkable, and how relieved he'd been to experience that hope coming true.

So, in his mind, Nud put himself back in that very same situation and imagined stepping through the very same actions. He concentrated long and hard. At first, he lacked focus: the emotions and sensations that he'd felt back at the pool were all over the place, evasive. Remembering simply wasn't enough. The events had to be *re-experienced*, like a recall.

That is what Nud tried next. Three times he recalled the events, and three times he analyzed each and every step of the process that led to illumination. Eventually, Nud discovered the secret combination, the key to unlocking the stone. And to his utter amazement, the bog stone flared up steady and bright to his command. After a moment's burn, it even went white, untainted: the true colors of the underground finally revealed.

At first, the light didn't last. Control dwindled as his

mind meandered to other thoughts. The essential ingredient to sustainment, he found, was to routinely revisit the thought sequence while otherwise engaged – a threading, if you will, of the mind's tasks, weaving them in and out of focus so that they could proceed together, without cancellation and without one dominating the other. If Nud could keep that up, the light would shine forth. When he lapsed, so too did the light.

The solution wasn't perfect – long and stubborn blackouts persisted afterwards. Thinking back to the original experience, he focused on good memories to bring back the light. Nud fondly recalled happy events with friends and family, and moments of glory. But darker thoughts always pushed their way in and interrupted the flow: When he called to mind Holly, her face melded into that of a bog queen. When he thought of his pals, a grisly image of pole-mounted bodies flashed in his mind, drifting at the bottom of the bog. Even Fyorn was not immune – he shifted into a rabid wolverine. When the distractions got out of hand, Nud's focus destabilized and collapsed. Worse, the degenerate thoughts turned in on themselves at times, causing the stone to go cold and dark. If that happened, it might take the better part of an hour to coax light from the stone and be on his way. Nud soon learned how to use distractions to reset his mood and remedy the situation.

Over the course of the hike, control of the stone's glow became automatic as the Pip devoted one small part of his mind to keeping the necessary thought-train active, freeing up the remainder to pursue other tasks. And he continued to toy with the light as he hiked beneath the Hanging City. Through subtle variations in emotion-stirring thoughts he modulated the flicker, changed the color, and even focused the light to a beam. With his newfound mastery of illumination, he explored from a distance the ancient city above him.

Why does a stone care about how I feel? he wondered. And not only to invoke light – Nud recounted how the watery motion in the dancing pool had been triggered by a deep and troubling despair. Surely, the leviathan had the answers, but not Nud.

*

The Pip had kept close to the left-hand side of the cavern wall as instructed, measuring step-by-step over a thousand paces from the Dim Sea entrance. Over the next hundred, the air slowly turned heavy and sulphurous, with a sharp, metallic tang that settled behind the tongue. It reminded Nud of that dry and biting odor on the wind that blew in from the smelters of the Bearded Hills every so often, teasing out metal from raw ore and puffing out the waste smoke.

Farther along, Nud began to suspect that, somehow, he'd missed his turn. The Pip had already traveled nearly double the distance estimated by the leviathan. He went over in his mind the exact phrasing: "On your left," the White Whale had boomed, "you will come upon a firelit haze and roads all leading into a large cave with much activity about it. You must bear towards the fires of Dromeron Odoon at that juncture, and ask those you come upon about your friend – news *flies* between the inhabitants there. *Flies.*" Nud scratched his head. *What did he mean by 'flies'?* The Pip titled his gaze up, but saw nothing special in the cavern heights.

After rounding a long bend, sheer and jagged bluffs rose up to either side and the ground began to slope downwards. Cracks and small caves gashed and gutted the bluffs, and only rock splits permitted passage between the freestanding fragments. In the distance, the path descended into a deep, open gorge. On the edge of that deeper darkness, a smeary red haze came into view, illuminated by a strange and uncertain light. Nud did a double take when he witnessed a dark shape fly out of that haze to disappear into the darkness. A small stream of the shadowy forms followed, zooming out together only to scatter erratically. Again, the shapes disappeared into the dark heights of the cavern, like a cloud of bats vacating their ancestral cave.

Nud took a deep breath and continued down the slope. The far-off clinking of metal on metal rang through the air, and a horn blasted out. But there was something else; something closer. The Pip pricked his ears to the faint sound.

Insect-like clicks and chirrs filtered into earshot, with varying tones, slow and rapid tempos, rising and falling volumes, and streams of varied and complex patterns. Some excerpts sounded like tapping; others mimicked the trill of a blackbird, the drone of a harvest fly, or the chirp of a cricket. The echoes played off the sheer terrain.

Nud couldn't be sure what type of animal was making the noise. *I need a better view,* he decided, so he scaled a rocky hill to its summit, pulled the leather cord up over his head and raised the bog stone. In his mind, he repeated the light-giving pattern to evoke the stone's brilliance: *thirst-hope-fulfillment-light.* But this time, his hope and fulfillment were heightened beyond compare by the prospect of being rescued at long last and reuniting with everyone he missed. The light flared up brighter than ever, a star in the palm of Nud's hand for all to behold. He gasped at the sheer intensity.

Nud caught a glimpse of the cave dwellers – a small group of them, making their way between the craggy hills and heaps of rocky debris that littered the cavern floor. They were *people*

– not animals. A rush of elation surged through his body. Head dizzy with delight, he called out.

"Hello there," he hollered, waving his arms frantically, "Over here." His cries went without acknowledgement, and the cave dwellers continued on their way. Nud slid down the rock face and hastened towards the group, winding his way between the rocky mounds until he came to an open area where the view was unobstructed. And there they were, on the other side of the clearing, about fifteen strong. At over a hundred feet away, Nud could make out that they were small and stocky – like shorter versions of Stouts – with rounded, hunched over shoulders, and dressed in drab clothing.

"Hello," Nud called again. Finally, they halted. "The light!" he said. "Look to the light!" A flurry of clicks, ticks and chirps erupted from the group. Heads turned this way and that way, before homing in on the Pip's position.

"Yes, that's it," Nud said. "I'm right here." He casually strode towards the cave dwellers, wondering how he might try to communicate. As the Pip closed in, he saw they were medium-grey in color, not albino like the ones he'd imagined. They were filthy too, with matted hair and covered in grime – not unlike Stout miners after a productive shift.

A particularly attentive member of the group carried some kind of contraption over one shoulder. He turned to face Nud directly. Even from a distance, Nud could see that there was something different about his eyes, but not like Kabor – they were … missing. The figure tilted his head side to side as if scanning the area around Nud. All the while, he let out a steady stream of sharp clicks. Then he turned to his companions and clicked some more, causing an uproar. They screeched angrily, shifted in place, nudged and pushed.

Nud felt a quiver in his stomach. Unsure, he slowed his

pace. "I'm lost," he called to them, voice wavering slightly. "Can you help me find my way?"

Without warning, two of the underground dwellers bolted in the opposite direction. Nud halted, raising his palms. "No, wait." A quick chase followed; one was caught and bludgeoned with a sickening thud, while a whip lashed out to take the other down.

Nud struggled to understand. *This doesn't look right.* He put the stone back around his neck.

Others joined in on the beating, swinging their short clubs at the runners.

No, not good at all.

Nud winced in disgust and backed away, slowly. Senses heightened, he watched curiously as the cave dweller with the contraption quickly erected a tripod. Another one nearby unslung a heavy tube device from their shoulders, and mounted it on top.

Whatever it is, it swivels, Nud thought. The device zeroed in on the Pip's position. The hairs on the back of Nud's neck stood on end. He immediately sheathed the stone, for cover of darkness.

A moment later came a metallic cranking sound, followed by a soft thwunk.

Nud's chest exploded in pain as a projectile smashed into his ribs, knocking him to the ground. He gasped for air; the wind knocked out of him. The stone flashed – unfurled by the hit. At his side lay the projectile … a long shaft with a heavy, pear-shaped ball on the end.

Thwunk! In came another, with a high arc. Netting ballooned out before it struck. Nud suddenly became entangled in some kind of ropey mesh. The more he fought against it to get up, the more tied down he got.

A cave dweller broke away from the main group and hobbled Nud's way, ticking in a regular beat. More followed.

Regaining his breath, Nud tore at the mesh covering him. He yanked where it hooked his clothes and tore free. The Pip sprung to his feet and shed the mesh. He grabbed his spear and scrabbled up the nearest hill. His pursuers – four strong – fanned out as they approached. Their chirrs and clicks grew louder and faster with every step; the sounds had a cold and calculated feel to them.

The light went dark.

Don't lose it now, Nud told himself, and redoubled his focus. He brought it to a flicker again. In abrupt flashes, he glimpsed the weapons they held: a whip for the lead, who was also the biggest, and leathery clubs for the others that flexed as their bearers swung their arms. And those eyes…

They're all the same.

Thwunk.

The next shot from the tripod device fell short. Nud set *Sliver* down beside him, then readied his bow. He took careful aim at the tripod operator who was in the midst of loading another round. Nud aimed low, waited for the next flash, and then released. The arrow plunged into the operator's leg. He fell to his side and rolled, chirruping in pain. Without delay, another took his place.

The assault team reached the hill. Nud fired another low shot as they began their climb, and took one down. Hands trembling, the Pip dropped his bow and picked up *Sliver*.

I can't fight them all, he decided, *but maybe I can outrun them.* Nud crouched, ready to dart. The crank grinded.

Thwunk.

Nud lunged to avoid the shot. Something smashed beside

him, like broken glass. A waft of foul air assailed his senses. He felt dizzy.

Nud stumbled, off-balance. Rocks slid as the dwarfish cave dwellers scrambled towards the summit.

Without warning, in that staggering moment, a giant bat with the wingspan of a rooftop dropped out of the black heights. Nud's heart seized in his chest. Like a blur, the cave creature flew straight at him. Worse, the Pip was seeing double.

As the dark form swooped in, Nud dropped hard to the ground. His attackers cringed, burying their heads in their arms. A rush of air blew past. Nud's heart raced as the shadowy thing arced up and away, melding into the darkness above. *That's not a bat.* He gulped air. *Shroud's Well. That's a damn huge cloaker.*

After shaking a fist at the monstrous cloaker, one of the attackers bounded up the slope, brandishing his club. He came at Nud swinging and clicking like mad. His angry face was deformed and terrifying. Nud jerked away and twisted to avoid the blows, blocking with his arm. He took a solid hit by what felt like a sand bag aiming for his head.

Adrenaline jolted through Nud's system. He sprang to his feet. Bracing with his legs and with *Sliver* in hand, the Pip grunted as he jabbed back – solid contact, but not penetrating. The force of the hit sent the muscled assailant stumbling backwards. He slammed into another coming up the slope.

Nud tried to scramble to his feet. Weak and light-headed, he collapsed as the world began to swirl. He lay there helpless, alone, and seconds away from being pounced on by a troupe of mad dwarves and a monstrous flying beast bent on suffocating its prey. If the cloaker were to spit fire at him, he wouldn't have been surprised.

Nud heard the flap of giant wings again. He felt a great push of air.

Desperate, he pointed *Sliver* straight up, with a mind to impale the beast as it descended upon him. At the last possible instant, the swooping cloaker abruptly changed course. Instead, it sailed over the heads of Nud's attackers. The mad dwarves cowered as the beast made its next approach and hovered over them, beating its massive wings. In a flurry of trilling protests, they backed away.

Then the oddest thing happened – the face sucking cloaker called the Pip by name, as it veered towards him. "Leno!" said the voice in the air. "It *is* you!" Nud heard the crank again.

Thwunk.

A balled spear zinged past the cloaker and over the hill.

Nud could hardly believe his ears. The beast's great flaps ballooned as they caught air and the creature floated to a landing. The wings fluttered on contact with the ground, and then conformed to it.

Again, the voice called out. "Get on, 'frog legs!' It's me!"

Nud could barely move or see. "Kabor?"

Thwunk – another miss.

"Leno, hurry!"

Barely lucid, Nud dragged himself closer. He gazed up at the blurry face of the rider, staring at Nud sideways. *It really is Kabor.* And there was another at his side – one of *them*, with grey skin and bat-like ears. Something else was odd about his face, but before Nud could take a closer look, Kabor's sturdy hand gripped the Pip's arm just under the shoulder. His mad dwarf companion grabbed Nud's other arm the same way. Together they hoisted the Pip up and hauled him onto the back of the cloaker beast.

"Hold tight," Kabor said, "especially on the spins." The

Stout's companion, who seemed to be in control of the creature, chirred in agreement.

"Spins?" Nud nodded and promptly clutched the straps of the flat-backed saddle.

"Wrap your feet in too," Kabor advised, glancing back.

Thwunk.

It was a net this time and it struck the cloaker, partially fouling one wing. Kabor's companion quickly unhooked it and tossed the net aside.

The giant cloaker's wings raised and beat fiercely as the beast lifted off. And as they gained height, the pilot directed his mount away, bearing towards the hazy lights of Dromeron Odoon. To a chorus of shaking fists, stomping feet, thrown stones and throttled curses below them, the three riders glided like magic carpet riders. They sped off into the chamber heights.

Nud felt the wind on his face and through his hair as they rode the air currents, as though in a dream. The cloaker swooped and turned sharply as it cut through billowing smoke. In the ambient light of the cave mouth leading to Dromeron Odoon, Nud caught glimpses of the fires within, but little more. Speeding on by, their mount effortlessly wove a course between the dangling structures of the Hanging City. At one point, the cloaker twisted along like a corkscrew before rolling into a steep dive.

Nud's stomach felt like something quite separate from the rest of him, with its own distinct inertia and resistance to every turn. Still weak, he redoubled his white-knuckled grip and kept his eyes shut for the most part. For a stretch, he heaved uncontrollably.

A few long minutes later, the beast righted itself and coasted to a steady glide. The motion felt a little like being on a boat ride along a fast river. When Nud's dizziness partially cleared, he brightened the light for a brief stint and watched as the ruins raced by. Some time after, the pilot gave the giant cloaker a few coaxing churrs and sharp tugs. In response, the beast spun into a shallow dive, righted itself again, and then floated to the cave floor on a cushion of air. Nud could smell water and hear it too as they neared the landing zone. His ears popped.

When the cloaker finally came to rest, it crouched low and hugged the stone floor. To Nud, the whole world was spinning. He let go his grip and rolled down a giant flap until he thudded on the ground.

Everything went black as he slipped out of consciousness.

CHAPTER X

The way

Nud awoke to the hollow sounds of Kabor up and about, busily minding his gear and muttering to himself. The Stout couldn't have had much to fuss over, only what he'd stuffed into his pockets that day at the Flipside. Still, every item counted in the dark zone.

Nud rubbed his eyes then opened them. A stream of blurry flashes lit up the cavern. He patted his chest and found that the bog stone was still in its place. Kabor must've unsheathed it while Nud was sleeping. When the Pip lifted his head, the world seemed to be on a slow spin around him. The giant cloaker was gone. That was fine by him.

Nud's voice came out weak and raspy. "Kabor?" he called.

The Stout was crouched near the river, washing something, perhaps. He turned to face Nud. "Good morning," he replied, "or 'Good evening,' or maybe 'Good afternoon.'"

Nud grimaced, half-heartedly. "I suppose you didn't make it out then, like we planned. Unless this is part of your grand rescue."

Kabor grunted. "Consider yourself rescued."

"At least we're both all right," Nud said.

"Yep." The Stout pushed himself to his feet, still messing with something in his hands ... his glasses, all bent out of shape. A long moment of silence passed as Kabor adjusted the metal frame and then tried them on. They sat crooked on his face. He looked the Pip up and down.

Nud wondered how he must've appeared to Kabor: dirty, thin, ragged and bruised, like he'd been through hell, and with a load of wood for a pillow. Not to mention the makeshift spear at his side. *Damn...* Nud quickly looked about. *My bow.* He'd left it behind, on the hilltop. The Pip bashed the back of his skull against his pack three times in penance.

"What's wrong?" Kabor asked.

"Never mind," Nud replied.

Kabor paused, then spoke earnestly. "I never thought I'd see you again. Figured you got caught up in that cave-in. I tried digging ..." He trailed off.

"How did you find this place?" Nud said.

The Stout smiled, and that's when Nud saw that Kabor was no better off. His face was cut and scraped, his hair matted and his cloak torn and soiled. He stood with his hands in his pockets, ragged and battered.

"Slid and flew here," Kabor said, a touch of pride in his voice. "How about you?"

"Kabor, where am I?" Nud asked.

The Stout winced. "You know about as much as I do, Leno. But we're getting out soon."

"Where's the pilot and the ...?" Nud trailed off. "Were you in Dromeron Odoon?"

"Dromodoon? Where the heck is that?" The Stout pointed

behind him with his thumb. "You must mean that despicable trash heap, thataway."

The constant flashing of the stone made Nud's head hurt and his eyes sore, so the Pip steadied its glow. Kabor jerked his head back and did a double take on the pendant.

"How did you fix the light?"

"I didn't *fix* it," Nud explained, "I just sort of figured out how it works."

Kabor met Nud's gaze. "How does it work?"

"I mean, I just figured out how to control it," Nud corrected.

Kabor just stared at the Pip. "How do you control it?"

"Mostly, I just think of being thirsty."

"What?" Kabor looked confused. "Can I try?"

"I don't know…"

"I'll give it back, I promise."

"Sure you will."

"Leno … that was different, back there. I'm just glad you got it back."

Nud hesitated for a long moment, grimaced, and then handed Kabor the stone.

Try as he might, the light continued to flicker on and off for Kabor in the usual way. His eyes widened when one flash went slightly longer the rest, but then it died – nothing out of the ordinary. The Stout shook his head. "I thought I felt something, but … I don't know … It's hard to be thirsty when you're standing beside a river." With a pinched expression, Kabor tried again. Absolutely nothing. He huffed, then slapped the bog stone back in Nud's hand. "Stupid thing."

"I guess it just doesn't work for you," Nud said, replacing the gem to its setting around his neck.

Nud never told Kabor that at one point, he nearly had it

– the stone had initiated a steady light. Amazing, really. And so soon. But Nud crushed the emerging glimmer with a single dark thought. One thing was for certain: the Stout's lackluster performance put the possession issue to rest once and for all. The stone was Nud's and Nud's alone.

The Pip rephrased his unanswered question from earlier: "What about Dromeron Odoon?"

Kabor grimaced. "Leno, they're not civil folks that live down here in the dark. Not most of them, anyway. I found one, yes, but most are very different. Their society is based on degrees of slavery. We can't go there."

"But Dromeron Odoon is the way out," Nud said.

Kabor removed his glasses and put them away. He looked at Nud sideways. "What makes you say that? No, Leno. We have to go this way." He gestured upstream. "Find the source."

"But the White Whale said—"

"White Whale? I don't think your head is right, Leno. And if that's the place you were heading to, Dromodoon or whatever, then you're nuts for trying. They enslave anything that walks on two legs or hops on one. They even sell 'em to the highest bidder. I know because I saw my fill of what happens down here and talked enough about it with … the pilot, as you say."

"Did you go there?" Nud asked.

"No," he replied, "but I saw some and I heard all I need to hear about it."

Nud was in no condition to argue. Plus, the encounter and his brief glimpse of the underground city supported everything Kabor was saying. *Then why would the leviathan send me there?* Nud still felt light-headed and so put off delving into that thought. The question lingered in the back of his mind though.

The light began to flicker again. Nud planted himself on a large rock. Kabor sat next to him.

"So, what happened to you?" he asked.

"Okay," Nud began. "Well, first I was chased down a tunnel by smaller versions of the beast that brought us here – cloakers, I call them. One was following us the whole way before … and it tried to smother me – that's what we saw near the pool, remember?"

Kabor nodded. "Stone ghosts."

"What?"

"I've heard old miner's tales about them. They call them 'stone ghosts.'"

"Well I call them 'cloakers,'" Nud said.

The Pip continued the story of what'd happened to him, but omitted any specific details about his encounter with the leviathan. When Nud was done, Kabor started his own story in a hushed tone. There was a waver in his voice.

"When the shaft caved in under me," he began, "I lost my footing and slid down with it for a ways. The light-stone just popped out of my mouth while I was scrambling to stay above it all."

He drew in a breath and puffed it out slowly. "Anyhow, I dug my heels in. The walls started falling apart above me too and it got real slurpy. I had to move my arms like this." The Stout waved his arms horizontally. "Like the butterfly – that time you showed me how to tread water, except tighter."

Nud nodded, eager to hear more.

"Well, the sloppy earth rose right up to my shoulders before it stopped filling in. Once it settled, I had to push myself up just a little farther, but it was pitch black. I tried digging to find the crystal and get back to you, but it was no use – too much earth and clay blocked the way."

"Then what?" Nud said.

"I couldn't go down, so I tried to go up, but I didn't get far – dead end. I didn't know what to do, so I started feeling the walls. I felt a really soft spot and started to push and dig. It was soaked through and gave way real easy." Kabor held his hands up and showed them to the Pip.

Nud winced at the sight them. The tips of his fingers were red and raw, and his nails worn and broken. The Pip showed his own hands. "I dug like crazy to find you."

They shared a chuckle, then Nud said, "So, you *dug* your way all the way here with your bare hands?"

"Not quite," Kabor said. "More like I poked my way into a parallel shaft, except it didn't lead to the same cave system. It took forever to make an opening big enough to get my whole body through, but eventually I forced my way in, pushing and clawing at the earth until it all gave way."

"Then what did you do?"

Kabor took a moment to compose himself. He sucked back a few deep breaths.

"Anyhow," he continued, "I pretty much crept, wriggled and slid after that, right down into this cave system. It's a rabbit warren up there – little tunnels leading every which way. When I heard rushing water, I headed for it. But I didn't stay long – had to keep moving. Had to get out. I felt like something was watching me the whole time though. It's odd when you think about it. What can watch you in complete darkness?"

Kabor paused, waiting for some acknowledgement that Nud was following his story.

Nud nodded to him, and neglected to mention how many animals can track in the dark by scent or sound. "What happened to you is a lot like what happened to me," he replied.

"I basically fell down a hole and landed in a stream, then followed it."

"My biggest problem was that I couldn't see anything," Kabor said. "I tried hitting two rocks together to make them spark so I could light up some cloth, but that didn't work. Just made lots of noise and attracted attention. I called your name, a lot, but …" His voice began to falter. "I thought maybe you got buried alive when the shaft collapsed."

"The slop piled in, but didn't fill the cave," Nud said.

"Anyhow," Kabor continued, "I started hearing noises in the dark. It scared the heck out of me at first. I followed the river and stumbled upon an odd sort of fellow banging away at rocks with his pick. I couldn't see him in the dark, but right from the start I could tell he was … different. He seemed decent enough though. Spoke with a Dim Lake accent, but with lots of weird beeps in between words. He knew what torches were, but didn't see the need for them apart from setting fires for cooking and metalwork and such. I couldn't see him at all until we passed near that fiery Odoon place. He didn't look right – all deformed, and his eyes were … I don't know. He was so grimy it was hard to tell."

Kabor turned away and peered into the vast darkness. He took a deep breath, and then continued with his story. "Anyway, this fellow gave me the run-down of the place and all the crazy things happening down here in the dark. It's like a separate little universe. I was so happy to be talking to someone. Said he was a 'slave driver.' Saved my life, no doubt."

The Stout laughed to himself. "I thought he meant he was in charge of slaves. You know, with a whip and all that, but after talkin' and ridin' with him, I find out he's a driver that happens to be a slave – he drives other slaves from place to place on his stone ghost – 'cloaker' as you say – and gets 'em to their work sites. Does some prospecting on the sly too, hoping to one day buy his freedom. There are whole flocks of them flying carpets in these caves, and lots of drivers – pilots – working for their freedom. Sometimes though, the cloakers *eat* their riders – dangerous business."

"You could have maybe mentioned that when you picked me up," Nud said.

"What choice did you have?" he retorted. Kabor paused, glancing upwards to the ceiling of darkness before tilting his gaze back to Nud.

"Anyhow," he went on, "I told him about you and he said I should try some place he called 'clickity clackity something-or-other,' but he said I couldn't go alone because of the slavers, so he was nice enough to bring me there and … I'd already given up hope."

Nud mouthed the word "Yep" and nodded. *Me too, for a while.*

"You see," Kabor continued, "like I said, that one's a slave too. I told 'Clickety-clack' – the pilot – to come out with me to the Hills, but he says they need him down here. Not his masters, mind you, but the other slaves he helps out. For some reason he gets lots of freedom and privileges compared to some, and that includes piloting."

"Unbelievable. You were lucky to find Clickety-clack when you did," Nud said.

"Anyhow, then I couldn't believe my eyes when I saw the bright light and the flickering … I guess it was the right thing to do because here you are and we're getting out now. By the way, that Clickity-clack told me about a way out, sort of. I'd never have found it alone in the dark though. But with your light, it should be easy enough to sort out."

"What was his real name?" Nud asked.

"The slave driver?" Kabor thought for a long moment. "Clack-click jitter-jit snap something-or-other pop," he said with a smirk, "… really. But he could speak our tongue as good as any Scarsander, except like I said he kept clickity-clacking between words, which was distracting at first, but I got used to it."

There was a long pause.

"Wow. Crazy," Nud said. "You're right. We'll get out together."

Nud could smell the vomit on his shirt. He glanced to the water. "I'm gonna rinse off," he told Kabor, and stood up slowly. He made his way to the river and cupped a small sip. The water had a metallic taste to it, but at least it wasn't salty.

"This water isn't clean," Nud said, as he took off his shirt and started rinsing it.

"Yeah – no good for drinking unless you'd die other-wise," Kabor said. "It's slurry: polluted runoff from a mine. That's what made me wonder if miners were down here. There might be arsenic and all kinds of chemicals and minerals in that water."

"Yuck!" Nud spat. "Thanks for the tip." With his toes in the water, small blind fish gathered around his feet, chasing the little bits of debris that Nud had stirred up from the bottom. They went so far as to nibble at his skin and toenails. The brave little fish were different from the ones in the Dim Sea, smaller and thinner for starters. They had no idea what Nud was – just random potential food to them, Nud imagined. He turned his gaze to Kabor.

"Did your gloomy friend say where this river leads?"

Kabor shook his head. "He just said 'falls.' There was never time enough to get into the nitty-gritty details. But I'd bet Gariff's hat that it leads to a mine."

Nud smirked at the thought of ending up at a familiar waterfall, but he knew by what Kabor was saying that they couldn't be anywhere near the bog. The closest "real" falls lay north, spilling out of Dim Lake.

Putting their worries behind them, with renewed hope the pair headed upstream. Nud brightened the light to its maximum intensity just once, stopped, and turned to take one final look back at the way they'd journeyed. It all seemed surreal to him.

CHAPTER XI

Spears of the gods

Giant, empty eye sockets kept watch over the great cavern. Below them ran a smooth torrent of swift water, out through a gaping maw.

"The jaws of gloom," Nud said, more to himself than to Kabor. The Stout stood beside him. Indeed, the thought of entering this new cave gave him the shivers.

"What is it?" Kabor said.

"Leviathan – it can only be a leviathan," Nud replied.

"They're just myths." Kabor gave the ornamental edging a sideways look. "That thing can't be real."

"No. I saw one," Nud countered. "I even spoke with it – the leviathan knew everything about everything, and it sent me to Dromeron Odoon to find you."

Kabor grunted. "Well, I wasn't there, was I?"

Nud let out a heavy sigh, and the two lost teens clambered up the bluff and over the edge of the plateau that bore the massive skull. Kabor knocked on it with his knuckles when he got close enough, and then made a "humph" sound.

The skull must have been the size of the entire Flipside Inn – larger even than the White Whale's massive head. The river they'd been following cut straight through its jaws, peaceful yet strong.

"C'mon Leno. A leviathan?" Kabor said. "You're not talking about the White Whale again, are you?"

"I think it *was* the White Whale – same as in the story."

Kabor tilted his head and paused. "Have you ever heard of a mirage?"

Nud firmed up his tone. "I know what a mirage is. It wasn't a mirage. Mirages don't talk."

"They do if you've gone batty."

"I'm not … I didn't … it was real."

"Stop blubbering and bring your light over." Kabor already had his glasses on, squinting as he examined the inner wall of the jaw closely. He ran his fingers along its edge.

"Humph," he said again, and then pointed to a smooth, wet section of the riverbank. "See that surface? That there is solid limestone – the stuff of the very first cave."

It looked like normal rock to Nud. "So? I couldn't care less if it were diamonds. I just want out … does it mean this is the way out?"

"Maybe."

Next, the Stout ran his entire hand along the inside wall. "This is the same stuff. The skull was brought here to mark the cave entrance, and the local stone shaped to make it fit perfectly."

Nud examined a section of the jaw carefully – where the transition was. There was definitely a subtle difference in shade and grain where, presumably, bone met stone.

Deeper inside the chamber, the natural cave narrowed and the flow of water turned violent. Bones littered the splattered shore: bear, deer and ox. Nud gazed at the rushing water, shrouded in mist.

The river had carved a passable tunnel through the rock. Beyond the bone chamber, smooth furrows, like rolls in a carpet, ran lengthwise along the ceiling. Roaring water noise from the tunnel suggested rapids might be upstream and out of sight.

"Only one path forward," Nud said. "I wouldn't call them falls though, like what Clickety-clack told you."

"Where else?" Kabor replied. "This must be what he meant." The Stout led the way.

Nud adjusted the straps of his pack and followed. Kabor glanced back over his shoulder. "Have you ever wondered what you'd do down here if your light went out?"

Nud hesitated. "Follow the watercourse upstream, like we're doing, I guess. The stone goes completely dark sometimes, but I've always managed to spark it up again."

"Like a fire?" Kabor asked, carefully choosing a sure-footed path.

Nud raised the light to help the Stout see what lay ahead better. "Sort of like fire, I guess," he replied. "Sparked by … imagination, fueled by…" Nud wasn't sure what to say.

"But a fire needs new wood when it burns low," Kabor added. "What would you throw into this flame if it went low? A new thought?" He chuckled, turned one palm face up where Nud could see it, and raised it.

"I don't know," Nud said, upping the brightness and sharpening the beam. "I'd certainly try something like that, I guess …" Nud stowed the idea away in the back of his mind, for later contemplation.

The farther in they got, the heavier the mist. In what seemed the opposite thing to do, Nud had to dim the light to see better. Otherwise, there was too much scatter. And as they pushed forward, the shape of the cave began to change: narrowing in, yet still tall. The current became stronger, and the rush of it grew louder in the confined space. Kabor raised his voice.

"We need to figure out a back-up light source, just in case." The Stout wiped droplets of mist away from his eyes. "And while we can still see."

Nud nodded, but without a single idea to offer.

The tunnel pinched in, the ledge-shoreline disappeared, and they were forced to wade in the icy water. The ceiling dropped as well, and the current ran swift and deep. Bracing themselves against the tunnel wall, they pushed forward until they came upon a veritable wall of water, splashing everywhere and all the way up to the ceiling. The skin on Nud's shoulder erupted in discomfort. Kabor saw him scratching.

"That's probably the slurry," he said, and smirked. "Frogs don't like it."

"Ha ha, very funny." Nud swept his gaze over what lay ahead. "Falls for sure. This might be our exit, but how are we going to get through that mess?"

The two of them stood there, scratching their heads and staring at the turbulent waters.

"I don't know about this," Kabor said, shaking his head.

More hungry than defeated, Nud hoisted himself up on a small ledge to get out of the central current. He fetched the last of the Dim Sea albino fish out of his backpack and split it with the Stout, who'd pulled himself up on the opposite side.

"We can try the Dim Sea cave," Nud offered, chewing. "There's food there, at least, and natural light. You might even be able to climb to the ceiling, to a daylight hole – you're a better climber than me. You proved that much when you stole that flag."

Kabor responded with a grim smile as he continued to stare at the water. Then he cocked his head and went still. A long moment passed.

"You're a better swimmer," he told Nud, without looking at him, "so maybe you can get us through this." He pointed to a spot in the torrent ahead.

"Look," he said, "Over there. The water sounds funny. Do you see anything."

Nud stared ahead into the mist and the swirling water. "It's just a wall of whitewater at that spot," he said, finally. "And some of the mist kinda swirls upwards." Nud paused. "You know, it doesn't really look like enough volume is falling for the flow I'm feeling."

"Exactly," Kabor said. "And I'm picking up a hollow sound from behind the falls. I bet that two streams collide there, a stronger current straight along the tunnel and another from above. Still, how could we ever scale the falls to see what's up there?"

"Wait, I have an idea." Nud thought back to the dancing pool when he'd controlled the water. But he didn't really understand how that worked. *I have to relive the experience,* he told himself, *just like I do to control the light.* Nud closed his eyes and slipped into recall.

"Leno, are you okay?" Kabor said, concern in his voice.

Nud ignored the Stout. In his mind, he brought himself back to the pool, to the watery motion ... to the trigger. *Yes. There it is.* He felt a jolt of emotion – the same feelings he had when tracing circles in the water. A heavy feeling surged through his body as waves of negative feelings pummeled him. Nud's ears pounded with the sensation. Good thoughts struggled to surface, but turned in on themselves to become twisted, dark thoughts. In the turbulence of the moment, Nud traced a circle in the air in front of him.

"Leno, what are you doing?" came Kabor's voice again. It sounded hollow and far away, as though in a tunnel.

Nud jolted once more, then opened his eyes wide. Ahead of him, the mist had begun to spin. The Pip held on to the feelings, the despair. He traced faster circles. Water swirled as heavier droplets joined in, rotating faster and faster. So fast, a gap punched through the middle of the falls. A hole. Nud felt a breeze rush through it. He broke his concentration.

The Pip took a deep breath as the heavy feelings washed away with the recall. After a long moment, he regarded his companion. "You're right," Nud said. "There's a pocket of air behind the falls."

Kabor just sat there, his mouth slowly opening and closing. His eyes were wide, still staring at the falls. "How did you do that?"

Nud shrugged. He didn't know how to even begin explaining himself. "I'll tell you later," he said. "Let's check out what's behind those falls." Nud slipped into the water.

Kabor grimaced slightly about not getting his answer, then followed.

"Wait here," Nud told him. "I can hold my breath for a long time." Arms braced against the tunnel walls, and with Kabor's hand steadying his back, Nud breathed deep and then ducked his head under. He pushed his way through the column of water.

On the other side, Nud surfaced into an air pocket, as expected. He wiped the water from his eyes and looked about. Kabor was right, there were two streams: one continuing along the tunnel and one dropping from the ceiling. His skin felt even more itchy than it had before. Tilting his gaze up, he saw a natural shaft. Water ran down one side of it, separating him from Kabor. The other side was open to air and appeared to be climbable. Nud ducked underwater, grabbed Kabor's hand and yanked him through to the other side.

"Look," Nud told him when he broke surface. The Pip created a narrow beam of light and directed it up the shaft.

Kabor rubbed his eyes and peered up. "How far does it go?"

"Maybe ten feet."

Kabor pushed at Nud. "Out of the way."

Nud stood firm. "No way. The last time you did this, it nearly killed us both."

Kabor scoffed. "This one's easy, and its solid rock the whole way."

Nud shook his head. "I'm going first this time."

Kabor glared back.

"… for luck," Nud added.

An awkward pause passed between them, until Kabor sighed. Then he offered Nud a hoist. Before stepping into the Stout's finger-locked hands, Nud reached behind his back to jam *Sliver* into his pack, tip first. Then he quickly untied the leather strap holding the stone and wrapped it around his forehead like a headband. Kabor boosted him up.

Once inside the shaft, the many rock ledges made for an easy ascent. Nud braced himself and then pulled the Stout up beneath him. As they scaled the shaft, it widened, and as they neared the top, Kabor climbed more beside Nud than below him. At the highpoint, a rim of stacked rocks lined the opening. One side had partially collapsed and the water poured through. Nud muscled himself up and out on the dry side, to a sitting position. Situated in the midst of a sparkling pool of water, Nud looked around him, the chamber glimmered and lit up like diamonds when the stone flashed.

"Whoa," Kabor said, as he felt out the final grip holds he needed to pull himself up.

The stone's luminescence found new and vigorous life in the glittering cave, dancing and playing on the moving water and complex cave surfaces of the wall and ceiling. Long, jutting crystals crisscrossed and collided in every direction, and the light seemed to converge at their tips, flashing like pinpoint stars.

Kabor pushed himself up through the hole and sat beside Nud on the stack. Squinty-eyed, he scanned the chamber. To one side, a thick column of glistening water gushed from the ceiling and into the pool. It crashed onto a pile of melded crystals that shot out like icicles, frozen in time. The walls sparkled and sent rainbows of refracted light scattering all around.

"Holly should see this place!" Nud said.

"Yeah, this is amazing," Kabor said. "We'll never see anything like it again in our entire lives, guaranteed."

"Too bad, she'd really love it," Nud said.

Kabor grimaced. "Holly doesn't need something this elaborate."

"What do you mean?" Nud said.

"A borrowed carriage and a picnic in a nice spot on a nice day would do the trick. It's easier and she'd appreciate the attention and convenience. She just needs enough romance to gab to her friends about – nothing so fanciful as an underground cave that you have to tread through miles of tunnels and slurry to get to."

"How the heck would you know?"

"She as much as told me to do it."

"She didn't."

"She did."

"All girls like crystals," Nud grumbled. He closed his eyes and generated a blinding flash.

"Ahh!" Kabor cried.

When Nud opened his eyes again, Kabor was rubbing his. "What was that for?"

"Oops," Nud said, apologetically. "It got away from me."

"C'mon Leno, you did that on purpose!"

Nud ignored the accusation and brought the light to a mid-range brightness. The steady illumination revealed more details and he let his eyes casually soak in the sights. Wide ochre veins stained the walls in sideways bands, while pure white crystals descended vertically from the ceiling, hanging like thin, squared-off icicles.

"A cave of giant spears," Nud said.

Kabor stood up on the rim of stacked rocks. He reached out and ran his hand along the length of an inclined crystal, the size of a young tree.

"Spears of the gods," he corrected.

There was more beauty and wonder to behold in that chamber than could be appreciated at once, like stepping suddenly into a room holding all the world's most fantastic art, but all crowded together and covering every square inch of wall space, ceiling and floor; one blocking the other. Kabor cupped a palmful of water to his mouth and slurped it down. He grinned.

"This water is good," he said. "The slurry must have come from the main river, below us."

At his urging, Nud drank deeply. The water felt cool and soft as it trickled down his throat. He felt it drain all the way down to his stomach.

Nud slid off the stack and waded through the pool to dry

ground. Feeling soggy and muscles nearly spent from all the climbing and fighting against strong currents, he shrugged off his water-soaked pack, set his spear on a lean against the cave wall, and found a comfortable place to sit. Water pooled at his feet as he waited for Kabor to join him. Nud took to playing with the flicker and the brightness of his bog stone. He stepped through the color spectrum with eyes darting about the chamber, admiring the light show and the unusual geometry of the crystals. Kabor made sideways stares this way and that way, hypnotized by the patterns of sparkle and refraction being cast about.

On a more practical note, there were no notable exits other than the one they'd arrived through plus the hole in the ceiling with water pouring out, which was impassable without rope or a ladder. After some time searching and poking around for alternatives, Kabor noticed some buried scraps of cloth and unearthed the complete skeleton of a smallish person. The body looked all twisted out of shape, with boney fingers still clutching a rusty pick – an old one but a good one, according to Kabor. Poor soul probably thought he'd found the "mother lode" as Mer would say. Then WHAM! That was it for him.

Kabor pointed to a long, broken crystal that pierced the skeleton's rib cage.

"Spiked by a giant spear," he said.

"The gods here had it in for him." Nud paused. A moment of solemn silence passed between them.

Using the heavy miner's pick, and after a good chunk of the ceiling crashed down not ten feet away from all the loud tapping and banging, they dug themselves out the same way the miner had come in. All the while, they stuffed their pockets and the pack with choice crystals.

While Kabor picked away at the last of the blockage,

careful not to tap too loud and set off another collapse, Nud grabbed his backpack and his spear. He stood behind the Stout, ready and anxious to get out.

"Move it," Nud said, finally, pushing him aside. Kabor got out of the way and the Pip scuttled through, guided by the light of the stone. He came to an opening on the other side, partially blocked. "What's this?" He pushed the debris out ahead of him.

Kabor followed on the Pip's heels. "You tell me."

Nud forced his way through, scraping his knees over the loose rocks. He crawled out and stood up, slightly hunched in a low tunnel. The stale, smothering air caught the Pip off guard. He coughed. Thick beams supported the sides and girded the roof – some broken or bowed, others shifted out of place.

The Stout poked his head out of the crawlspace. He scanned the rough rock-and-dirt walls of the passage both ways, then sniffed. Kabor grinned widely. "It's a mine all right."

A wave of relief poured over Nud. "We're on the home stretch now."

No doubt, the passage they'd entered was darker and gloomier than any other mine Kabor'd been in. Not one torch or lantern lit the way. But a mine has a clear way in and, more importantly, a clear way out.

The Stout chose their direction and they started along it, single file and along the middle of the tunnel where there was less debris and the ceiling was highest. Their footsteps echoed ahead of them.

Before getting far, they heard a clicking sound…

CHAPTER XII

The eyeless Glooms and Isotopia

The strange noises began to fill the passageway. Nud had heard them once before.

The Pip's body tensed. He backed away.

Kabor, a step behind, pressed his hand firmly to Nud's spine, stopping him. "Wait," he urged. "Maybe they can help."

"No way," Nud said, responding in hushed tones. He wriggled sideways to free himself from Kabor's hand. "Not after what happened near Dromeron Odoon."

The stream of sharp clicks grew louder. The noise mingled with the patter of soft footfalls. They were getting closer. Nud's breaths caught in his chest as he raised his spear and stiffened his stance.

"Relax," Kabor pleaded, whispering back. "They're probably just a bunch of miners. You know, slaves … nothing like the mad dwarves that you met up with."

Nud cast him a sideways glance. "Who do you think keeps them in line?" Then he fixed his gaze straight ahead.

Kabor blinked at the suggestion and provided his best counterpoint. "Probably a few guards at the surface and a dozen or so patrolling the whole mine. I don't know what they're going on about, but all the chatter sounds a little lively for security."

Nud paused and tuned his ears to the noises. He breathed a little easier at what he heard – there did seem to be a kind of excitement or thrill in the rise and fall of the staccato exchanges, as though engaging in banter.

"I guess you're right," he conceded, continuing to whisper. "Still … let's just wait."

The pair held steady as the twisted and deformed shapes slowly came into view, hobbling in from the edge of darkness. They held steady and they waited for the nightmarish and malformed faces to take note of the displaced above-worlders. But they didn't, at first. At first, they just continued towards the teens, preoccupied with their conversational chirps and beeps to one another. The creatures stood vaguely Stout-like, nearly a dozen in all and covered in grime, males and females nearly indistinguishable. They carried picks, shovels, and hammers; and they dressed in long, drab robes that nearly matched their greyish skin. Most lacked footwear, but some wore crude leather sandals.

Remembering the others hadn't reacted to light, Nud brightened the stone and focused on their eyes.

But there weren't any – just like the others. He gasped.

All of the other normal features of a face were present – nose, mouth, ears and hair, but wholly unkempt and lacking in basic symmetry. But the place where eyes should be was grown over.

Suddenly, the cave dwellers stopped. A chorus of clicks and trills erupted in the tunnel. Nud's heart pounded. A sudden impulse shot through him.

"YAW! STAY BACK," he shouted, brandishing the spear.

Kabor huffed loudly. "Leno! Put that thing down!" He stepped beside Nud and reached for *Sliver*, but the Pip shouldered him out of reach.

The group chirred in heightened tones, pointing their fingers and waving their arms, clicking and clacking in rapid bursts. The crooked creatures shook their tools at the intruders, until one trilled so loud Nud's eardrums nearly burst. Then, for a long moment, there was silence.

The same individual advanced a few cautious steps. Hairy, bat-like ears angled this way and that way as her misshapen head tilted left and right.

Nud feigned a short thrust of his spear. "Kabor," he said, nudging the Stout with his elbow, "we should go now."

The cave dweller halted.

Nud thrust again. "They look angry at us. We can still make it back to the crawlspace and escape down the shaft."

Kabor wouldn't budge, nor did he protest. Nud edged back towards the opening, then yanked at the Stout to follow. Kabor stumbled back with him.

The creatures of the gloom followed in step. When Nud reached the opening, the chatter amongst the group rose alarmingly. They shook their heads and waved their hands frantically. Some lowered their picks and hammers.

"Leno, they don't want us to go," Kabor cried.

The Pip stopped, undecided. He felt trapped.

Kabor's tone turned calm and focused. "Leno, take a look at what they're carrying – work tools. These are the slave sorts, like Clickity-clack. They're not out to get us and they're unarmed. Really, there's nothing to worry about."

The Stout had a point. Their sheer ugliness couldn't be considered a weapon in-and-of-itself, nor could the unfamiliar sounds they used to communicate. Even Nud got the sense these miners were trying to protect them from entering a danger zone.

As the above-worlders stood firm, the "slaves" studied them with quizzical looks, incessantly chittering louder and louder until the triller swung her head around to face her brethren. She let out a second ear-piercing blast. The others hushed. All faced Nud and Kabor, clicking softly, expectant.

The Pip sighed heavily, then lowered his spear point. *Kabor's right,* he thought. *They're not after us, not like the slavers near Dromeron Odoon.*

Kabor spoke softly, "Do you think they're waiting for us to tell them something? Like maybe what to do – after all, they're trained slaves."

Nud snorted. "That's just stupid."

The miners stood and waited, shuffling in their places, each one badly hunched and warped in limb. Loose, wrinkled skin marked where eyelids, lashes, and eyeballs should've been, grown over with dullish grey flesh. Bristly hair grew over the vacant eye patches. Indeed, they were the epitome of utter gloom, and pitiful to behold. But they were not monsters. They were people.

"Put the spear on the ground," Kabor said.

Nud hesitated. "This better work," he gruffed, and laid it down in front of him. He stepped back from it.

The gesture seemed to excite the gloomy onlookers, who went on to wave Nud and Kabor down to adopt a more hunched stance, like them. "Eye to eye" so to speak.

"See," Kabor said. "They don't want a fight." The Stout put on his spectacles.

The loud triller of the lot spoke in a husky voice. She used common syllables.

"I-so-top-i-a?" she said, amidst a flurry of clicks and ticks.

"I-so-top-i-a?" repeated another, sprinkled with the same sounds.

Others joined in, each repeating the same word again and again, louder and louder to be heard above the others. They crowded in closer, hands groping at them.

Nud and Kabor raised their palms to stay them. Neither tried to answer, or even knew how to answer.

"Give them something," Kabor said.

To divert their attention and perhaps gain their favor, Nud slowly reached into his pack. He brought out a sturdy piece of deepwood, then looked to Kabor.

Kabor nodded. Nud regarded the miners and addressed them.

"I am Nud and this is Kabor." He stretched his arm out to the loud triller. "Please accept this small token of friendship, from both of us."

The group went quiet again. Clearly, despite lacking eyes, they could track his movements. While clicking sharply, the triller reached out and ran her fingers along the wood, grasped it, and then pulled it back. She tested its sturdiness against her thigh, and then nodded her head in approval. Nud gave out two more pieces and added a handful of cave crystals for them to split. Her companions accepted, exchanging excited clicks as the offerings changed hands from one to another.

"Can you lead us out?" Nud said to the triller. "We live above the ground ... outside ... under the sky, the sun, and the moon."

"And clouds," Kabor said. "And rain and stars."

"And comets," Nud added.

"Comets? <click>" said a cave dweller.

Some of the others chirped inquisitively. One of them, with an oddly-spotted head, seemed to have acquired some measure of understanding. "Nud," he uttered, and then clicked. Ever so cautiously, he advanced towards Nud and took him by the wrist. Another, smaller than the rest and attentive, called Kabor by name and grasped his arm the same way. They gently tugged at the pair to follow.

With Nud and Kabor in tow, the miners started off back they way they'd come. One scooped up *Sliver* and carried it along, while another relieved Kabor of the pick he'd found. They moved together as a group with the two surface dwellers in the middle. These "Glooms" – as Nud and Kabor began to call them – were friendly.

*

The Glooms had much to discuss among themselves, but not so much with Nud and Kabor. All attempts to make small talk came up short. And as the miners shepherded the pair of surface dwellers through the dark maze of cramped mine workings, clicking and chirring between them, Kabor and Nud spoke openly about their escorts.

"They click to talk and they click to see, don't they?" Nud said.

"That might be it – something like bats," Kabor replied. "But I don't know if we can hear all the sounds they make. Just look at those ears."

Nud shifted his gaze to the nearest Gloom and stared at his pointed, active ears, angling about in the flickering light. "That's sort of like turning sounds into pictures, isn't it?"

Kabor winced slightly. "Maybe they can blend words and pictures when they talk, by imitating the reflected sounds."

"I don't know how that would work, really," Nud said. "I would think they converse normally and sense the layout by the way the conversation echoes – kind of a background processing thing. Besides, just because I hear a sound, it doesn't mean I can imitate it perfectly to tell you about it. So, when they 'hear' the image of some object, they still might not be able to convey exactly what they 'heard.'"

The Stout grunted. "I didn't say it was perfect."

Kabor's idea got Nud thinking though. "I wonder if they get mixed up. Like if their words bounce off things and get twisted into pictures in their minds, muddling up the conversation."

"Or," Kabor quipped, "if sometimes one can't 'see' because the other won't shut up." They shared a chuckle.

A Gloom miner passed the two of them a disapproving look. Already, Nud had learned to read the mouth and brow for signs of emotion, as opposed to the eyes. Not quite sure what they might've done wrong, both Kabor and Nud hunched a bit more and trudged alongside the miners in silence for a long while, soaking in the lulling drone of their chatter and curiously eyeing the rough rock and dirt walls.

Nud noticed an iron ring jutting out, pitted with age. He steadied the light and illuminated the object, then swung his gaze to Kabor. "What's that ring on the wall for?"

"To support a torch, that's all." The Stout pointed to a scattering of smashed glass and twisted metal on the floor, amidst loose stones. "Or to hook in a lantern. Good eye. It means somebody needed light down here at one time."

Kabor looked about the passage and gestured to more of the same. "These are very old workings," he went on. "Those sconces are from the Hills, but no one makes them like that anymore. I can't think of any mine that would be quite like this one. I think we're deep, really deep, and that we've strayed north."

"What makes you think we're so deep?"

"The rock," he replied. "I've only ever seen anything like it once."

Kabor went on to describe the geology of the Bearded Hills, and precisely how the rock they were walking through might fit in. Nud didn't quite understand what he was saying – the jargon was all foreign to him. He got the impression that the layer of rock they were in somehow intruded into a layer Kabor had seen on the deepest level of a Stout mine he once worked in, and that the angle of intrusion told him something about the bearing. So, by the Stout's reckoning, they were down and north of that part of the mine – towards Harrow.

As Kabor talked, the Glooms led them on through many low and dark passages, with puddles and wet walls that glistened in the light and piles of rocky debris at every turn. At one point, they were forced to crawl past a rubbled section of the mine – a partial cave in. After that, the tunnels widened slightly. Kabor mentioned that, although they'd gone up and down regularly, it seemed to him there was more up than down lately, and overall, they must be getting closer to the surface.

For the first time since their flight from the bog queens, Nud really felt like every step was getting him one step closer to home. He found himself wondering what Paplov was doing back in Webfoot, and how his friends had faired against the hags. He daydreamed about reuniting with them all: Gariff, Bobbin and Holly at the Flipside, along with Pops, the innkeeper and his wife, laughing and cheering as Nud and Kabor unexpectedly barged in through the great room door. And then Paplov in his workshop, looking up and smiling when he saw Nud, relief washing over his face. All these things he could picture vividly in his mind.

Eventually, they came to a dead end. Not quite a dead end, as it turned out, but they were forced to squeeze through a small, vertical crevice in the rock. On the other side, they entered a wider and taller section of the mine. Metal on stone clanged in the distance, and faint clicking noises echoed through the tunnels – more Gloom miners, surely, busy at work. They hadn't heard any activity or seen any other workers up until that point.

Nud felt a pang in his stomach in anticipation of fresh air and the warm light of day, or perhaps a crisp, starry night lit by a half moon. Either way was fine with him.

Kabor, too, had a noticeable spring in his step.

The dream was nice while it lasted.

As they were about to round a corner, their escorts suddenly froze in their tracks, silent. Those ahead dropped what they were carrying, fell to their knees and bowed down. The rest quickly followed, tugging at Nud and Kabor to do the same.

Nud's mind raced through the possibilities. He didn't know what to do. As he stood there deciding, the small, attentive Gloom that had taken Kabor's hand frantically waved at the Pip and the Stout to get behind him, against the wall. Nud made a split-second decision and hustled in that direction, picking up the discarded *Sliver* along the way. He passed the Gloom, shrank flat against the wall, and sheathed his bog stone. Kabor crept in close beside him.

CHAPTER XIII

Never forget, never forgive

Torchlight filtered from around the bend in the old workings; a host to dark phantoms in the shadows cast. The walkers were silent.

A dark, hooded figure was the first to appear, his thin frame crimped like a tall man bent over. Clawed, spindly fingers jutted out from the wide-sleeved robe he wore. One hand gripped a long shaft, capped with a curved blade that gleamed in the firelight. Nud recognized the looming apparition from his dream.

The figure swept his gaze over the prone and vulnerable Glooms. His eloquent voice soaked the air with venomous pleasantries. "Now this is just lucky," he said, "as I am famished." He sneered to his companions, still mere shadows on the wall to Nud's eyes. "How long since we last feasted?" Their murky heads turned to one another as words hissed between them in an unfamiliar tongue.

After a long moment, the tall, bent figure beckoned one forth – a torchbearer, who set his torch on the nearest sconce, and then lit another to hold. Three others glided past him as they entered into view. An icy presence chilled the hallway.

The four new walkers reveled in the implications of their leader's words. Glooms whimpered and squirmed.

"Too long," the torchbearer replied, his voice hoarse. "Our servants have been overly obedient of late … until now."

The leader – clearly the sort of slave master Nud had speculated about earlier – responded with a slow nod. "Too long indeed." He raised his voice to address the Glooms. "Is that what you think, Gropers? I, for one, believe it is true – you have taken your obedience too strongly to heart."

The dark figure glanced to his companions, as grim and dreary as he. "And my own congregation – you have also served so very well of late, like true masters of vengeance. Where does the balance lie?" He pondered the notion for a long moment, until the answer came to him.

"Gentlemen and lady, you must show restraint nonetheless."

Relief-laden chitter spread among the Glooms, while in tandem a subtle but sick anticipation began to grow among the ghastly crew.

Slowly, the torchbearer raised a single, dagger-length claw. He looked to the slave master for approval.

"Oh, very well then," his superior responded, addressing them all. "Each may take ONE for their pleasure and sustenance. But leave the tag-alongs for me." He swung his cold stare to Kabor for a long moment. Then, as the hood turned towards Nud, the Pip looked away. "Yes, little ones … I have noticed you there." He spoke with a gentle sleekness. "You cannot meld into the wall."

"Who are they?" hissed one of the four – a female's voice. Her frame was indistinguishable from the rest and her face was shrouded.

"So sweeet," wheezed another.

One Gloom – the smallest of them – responded with a flurry of clicks. He frantically waved a stick of deepwood above his head.

The torchbearer narrowed his eyes at the piece. "Curious. This one is trying to tell us something." He shifted his gaze to the leader. "He's being … helpful. Yes, very helpful indeed." He addressed the slave next. "These items were found on the Outlanders, weren't they, Groper? … I'll bet they stole them."

But we're not Outlanders, Nud felt like saying. Of course, he said nothing. He said nothing, kept his head down and avoided the robed figures' gazes. He didn't know what else to do.

The Gloom responded with more clicks and chirrs, accompanied with nods of his head.

The leader nodded slowly. "Yes … they might know something important."

His grim crew then proved themselves truly evil and merciless, for what happened next was that and more – undeniably despicable. It started when the torchbearer set his blazing stick on a second sconce, to free his hands. Then, the slave master addressed the Glooms, his viperous voice smooth and penetrating.

"Slaves! Mongrels! Take heed! Those among you to be spared shall bring these *prisoners* to Taeglin at once, or suffer the fate of those who are not spared. You must take ALL of the items along with them – I have made note of that rusty old pick, the makeshift spear, and the stolen crystals bulging out of the Outlanders' pack. Let him know of your insolence as well. Any disobedience will mean a feast – ten of your brothers and sisters to every one of you that crosses me!"

Nud glimpsed a vile grin creep across the speaker's face, smug as a snake in the confines of that cowled hood.

"In return for your obedient service," the leader continued, "we promise to take no more of you than we absolutely need … this day."

Nud's gaze darted over his eyeless companions. *Why don't they run? Scatter?* he wondered. But the Pip knew in his heart that the cowering Glooms were not only too terrified to move, but too slow on their feet as well – the shadowy beasts would gain on them and take as many as they desired. And although it sounded like Kabor and Nud would be spared, the young diplomat didn't wholly trust the slave master's intentions.

The four grim figures nodded in agreement with their leader before sizing up their prey. As they deliberated in foreign words, the hairs on the back of Nud's neck stood straight on end. And when they started pointing with those long, clawed fingers, an icy feeling swelled in his chest. His pounding heart sent the chill through his veins to every part of his body. The Pip averted his eyes so that he'd catch only side views, but he could still feel the probing gaze of one walker in particular, measuring out his portions and visually gorging on his flesh. It made Nud's skin crawl. Slowly, the figure swayed left and right in a rhythmic, fluid motion. The body swayed, but the head remained fixed, as though floating above it. Just as the others began to close in on their chosen game, that one took a cautious step towards Nud, muttering with a gentle rasp.

"Sweeet," said the shadowy form, nearly under its breath.

The slave master responded in a calm but firm tone. "Not that one."

"So sweeet," repeated the aggressor, "so tenn-der, so sweeet."

The dark figure stole another step forward. Kabor glanced over to Nud, jaw hanging and eyes screaming pity. But the grim master would not stand to be disrespected. He raised his black metal blade in warning and screeched.

"NOT THAT ONE!" The slave master's voice was murder, torture and defilement all in consonance. The cowering Glooms shrunk into small, quivering mounds.

The shadowy, insubordinate figure backed off, but his torturous desires could not be quelled. He immediately turned to glare at another would-be victim – the closest Gloom to where Nud happened to be crouched. The one that had grasped Kabor's hand and led him along.

"I am glad you found these wretches," the leader said to the Gloom that had waved the stick of deepwood. "But you should not have come so deep. There is no active mining from whence you came … I know where you have been, you fools."

His last words hung thick in the air. Nud couldn't be certain whether the slave master was irked or banefully glad, or what it might mean either way for the fate of their new companions. This vile thing seemed to revel in dangling kindness over the thralls' heads, while at the same time keeping terror close at hand, never further than a dark whim away.

"Now I will spare you, and I mean you only, due to your tremendous good fortune and good sense in bringing the Outlanders to us. But, unfortunately, someone must pay … no … many must pay dearly for the larger insult."

Please don't harm them, Nud begged to the gods, old and new. But this was not a negotiation. An urge to stand welled up inside, but then came the counter voice. *What good would come of it – drawing attention to myself?*

The urge to act rose again. *Surely, the bog stone… it must …*

But then Nud thought back to the incident with the bog queens. *I'd just get more of us killed.* The Pip wished he could fade into the wall or sink through the floor. *Why am I here? Why are we all here?* He felt out a crevice and did sink into the wall, it seemed … just a little. But he found no comfort there.

The slave master's voice lashed out once again, loud, smooth and commanding. "NO ONE IS TO COME DOWN TO THIS LEVEL. IS THAT CLEAR? Take that message to your sneaking brethren that call themselves prospectors!"

Meanwhile, the shadowy figure that'd chosen Nud played a sick mind game. He abandoned the Gloom closest to him and pointed to one quivering miner after another, glancing to the Pip for approval as he pondered each selection. The Pip didn't move or even flinch. In no way could Nud bear responsibility for the insinuated authority put upon him. But each round, the cruel man – if it could be called a man – shook its head, as though Nud had responded "no." In the end, the thing shrugged its shoulders and settled upon the original choice – the Gloom nearest.

That fiend would be the first to bear down upon a Gloom.

A simple touch was all it took to subdue his prey. Even then, he continued to fix his gaze upon Nud. The Pip squeezed his eyes shut, fearing the inevitable, unable to bear the everlasting impression such horror would leave on him. Pips never forget that which they witness, even when they want to.

Then Nud heard the grind of boots scuffing over loose rocks.

Kabor?

The Stout was about to do something stupid. Nud opened his eyes and shot his friend a firm look. "Kabor don't," he whispered. But Kabor was braver. Always braver.

Kabor stood up anyway, without so much as a weapon to hold. Well, he had a rock.

The creature – crouched over its prey – had heard Nud's whisper and tilted its deathly glare to the defiant Stout.

Nud bit his lip hard and scrambled to his feet to stand with his friend, *Sliver* in hand. He grunted as he braced himself solidly, pointing the spear's tip at the aggressor.

"Leave him be," Nud said, his voice firm.

Kabor pulled his arm back, ready to throw hard.

One swipe from their foe was all it took. Kabor stood still for a moment before his rock dropped. Nud's spear dropped with it. The clawed strike had drawn blood from the two of them. Nud's heartbeat raced inside of him, erratic. He felt a tingling in his hands, and watched as blood dripped from his elbow to the floor. They both stumbled. Numbness spread like wildfire. Kabor collapsed to the ground and Nud fell backwards against the tunnel wall, then slid to the floor, propped up against the rock. The fight was over before it could begin; the rebellion quelled the instant it'd started.

Nud sat motionless, unable to move. He couldn't see Kabor even though the Stout was right beside him. The Pip couldn't even close his eyes.

"Enough!" the leader scolded.

The taunting figure near Nud turned back to its prey and continued from where it'd left off. A sickening scrape sounded – claws ripping into flesh. The unfortunate Gloom remained silent throughout the gorging, even when dragged, twitching, directly in front of Nud's field of view. In what followed, the Pip – unable to look away or shut his eyes – bore witness to unimaginable gore. For mercy's sake, Nud could only hope that the gentle Gloom was no longer aware of what was happening to him, and that he couldn't comprehend his half-devoured state.

The other two shadowy forms in Nud's vision took a more cool and calculated approach, going so far as to court their victims. He wished he could turn away as each stroked its chosen one on the back of the neck ever so gently, as though scritching the family pet. One – the woman – gently lifted her prey and began neatly gorging. The second fed in a rough, whirlwind frenzy. Blood and guts hurled in every direction.

Scythe in hand, the slave master waited patiently while the others fed. He seemed to revel in the gruesome show of gore put before him. And when his crew had gotten their fill, the slave master took his time to step carefully among the survivors, still prone and cowering, tapping each one with the butt end of the shaft handle. He prodded some in a way that spoke to testing plumpness.

Finally, he settled on the innermost Gloom of the group. Nud watched in horror as the leader set his polearm down beside the poor creature and crouched over him. The Pip wished he could run and grab the weapon, then bear it down upon the slave master.

Nud's finger twitched. *The paralysis … it's wearing off.*

Nud tried to open his mouth to scream "NO!" as the slave master grasped his prey, but only a bubbling "Ahhh" wheezed out. The leader hesitated at hearing the sound, then turned his gaze to Nud and Kabor. That very moment, Nud noticed a faint flicker on the wall. *My stone.* It must have shifted in the fall and was about to slip into full view.

So, to quaff the light, Nud raised his darkest thoughts and dwelled upon them – that much was easy, given his present company. The stone burned cold against the Pip's chest. And even though it was not the stone's sparking light that illuminated the tunnel, the entire room flickered. The dark only lasted an instant, as though a wayward gust had snuffed the torches. And when it was over, they still burned with their usual glow.

The foul creature glanced at the sconces on the wall, shook his head, and then returned to his foul business. The others looked this way and that way for a brief moment, but soon carried on.

The leader returned to stroking the neck of his chosen Gloom in long, slow draws. Nud knew what was coming. He fought to close his eyes. It was no use.

Lifting the compliant Gloom gently in his arms, the slave master whipped his head back. The motion threw off his hood. The face beneath was corpse-like. Long, thin fangs pierced the flesh of the helpless victim. The slave master simply tore the poor, obedient thing apart.

Blood and bits of flesh spattered the hallway. The cringing Glooms whimpered as the frenzy played out – horrified, but subdued. When it was over, the leader wiped his mouth clean with his sleeve. He pulled the hood back over his withered skull and called to the others.

Smooth as silk, the grim walkers retreated the way they'd come. Their shadows shrunk into the receding torchlight.

*

Of the original eleven, only six slaves survived the encounter, as each foul master had chosen one to devour. Those spared from the dreadful feast took leave to mourn over the dead. With heavy footsteps and dull chatter, the Glooms collected what scraps remained of their kin and heaped them in the middle of the tunnel.

Dragging his feet, with palms raised to detect the heat, the miner with the spotted head felt out the location of the torch left behind. He proceeded to ignite the torn clothes of his fallen comrades, all the while emitting low, muffled clicks and taps.

"Isotopia," a female Gloom said angrily to another, when the deed was done. Smoke began to choke the hallway. Boney fist raised, she pelted the other in the eye socket. The injured

Gloom yelped as he dropped to the ground, hands covering the vacant patch. He rolled back and forth in agony, and then sat still for a long minute. Without so much as a click or a clack, the fallen Gloom stammered to his feet and wandered off listlessly, bumping once into the wall before setting himself straight, back the way they'd come.

The rest gathered their belongings and hastened out of the bloodied hallway before the fire burned high and the smoke became too thick. Kabor and Nud leaned heavily on the sturdiest Glooms as they were half-led, half-dragged along. Eventually, the poison wore off and the pair fell into proper stride.

The level of chatter between the miners, once lively and full, had dampened with their spirits. Only the occasional low volume, sporadic burst broke their muted silence. Nud surmised that it was just enough to allow for minimal navigation and little or no conversation. In time, they passed through a doorway with a heavy stone door and a rusty bar latch. The mechanism allowed for the bar to be raised and lowered from either side. Once through, the rearmost Gloom slammed the door shut behind them and dropped the latch.

Kabor was the first to regain his ability to speak. "Wha' were w'ey?" he asked the Gloom with the spotted head.

Nud's own mouth was too numb to form words.

"Wraiths," replied a different Gloom, between muted clicks. It was the same miner that'd first inquired about Isotopia – the loud triller. The one with the spots on his head nodded in agreement.

CHAPTER XIV

Interlude - Nekenezitter

Ahh … a break in the storm, no less. But temporary. A perfect time to propel you to the next phase of this tale, before the winds and the rains return…

*

Nekenezitter was a Gloom with eyes. It happened every few generations.

I learned of this Nekenezitter because of the small part I played in his journey – a great journey, ongoing even today – and because of the time we spent exchanging views. I was the first to teach him the meaning of dawn and dusk, and the names of the colors of the rainbow. We discussed common uses of words on paper, and the notion of "capturing" a scene on canvas, and of maps for navigation. The notions of light reflection, translucency and scattering were familiar to him, in as much as they related to the soundproofing qualities of certain materials.

All of this took place over too brief a time. My quick

lessons about life aboveground were but a trifle considering the debt that I owed him, for who knows what would have become of Kabor and I if Nekenezitter hadn't acquired clothing and a spare cell key from his kin, and suddenly showed up to lead us to the upper world by a secret way. I might've been wrapped in bark much sooner, were it not for him.

Nekenezitter was born in as common a manner as any other of his brethren, who call themselves "Il'kinik," amidst the choking fumes and perpetual darkness of Dromeron Odoon. But as he matured, it became obvious something was different about him. The Gloom perceived things others did not. At first, he couldn't even begin to convey his perceptions in terms any would understand. What he described was nothing like the rumble of a cave-in, or the wind whistling through tunnels, or the gurgle of flowing water, or the clank of hammer on anvil. Nor was it anything like the echo of a column, or boulder, or cave icicle, or breach in the stone. It had no feel, smell or taste to it. The closest sensation he could give them was that of heat, for he first perceived the fiery glow of the forges where his parents and siblings labored. His family was a mere station above the status of Bound Ones. "I can *hear* the heat," he would tell them, beyond the audible roar of the coal furnace.

After first making contact with the old-worlders of Dim Lake, it took years for the Glooms to learn about this extra sense. Those who believed in extra-sensory perception dubbed it "The Fifth." Of course, this refers to a fifth sense. Those who would deny the ability called it nonsense.

Nekenezitter seemed destined to become a great teacher and leader of his people. Already a vocalary, philosopher and prophet in their minds ear, he was encouraged by his elders to travel the world above, a world sounded out as a veritable hell in traditional teachings. The recent experiences of slaves returning from Harrow after being sold into service – the so-called Bound Ones – only reinforced such notions. They spoke of Taradin's demons in the catacombs under the Iron Tower: beasts of the upper world who kept the order and wreaked havoc among them. And they spoke of old-world secrets, best left undisturbed.

Yet, as decreed by the elders of Odoon society, "the child must learn the way of The Fifth, and this, he must do alone." And so, Nekenezitter received the finest education of his people before embarking on his solo journey, including teachings of all the known heritages of the upper world, their ways, customs, and languages. These were limited, though, by what could be gleaned from his people's interactions with Harrow, abandoned mines that the Glooms had stumbled upon, and lost surface-world items in their possession. For the most part, what they found only served to confuse them.

It became evident to the elders that none among the Glooms truly could prepare Nekenezitter for his quest, and so they turned to the being they held as divine. "Kechekenibek" – commonly known as simply "Kech" to the Glooms – heard their request and agreed to provide the additional tutelage. The huge, watery beast proclaimed, however, that the entire undertaking was to be held in the utmost of secrecy, for sanctioning a journey to "Hell" and back would meet resistance and could cause unrest among the worshipping populace. "Huum haa, change must be gradual," Kech boomed.

Now there was an ulterior motive to the mission, which Nekenezitter also kept secret – nearly secret that is. The gifted Gloom also took on a personal quest to discover the truth about another great mystery of his people. It was the Bound Ones – like his parents and siblings – who often whispered of a land they called Isotopia. To them, it represented heaven in earth. They held to the prophecy that someday, one with The Fifth will deliver their people to its bountiful caves.

Some say the slave masters fabricated the dream of an underground paradise as an instrument of control to prevent the Bound Ones from committing suicide. Isotopia gave them hope for a better existence, so they'd never succumb to ending their dismal lives and thereby decrease productivity.

The day finally arrived when, armed with knowledge and burdened with duty, Nekenezitter departed Kech's side on the turbulent shores of Gusher Run, on a personal path of discovery and enlightenment. It happened to occur only a short time after my own visit to the Dim Sea...

CHAPTER XV

Break-out

From his seat on the lower bunk, Nud stared at the barren wall across from him. His circumstances could be worse – chains with handcuffs and ankle cuffs dangled there, empty of limbs. The rough rock of the windowless cell was gouged and scraped with messages to no one in particular. Kabor sat on a low wooden table – the only other piece of furniture in the small room. It was bolted to the floor. A septic smell wafted up from the barred hole tucked in the corner. Inmates in the adjacent cells muttered and swore.

The jingle of keys sounded. Footsteps echoed along the walkway. The moment had come.

Nud had no idea what he'd say to this "Taeglin" that the wraith had gone on about. He'd heard the name before, from Paplov's political circles. Fyorn had mentioned him as well and both regarded the man with contempt. Other than that, Nud didn't know what to expect.

The Pip shifted his gaze to the hallway. He blinked and did a double take.

"That's no guard," Nud said.

Kabor tilted his head up. "What the heck?"

An odd-looking Gloom approached their cell, with a fist full of keys in hand. "What your names <click><chirr>?" he asked.

As misshapen and disfigured as the cave dweller was, he was different from regular Glooms. Very different. This one had eyes – large and bulbous.

Nud got up off his scratchy blanket, shuffled to the gate and peered between the iron bars. He grabbed the cold metal exactly where they were worn shiny. Behind him, the table creaked and groaned as Kabor pushed himself up to follow.

"My name is Nud," the Pip said. "Nud Lenokin ... from Webfoot. And this is Kabor Ram. He's from the Bearded Hills."

A mechanical clink sounded. Before Nud could explain the wrongfulness of their incarceration, the lock had been sprung.

"Kech <tick> sent me," said the Gloom. "His <click> design dictates we help one another <clack>." He extended a handful of robes through the open cell door – Gloom robes. "I am <click> Nekenezitter <tick-tick>," he continued. "Put these on. Hurry <chirr>."

Kabor and Nud quickly donned the clothes over their own, then followed the hobbling Gloom down the hallway, past the other two cells in the "political" block, and out the door. Nud looked closely at the long and drawn faces of those incarcerated as he strode by with slow steps, just in case. Hoping. But none were even Pips.

The two teens reclaimed their belongings from behind an unmanned desk along the way, including *Sliver*, *Shatters* and Nud's backpack, but minus the cave crystals and glassy tablets that were nowhere to be seen. It was a small price to pay, considering.

Nud knew the rescue could only be the work of the Dim Sea leviathan, and that the name of the loremaster he'd met had to have been "Kech."

*

Nekenezitter led the above-worlders through secret dark ways. And when they finally reached the surface, Nud and Kabor watched, through watery eyes, the magnificent sun sinking over green, rolling hills. The forgotten music of birdsong and buzzing insects filled their ears. Fresh air filled their lungs. Nud heard the wind in the treetops. They'd come up just outside Harrow's city wall.

As Nud savored the last hints of daylight, he turned to Nekenezitter and asked a simple and naïve question about the search the Gloom had talked about along the way. "Why would you go aboveground to find this Isotopia place if it's supposed to be underground?"

The Gloom paused for a brief moment, as though in perfect stasis. He was curious to watch, standing so still he could've passed for a statue. Nekenezitter didn't shuffle, or breathe or fidget while he searched for the right words in our awkward tongue. His expression mirrored the placidness of a lake on a windless morning when the water is glassy.

"I <click> begin <clack> search where no one <click> look before," he said. It was that simple.

The Gloom gazed at Nud squarely with those large, unseemly eyes, and chirred. "I do this <click> for Bound Ones. <tick> They are my brothers and sisters <trill>."

Nekenezitter went on to explain that the dream of Isotopia emerged decades ago, maybe longer, but that no true evidence of its existence had ever been found, despite "many, many costly attempts." A disconcerting outcome, for if anyone knows where to look for a hidden underground city, it would be the slave miners.

"How <clack> I hope to do better than they?" he continued. "<click> I take different approach <tick>; one they never take themselves <chirr>. Aboveground <tick>. Kech advised me so."

As they stood in the twilight of the world above, ready to part, the Gloom had some final advice. It came in part from the leviathan and in part from him, personally. When he spoke, the usual Gloom noises punctuated his words.

"Steer clear of crowds <click> on way home <clack>. Half city search for you <chirr> when wraiths <click> learn of escape <clack>. Label you thieves, assassins; they will <tick-tick>. Hunt your blood <tick> until Kech's word <click> reaches Taradin, they will <chirr>. Be watchful, ready."

The leviathan was more connected and helpful than Nud ever could have imagined.

In return for his guidance, the two surface dwellers gave Nekenezitter some of their own advice. They pointed him in the direction of a good place to begin his travels. Nud used a stick to draw a quick map in the earth, and then directed him towards the Bearded Hills. The miners and prospectors there might be able to help him. He even gave Nekenezitter the name "Mer Andulus" and told him to tell Mer that Nud Lenokin and Kabor Ram sent him.

The bog lands and Turnsby were also on the map that Nud had sketched for him, as well as locations east to Gan, south to Fort Abandon, and west towards the Scarsands. "Wherever you go, don't go west," Kabor told him, "or too far east, beyond the forest."

Nekenezitter looked up from the scratchings. He gave Nud a concerned look. "You say you live <clack> in a bog <chirr>?"

"That's right. Born and raised," Nud said.

"Hmm <chirr>." He sighed heavily.

"What is it?" Nud said.

"In Iron Tower <click>, hushed talk about bog <clack> overheard. Old-worlders not know how good are Il'kinik ears. Taeglin <click> ordered <clack> Tor Lord to drain bog <trill> … dig out for mining. Equipment <click> gathered <tock> Western Tor."

Kabor and Nud exchanged glances.

"HME," Kabor said.

Nud nodded. He regarded the Gloom. "Why would Taeglin want to drain the bog?"

"Which Tor Lord was he talking to?" Kabor added. "Nothing's there 'cept bog iron and bog bodies."

"I <click> don't know," Nekenezitter said. "But he wants <tick> something buried there <clack>. More, <chirr> I cannot say, except sounded … urgent talk."

"I don't think they can do it," Nud said, calling to mind his lessons on treaties and agreements. "The Non-aggression Treaty clearly states that neither Harrow nor Gan can occupy the Tri-town region – that covers Webfoot to Turnsby to the Bearded Hills." But even as Nud recited the words, he knew they were empty. *Harrow takes what Harrow wants.*

Just before parting, Nud tried to explain a bit more about directions. Nekenezitter was not accustomed to having so much choice in the matter. The Gloom showed the Pip his compass though, and demonstrated that he was well versed in the use of a lodestone, and that he knew which way was north.

That helped; otherwise, it would have been far more difficult to explain how the sun moved.

Kabor and Nud didn't have the luxury of time to play with; daylight had faded and the wraiths would be on their trail soon, if not already. The beaming tower light of Harrow had been lit for an hour, and already burned bright in the distance.

They had to make a run for Deepweald to cross the line of control.

CHAPTER XVI

Sacred grove

Gasping for breath and legs nearly spent, Nud crashed through the dark forest with Kabor on his heels.

"How did they find us?" the Stout puffed.

Nud replied between short breaths, "I don't know." His heart pounded. "Where are they?"

"How should I know, I'm half-blind." The Stout glanced back anyway.

"We should hide," Nud whispered. He dropped flat behind a fallen log and Kabor ducked down with him. They gulped shallow breaths to keep quiet. The Pip's heartbeat raced. He pricked his ears to the sounds of pursuit. Wind hushed through the branches; tall trees creaked and groaned as they rocked. The creatures of the forest had all gone silent.

Nud spoke in a low whisper. "Do you hear them?"

"No," Kabor replied. "Did we pass the line of control?"

"I'm sure of it. We're in Wilder territory now, but I don't know if that will stop them." Nud shifted his position and peered over the frayed bark, into the gloom of the woods. "I don't see them either. Maybe we lost them."

The wraiths didn't move like regular old-worlders. Their motions were fluid and silent – only the whipping sounds of branches in the dense bush confirmed that they'd followed Nud and Kabor into the forest. Before the sun was even fully down, the grim walkers must've learned of the escapees' bearing or had guessed it. They'd moved unseen and unheard, picking up the teens' trail on the eastern edge of Harrow, somewhere near the docks. Nud could've kicked himself – the price paid for having lingered a precious few minutes too long with Nekenezitter. The two of them had fled into the forest with a good head start, but the wraiths were bigger and faster, and they pursued their quarry with cold determination.

The flap of wings sounded – a screeching bird scared up into the branches.

Nud ducked down again. "They're close," he whispered, then shrugged off his pack. It was slowing him down.

"How many?"

"I don't know. I didn't see a thing." Nud retrieved *Shatters* from his pack and tucked it into his belt, then gripped *Sliver*, balancing it in his hands for a throw. "Two of them, at least."

"I thought I heard three," Kabor said.

"Maybe."

The Stout grimaced. "We should split up," he puffed. "If one of us can get out—"

"No way. You saw what they did to those Glooms, didn't you?"

"They won't kill us. One of us needs to get out, to get help…"

"I don't know." Nud didn't like the suggestion, but the

more he thought about it, the more it made sense. The situation was hopeless. Splitting up gave them the best odds.

Branches whipped. Nud's head jerked up. Eyes darting, he detected movement in the woods. "They're coming."

Nud and Kabor scrambled to their feet. In a desperate attempt to foil their pursuers, Nud launched *Sliver* into the dark where he thought they'd be. He didn't even wait to see where it landed. A woman's baneful screech sounded.

The two friends glanced to one another. A bitter grin and a knowing nod passed between them. *Goodbye.* Nud dashed left; Kabor dashed right.

The going was suddenly good for Nud, as though the forest had opened up in front of him. The Pip leapt from one stone or log to another almost silently, and jumped across a ravine before heading straight up a hill. He heard Kabor's blind crashing through the bush behind him. Then came a loud thunk and sounds of rolling, followed by screams in the dark. Nud halted.

What have I done?

Last came the ominous silence, heavy as though the night had mass. All manner of terrible images came to mind.

Without warning, branches whipped from behind. Nud gasped. *They're coming.* Adrenaline jolted him into action; the Pip bounded up the rocky slope.

Kabor was as good as dead and those that'd struck him down were gaining on Nud. The Pip didn't look back. Dead ahead, a thick stand of young cedars blocked passage. Hoping for the best, he braced himself to barrel through. It could lead off a cliff for all he knew.

Unexpectedly, the cedars parted for him. Nud dove between the branches, unimpeded, before they snapped back into place. The Pip tumbled into a wide clearing at the crest of the hill. Standing before him was a warrior, facing from the heart of the grove – no, stationed there – stationed beside a mammoth stone monument with runes inscribed upon it. Ordered rows of maples, elms and oaks stood behind him, like troops in reserve.

The warrior didn't quite look the same as kind old Uncle Fyorn, the one that Nud had known for so many years, for the light of the Elderkin shone from his fierce, wild eyes. He stood tall and straight in a mail vest that shimmered in the moonlight. And he wore a silvered helm in likeness to a ferocious wolverine. A great tree insignia covered the front of the Kith ranger's vest, with silvered branches and shining green oak leaves. The Pip darted to one side, not knowing exactly what to make of him.

The woodsman unsheathed a large sword in one hand and held his trusty hatchet in the other. The hatchet Nud recognized well. The sword he'd never seen. The white metal of his weaponry gave off a pale sheen in the moonlit night.

The wraith cursed and fought at the barrier of branches, hissing and clawing and pushing aside the grabbing twigs.

Fyorn shifted into a readied stance – bent knees, left foot ahead of the right, eyes focused on the cedar hedge. He raised the sword high above his head. Nud's heart skipped a beat and the Pip feared the swordsman's rage, but for a moment. With a sharp "fvit-fwit" and a quick shake of the axe, the Wilder gestured at Nud to move the hell out of the way.

Nud scrambled aside as the wraith tore and cut its way through, clinging to the shaft of its long scythe. The grim walker entered the grove in a crouched pose.

Nud froze, utter dread overwhelming his senses.

It was the slave master.

The wraith leader glanced to Nud first, but quickly turned its burning gaze to the armored Elderkin.

The foul creature sniffed at the air in Fyorn's direction. From behind its dark hood, a liquid voice poured out into the grove, cold and fluid and hateful. The words surged through Nud's spine in a shiver and permeated his being.

"Mut!" slashed the terrible voice. The thing moved slowly in tight arcs as it gauged its opponent, back and forth with smooth, gliding steps. "You don't fool me. I've smelled your false flesh before; the stench you left behind at Harrow's Gate."

Fyorn's stone-cold expression broke, his jaw clenched, and his eyes went wide and dark. The woodsman tilted his head slightly to one side, lips pursed, defiant.

The wraith worked his forked tongue. "Yes, I was there so long ago now," he hissed, "I know … I know … I am the one you should hate."

The vile creature then pointed a long, clawed finger Nud's way. "There's no more life in a mut like you than there is in this half-sized wretch, or his wretch of a father. But his mother … now she was fine wine, and her unborn child a delectable morsel. So, Half-Elderkin, I'll take this wretch's life just the same, and yours too, if only to savor the sweet intoxication of it."

Mother? Father?

Fyorn roared as he charged the beast with unchanneled aggression, bearing the sword down and hard in a wide arc. He followed through with a quick swipe of the axe. The wraith dodged the attacks with effortless, gliding motions. The dark, loose robe it wore flowed like a trailing shadow behind it.

"Look out!" Nud hollered when a second wraith appeared at Fyorn's side, stepping out of the long shadows of the grove's perimeter. In a flash, the woodsman turned and cut the creature down with his long blade. At the same instant, with his axe, he parried a would-be deathblow from the slave master's swiping scythe, and shoved it off.

Turning his fiery gaze back to the slave master, axe spinning in his off-hand, Fyorn rushed the creature. A fast, two-handed blow from the scythe kept him at bay. He tried again, with the same result. The wraith was being cautious, taking advantage of the extended reach of his weapon to wear down the woodsman's aggression. And the wraith never stood its ground for an instant. Neither did Fyorn for that matter. Each tried to outwit and outmaneuver the other in a swift and deadly dance to gain the upper hand.

The Pip tried to warn Fyorn several times when he saw a strike coming, but each time the woodsman reacted before Nud could even get a word out. Fyorn was fully immersed in the heat of the moment – the battle rage. Nud was just an out-of-breath onlooker.

I have to do something. The Pip's mind raced through the possibilities: sneak attack from behind, hurl a rock … Nud watched in awe the foot movements, the feigns, the precision of thrust and slash. He witnessed subtle lures not fallen for and missed opportunities. Time seemed to slow seconds to heartbeats.

No, I'd only bring greater peril to Fyorn. This fight was clearly out of Nud's league. His reach was less than half that of the long-limbed, lanky creature, which made him an easy target, a liability. *Think. What can I do?* His stomach hardened. The answer came to him in the most unsatisfying way. *Wait.* It was all he could do. *Wait and be ready.*

Nud drew *Shatters* and watched for an opportunity – a misstep. Something.

Fyorn's axe made first contact during a clash of sword and

scythe, cutting into the shoulder of the wraith. Green sparks flashed where white metal met flesh. The creature had been blind-sided. But the axe didn't release when Fyorn tugged it back. It stayed wedged. And the slave master hadn't reacted to the strike as one might expect – he barely flinched. Rather, the wraith used the momentary hold-up to advantage.

Still wrestling scythe against sword, the vengeful creature caught Fyorn's leg with a swift kick, causing him to stumble. The woodsman maintained his balance, partly leveraging the axe still embedded in the wraith's shoulder to do so, even as the fiend writhed to break free.

But the Wilder had made a fatal miscalculation. The wraith unlocked its jaw and snapped down at Fyorn's out-stretched arm, sinking its teeth deep into his wrist. The woods-man jerked back, grunting in pain as the axe sprung free. Next, the wraith lashed out at the woodsman's face with one clawed hand, while the other kept a firm hold on the scythe to brace against the sword. As Fyorn spun away to avoid the wraith's strike, long black nails scratched beneath the protec-tion of the ranger's helm. Trails of blood streaked across his chin and neck.

Nud gasped. *The touch… this could be over.*

Now as Fyorn spun, he yanked free the entangled sword in that same whirling motion. Leveraging his pivot, he stole a swing – a near miss. The wraith sprung back and avoided the cutting force of the blow. The follow through of that failed attack put the woodsman in yet another vulnerable position. He stumbled close to the tree line.

Fury welling up inside, Nud tensed his grip on *Shatters*. Fyorn could be going numb, and if that happened…

The Pip charged into battle, screaming bloody vengeance. With another swift kick, the wraith sent him flying backwards.

In a flash, the scythe rose high against the bulging moon, and the slave master readied a deathblow against the sprawling Wilder.

At that pivotal moment, time stood still. The Pip experienced a sudden rush of energy. First, a wide pulse tingled up his spine. Then it fanned out, coursing through his trunk to every limb, finger and toe. Fully connected to the energy of the living forest, Nud unsheathed the bog stone, light pulsing in pale red flashes. He focused his mind to a point and imagined the trees lashing out in vengeful fury. The memory, the motion and the *e*motion all intertwined in a split second to become one.

Nud whispered into the wind: "Strike."
SNAP!
Branches whirred out and lashed at the slave master from behind, knocking him off balance. He hissed as the force hurled him directly into Fyorn, just as the scythe was bearing down. The disruption was all that the woodsman needed. As the wraith attempted to adjust his swing, he missed a beat, giving Fyorn just enough lead-time to dodge the plunging strike. Fyorn dove to one side and then rolled. The scythe dug into bare earth, clanging on buried stone. It glanced and hooked on a root.

From all fours, Fyorn scrambled towards the monument. He leapt over it to the other side, landing squarely on his feet. In that time, the wraith had pried the scythe out of the ground, and then launched a flying attack at the woodsman. But Fyorn was fluid and quick to counter. He toyed with his opponent around the stone slab, playing a child's game of elusion that kept the rock between them. It seemed as though he could have danced merrily around the monument all night until sunrise, if need be.

A mischievous grin appeared on Fyorn's face during that dance with death. Nud had seen the look many times before — the moment he knew the game was his.

But the wraith was not impressed or amused, and grew angry and impatient at Fyorn's mockery. The shadow in the night threw up its arms and shrieked in frustration at the hopelessness of the chase, while Fyorn spun his axe tauntingly.

The fight turned, unexpected. In a move of cold cunning, the wraith threw back its hood and jerked its gaze to Nud instead. The slave master unleashed a horrific hiss before lunging.

Nud gasped. Heart pounding, he braced himself for the impact and readied his deepwood club for a strike. But Fyorn came upon the wraith so hard and fast, his timing bordered on precognition.

The woodsman had made his own lunge with lightning speed and immeasurable ferocity. In a flash, he'd sheathed his sword and vaulted over the edge of the monument, tackling the charging figure. As one they rolled on the hilltop. In the scuffle, the wraith dropped its scythe. Fyorn gained the upper hand and pinned his foe to the ground. Desperate, the creature grabbed for the handle of the woodsman's axe and wrestled for control. Raging, hissing, and cursing, the vile thing jerked violently to be free of Fyorn's heavy-handed grip. But the woodsman wouldn't relent. He would never give in.

The shadowy form was slick though, and in a wiry way managed to twist free and stand. It reached to regain the scythe, one hand staying the axe. But during the tussle, Fyorn had found a moment to draw his sword. And with what looked to be an awkward swing that started with the sword lying flat on the ground, he slashed into the slave master's mid-section from the right flank. The wraith's body bent into the blow, and its clawed grip on the woodsman's axe went limp. The sword dropped to the ground as Fyorn regained his footing and moved into a low, balanced squat. Without hesitation, he raised his hefty axe in two hands and hacked down on his opponents exposed neck, severing it. The gruesome head dangled, bloodless, held by a mere thread of flesh. And when the creature fell to its knees in front of Nud, the body remained upright. The head spun freely and the eyes rolled to and fro, mouth open wide in a silent scream. Nud backed away.

Fyorn stepped back as well when the headless body began to flail about. It twitched and spun wildly in what could have been a morbid dance, until stopping abruptly in place. The creature's own hands cradled the dangling head, and held the face so the eyes could gaze directly at the Pip.

And then the thing's lips formed a grim, half-crazed smile. Dark eyes dug deep into Nud's soul and tore away a piece of it. The wraith had chosen to mock the Pip in its final moments, as though somehow it sensed Nud was doomed anyways. The smile drew thin into a silent laugh. One hand reached out with long, skeletal fingers to pull Nud in close. It was slow moving, and Nud easily sidestepped the grab. Having had enough of this wicked beast, the Pip stepped in and swung with all his might. He bashed the head with *Shatters*. Its tether snapped, and the hoodless skull went flying into the night. It sailed across the grove, deflected off a tree and crashed into the brush beyond. The decapitated body fell forward, hitting the ground with a thud.

A wave of relief washed over Fyorn's face. Then he gave Nud an odd look, a sense of urgency upon him. "We have to burn the bodies now," he said. "NOW!" he shouted when the Pip didn't move within half a heartbeat.

His body shaking, Nud fumbled through the pockets of

the robe Nekenezitter had given him, and produced a handful of sulphur sticks. *Somehow, he knew,* Nud thought. Too
disturbed to start the flames himself, he tossed them over to
Fyorn.

"Here," was all Nud could manage to say.

Nud's former uncle handled the deed, first setting the
wraith's robe on fire and then adding dry wood to the flames.

"Get the head," Fyorn said as he fussed over the fire. The
woodsman left his handiwork to gather the second wraith.

With *Shatters* tight in his grip, Nud cautiously made his
way to the edge of the grove where the head had sailed. He
peered into the brush. Dark shapes and darker shadows met
his eyes. Anything could be lurking amidst the thick foliage.
He feared stepping in, but knowing the importance of his
task, the Pip called on the bog stone one more time. A narrow beam focused ahead of him. He spotted the disembodied
head, only a few steps in. It wasn't moving and seemed dead
enough, so Nud approached the vile body part. He reached
out and grabbed the bloodless head by its stringy hair, then
raised it up high and held it away from his person to the limits his outstretched arm would allow. Stepping back into the
grove, the Pip called to Fyorn.

"Head's up!" he said, and then bowled the head towards
the woodsman. It was a good enough roll, stopping only a few
feet short of Fyorn's boot. The woodsman gave Nud a steady
look, and then side-kicked the head into the fire.

The Pip let out a heavy sigh. Exhausted, he sheathed his
stone and lumbered to the fire. The air soon became thick
with billowing, dark smoke and the smell of burning flesh
as the fire crackled on. Flames danced merrily over their rich
sustenance.

A gradual movement in the dark caught Nud's eye – it

was the trees. Rows of young maples closed in, ever so slowly, eventually forming concentric rings around them. The inner circle included the fire and the rune stone, with additional layers extending to the edge of the clearing. Branches intertwined into a contorted mesh. From above, the light of the moon filtered in, illuminating the rising column of smoke that passed through an accommodating gap in the crown canopy.

The deed was done. And of the remaining wraith or wraiths in the woods – naught to worry…

Janhurl

Flames roared and the fire crackled violently, taking deeper root in the blackening remains and throwing off a burnt meat smell. Fyorn tossed in hardwood to keep it steady – larger pieces of dried maple. A loud hiss rose from the fire. No doubt, it would consume the remains through and through.

Fyorn doused his injured wrist with whiskey, and began wrapping it. Blood soaked through the material.

"Kabor's still out there," Nud said, resting against the monument.

Face aglow in the firelight, Fyorn swung his steady gaze to the Pip. "Anyone else?"

Nud sighed. "Another wraith," he added, based on the scream he'd heard in the woods when he'd thrown *Sliver* and the fact that neither of the burning corpses were female.

Fyorn's expression softened. "You sent her fleeing back to Harrow with her tail between her legs, and less an eye." The woodsman was almost smirking. Suddenly, beneath the ornate helm and shiny armor he seemed like good 'ole Uncle Fyorn again.

Nud didn't question how the man knew. He always knows. Fyorn had more to say. "Kabor has been located. He's safe and in good han – limbs. He'll be with us shortly."

For a long minute, the Pip just leaned back against the rock and stared at the building fire. The dry heat bade him to stay put. His body ached, he was hungry, and sweat stung the many scratches and scrapes that he'd suffered while running through the woods. There'd be serious bruising on his ribs where he'd been kicked. But at least there was the fire – bright, warm and inviting, in as much as charring wraiths can be inviting.

The woodsman spaced out the new fuel with a makeshift poker. Nud could still discern some of the grisly contents of the fire, and found great satisfaction in the flames' permanency. The Glooms had been avenged and there would be no more grim demons in the night.

Satisfied with the arrangement of all things burning, Fyorn made his way to the large rock in the clearing and plopped down next to Nud. The woodsman-turned-warrior finally removed his helm and set it next to him, then wiped the sweat from his brow with the back of his sleeve. He'd already returned his sword to its scabbard, wiped clean and sterilized by fire, and had left it to lean casually against the monument. His axe, similarly treated, lay flat atop its rough surface.

Fyorn said nothing for a long minute, drawing in deep breaths and gazing up through the smoke hole to the starry sky above, legs sprawled out in front of him. Nud suspected that the Elderkin pondered his mortality, as Nud pondered his own. It'd been a narrow escape.

Nud broke the silence. "Thanks," was all he said.

Fyorn only nodded. Nud had never seen him so winded.

"One less eye? Really?" the Pip added.

Fyorn nodded again. Between breaths, a silent "Yep" formed on his lips.

"Lucky shot," Nud said.

Finally, the woodsman spoke. "That wasn't luck, Sir Nud. *That* was deepwood."

The Pip paused. "Lucky I found this place, then."

"Not really," the woodsman replied, that smirk building once again. "Not much luck there either, I'm afraid. The Hurlorns guided you here. I know because I asked them to."

"Holly, Gariff, Bobbin…"

"They're all safe."

A wave of relief welled up inside, carrying a rush of emotion. Feeling overwhelmed, Nud buried his face in his hands.

Fyorn took notice. "It's okay, Nud. You did good." He patted the Pip on the back. "Bravery and good sense in a pinch are hard to come by. You have it in you to make your mark on the world, on the strength of those pillars alone."

"How—" Nud began to ask. He choked on his words.

"It's a long story."

"And how—"

Fyorn sighed. "I read the rustling of the leaves and the whispers in the wind," he said, breaking into a smile. That was always his answer. But the smile quickly turned sour. The woodsman's gaze fell to his feet. He shook his head, then tilted his stare forward and firm. "Tragically, your lost guard was not so lucky."

Nud squeezed his eyes shut for a long moment. *Poor Jory.*

He and his "uncle" sat silent and still again, taking in the cool, night air with heavy breaths, lost in thought.

Fyorn cocked his head, followed by a sideways glance while he listened intently.

"Kabor?" Nud whispered, and then stood up.

Fyorn shook his head. "Holly," he muttered, nearly to himself.

"Holly?"

Sure enough, the trees parted and the Flipside hostess strode into the grove like she owned the place. She wore a worried look on her face, and carried her exceptional cloak in one hand. Her hair shone and sweat streamed down her cheeks. She looked radiant in the smoky moonlight, as radiant as the first night Nud had seen her at the inn.

"They wouldn't let me in here until I took off the cloak," she complained, gesturing to the ring of trees. She tugged on the shoulder of her shirt. "They kept hooking it." Holly brushed the leaves and crud off her clothes, then shot Nud an easy smile and rushed over. Her embrace was long and sweet and heavenly. She smelled of lavender. Grasping his hands and squeezing them tight, Holly stepped back to gaze upon Nud. Her eyes were the forest moss and her hair the finest silk.

But it was Fyorn's voice Nud heard instead of hers, speaking in a firm, fatherly tone, blending annoyance with concern. "Is Janhurl coming?"

The two Pips broke off their greeting, all too soon in Nud's mind. Holly regarded Fyorn.

"Janhurl's moving at a snail's pace. She has Kabor. He isn't feeling well. In fact, he looks terrible." Holly's jaw dropped and her eyes went wide. She puffed air. "It's sooo eerie out there in the dark ... there are all kinds of *noises*."

Fyorn grimaced slightly. "No doubt, you were the loudest among them – the cloak can't hide your crunching footsteps.

Those wilderness noises are a good sign. It means things have returned to normal."

"There's more than just a little eeriness right here," Nud said, gesturing to the burning corpses. By that time, the flames had consumed the bulk of the bodies and, with all the wood stacked on top, they were unrecognizable.

Holly closed her eyes, turned her head away from the fire and held one hand up. "UGH … Don't even tell me what that is – I don't want to know. I heard all the clanging and grunting. And I could smell … never mind."

Fyorn planted one hand firmly on Holly's shoulder, with the other he pointed to the flames. "Your Nud here finished off a vile and dangerous enemy – a ferocious beast – and sent another fleeing back to Harrow."

She glanced to the fire in disgust, then swung her gaze to Nud and looked him over, as if trying to see something that wasn't there before. Nud didn't correct the woodsman's account of things, or try to be modest. Surely, knowing Holly, she'd eventually pry every minute detail out of them anyway. For the time being, the Pip simply basked in the glory of a borrowed victory.

"What happened to Gariff and Bobbin? Didn't they come along too?" Nud said.

Holly answered. "They went searching for gossip about you two lost pups in Harrow. Since there were no *whispers* about your disappearance, Fyorn thought you might've somehow ended up there."

"He was right," Nud said. When the Pip looked to Fyorn, the woodsman winked. Something about the way his eyes sparkled told Nud that he'd known more than he'd let on to Holly.

Fyorn said, "We'll meet up with them back at the cabin

tomorrow morning. I had to call back Janhurl – who'd brought them there. Gariff and Bobbin have more than enough coin for a decent inn."

While they waited by the fire, Fyorn waved the rings of trees off, which he referred to as "Sleepers." As they redefined the grove, slowly backing away into their ordered rows, Nud recounted the details of the chase. He then explained how he and Kabor had come upon the wraiths in the mine, and of the premonition he'd had earlier, in a dream. But Nud couldn't do so without recounting nearly everything about their adventure in the Hanging City, the catacombs beneath Harrow, and their short stint in the Iron Tower. Fyorn and Holly both listened intently until the fire burned low, nodding and shaking their heads. Holly even sobbed when Nud mentioned how he'd thought Kabor had been buried alive.

Nud left out the White Whale for the time being, saying only that a solitary and very knowledgeable underground dweller helped to guide his way. By the time Nud finished, he and Kabor were heroes in their minds.

After the tale had settled and their stares had fallen to the dwindling fire, a loud crashing sound startled them. Fyorn leapt to his feet as a thirty-foot tree strode into the clearing. Nud jolted into action, calling to mind his experience with the box in the attic and the spider-thing. He sprung up and tried to yank Holly up with him.

She resisted. "Relax, Leno," she said.

The tree's long strides whipped curled roots over the hilltop and stirred up leafy debris. Unlike the normal sorts of Hurlorns that grew in these parts, this one had a kind of face – feminine in certain qualities, but twisted in on itself with features all knots and burl wood, and a hollow for a mouth.

Black knotty eyes shone like polished ebony from inset eye sockets.

Fyorn greeted the tree creature with a nod of his head. "Janhurl," he said.

"Fyor-yor-yor-yorn," the Hurlorn replied, with a voice like a flute in the wind.

Janhurl bore Kabor in her limbs, wrapped in a cocoon of leaves and a nest of woven branches. The Stout was pallid and shivering feverishly. She gently laid him down close to the monument, mindful of the fire. Holly hastened to Kabor's side and, down on one knee, threw her cloak over the Stout's trembling body and made him comfortable.

The rest of the conversation between Fyorn and Janhurl was foreign and musical. The Hurlorn's voice rang out mellifluously as a rich, resonant buzzing of notes. It wasn't proper speech by any stretch of the imagination, but Fyorn seemed to understand it. He gazed into those dark eyes and nodded in acknowledgement as she winded on, and on … and on. Holly and Nud kept their distance, tending to Kabor while casting curious glances at the tree-creature and to one another.

After a long pause, Janhurl passed one final message to Fyorn. Her tone changed to one more hushed and somber, and she made passing glances Nud's way as she spoke her Treesong. The woodsman and the Hurlorn said goodbye to one another in the customary way of the woods.

Janhurl fluted her part, incomprehensibly, to which Fyorn responded,

"By sun, wind, rain and earth."

They all watched as the tall Hurlorn strode across the grove, west towards Harrow. She stopped to glance back. Janhurl's measuring gaze found Nud's for a long moment, before she turned back to her route. With one giant stride, she stepped out of the grove and out of sight.

Fyorn made his way to his backpack near the monument, pulled something out and then ambled over to the firepit. "Holly, can you get Kabor some water?" he said, then turned his attention to Nud. He spoke in low tones. "We need to talk."

Nud nodded and Fyorn led him to the other side of the pit. He stooped to eye level, facing the Pip directly. His huge hands reached out and gripped Nud's shoulders firmly.

"I'm sorry to be the one to have to tell you this," he began. "Dark news – a whisper out of the alders, rushes and reeds of Webfoot."

Fyorn paused.

Nud felt a shakiness in his limbs as the shadow of dread crept over him.

The woodsman continued, "Your papa is seriously ailing; he may not make it through the night."

It was like the news had come out of nowhere.

The words seized Nud's chest like a ghostly fist. He searched Fyorn's eyes for the truth in them. The man's gaze was a calm sea of blue, his pupils sparked with flames from the bonfire.

Nud looked away.

The woodsman talked on, but Nud wasn't really listening as he struggled to understand how Fyorn's bad tidings could be true. How this could be happening. The water welled up behind his eyes as the woodsman made mention of a long and successful life, and something about Paplov using his time well, and wisdom. When finished, Fyorn let go his grip and handed Nud a rolled sheet of black leather. It was familiar to the Pip – an official document from Paplov's desk.

Holding the scroll close, Nud turned and stared into the heat of the bleary fire. He brushed a tear away. The flames danced on what was left of the burning wraiths. His heartbeat suddenly quickened, his lifeblood pumped nervously. Nud felt the fluid suck in and spill out in its vital rhythm, the body fully aware of what the mind had willed away by denial.

Flames consume all.

The woodsman spoke again. "I'll send word that you and the Stout have been found alive and well," he said. "Your papa will hear those words tonight. That will put his mind at ease and lift his spirits. He never gave up hope."

Nud nodded, numbly. *He never does.*

The Pip went over recent events in his mind leading up to Paplov's condition. He'd been sick on and off for some time and … the Turnsby trip was hard on him … and … *I should've carried more of the load. I shouldn't have given him such a hard time.*

The tightness in Nud's chest squeezed full force as he mulled over how much Paplov had stayed in lately, curled up in his chair with a blanket and a book. Nud thought of how he'd missed several meetings lately too, and how he'd passed important duties to other council members, and how he'd tried to do the same to Nud. The signs were all there, Nud just never put them together. *Did I care enough?*

Time was short between that and the next setback.

"That's not all," Fyorn said. "Holly, you need to hear this too." He waved her over, then spoke in a hushed voice. "I don't want to alarm anyone, but Bobbin and Gariff haven't been heard from since early evening. At this point, Janhurl is optimistic, but she's being cautious nonetheless. She'll look into it and we'll know more in the morning. Hurlorns are on the watch tonight."

"They probably just took a meal and a room for the night, that's all," Holly said.

"I think so," Fyorn replied.

Nud sighed. Maybe he'd learned to think the worst, but somehow, Fyorn's optimism rang like dissonance in his head. *It never rains, but it pours.* Paplov had repeated the phrase many times, whenever worries started multiplying.

Paplov…

Nud turned away from the others.

"Leno?" Holly reached out and brushed his shoulder just as he started off.

"Let him go," Fyorn said.

Nud kept going and strode to the edge of the hilltop. He stared out over the forest. The wraith had stirred a great many memories, and Fyorn's words resonated in his mind … *He never gave up hope.* Nud savored the thought of his grandfather and slipped into recall.

CHAPTER XVIII

Night watch

When the town officials came through the gate, Nud was waiting on the stepping stone path outside his hut, as he'd done each and every day since his parents' disappearance. He'd hoped to be the first to hear the good news that they'd been found; that they'd taken a wrong turn, gotten lost, and ended up in Deepweald Forest or some other unlikely place.

Paplov sat in his favorite chair inside, plotting his next traverse through the bog, when Wyatt and the other town officials greeted Nud with bitter smiles. They walked on by and knocked on the front door. Paplov invited them in, and as they shuffled into the kitchen, Nud padded softly to stand near the open window where he could hear everything.

Wyatt started off by conveying Old Mayor Flosh's condolences. And then, with heavy reluctance in his voice, he informed Paplov that the search couldn't be kept up any longer. "The town had done everything it could," he said, "and the mayor believes that it's time for people to get on with their lives."

He went on to say that the volunteer search crew would be disbanded after an extensive, three-week investigation that had turned up nothing on Paplov's daughter and son-in-law. Despite the Council's ruling, in sympathetic tones Wyatt vowed to keep searching on his own time. He'd already secured a blue tail for the next few weeks.

Nud cringed at the shouting that followed. His grandfather was furious over the decision and tore into those who'd showed up. Wyatt sympathized, calling himself "the messenger" in this ordeal, and saying that half the town was still fuming over the incident and the botched efforts that followed, and so was he. With heated words, Paplov summarized it all for the officials standing there: The Bearded Hills and Turnsby had offered up help that Council largely ignored, stating their own people were best equipped to handle the situation and that bringing in outsiders would just complicate matters. Then came "volunteer" searchers from Harrow – soldiers. They'd received a hero's welcome. Yet, less than a day in, the Harrow crew had announced that the search was hopeless. Sadly, the entire operation was a mess, and poorly handled.

Paplov had his own ideas about where the delegation was last seen and their heading. Why there'd been no sign of Nud's parents or the other delegates was puzzling to the point that he suspected foul play. Harrow claimed they never received their "guests," but not all Webfooters trusted the word of the dominating power, especially not Paplov.

After the officials left, Nud lingered in the front yard under the willow for what must have been hours. He didn't go inside for lunch and Paplov didn't make him eat any dinner … both dishes sat full, nothing touched.

The days that followed were quiet and solemn. Paplov spent most of his time out and about with Wyatt, while Nud stayed home and ate meals with the neighbors. They were especially kind to the young Pip, and they were always so sure that his parents and the others soon would be found – the next day, the day after that, and the day after that. But even at a young age, Nud could see their smiles wearing thin as the days rolled by, and he caught how their expressions changed when they looked away after saying it.

Nud never stopped believing that one day they'd return – that Mother would come running through the gateway towards Nud with arms wide and a big smile, and give him the biggest hug and tell him how much she missed him. His father would come strolling up casually behind her. They'd never leave him alone like that again … Nud supposed he was never quite alone though. He'd always had Paplov.

*

Nud jolted back into reality with a gasp, Paplov's scroll gripped tight in his hand. He rubbed his forehead, and then stared at the scroll for a long moment. Slowly, he unraveled the leather, soft and worn. Then he held it facing the fire to read by the flames' unsteady glow. Nud recognized the document fully. Paplov traveled everywhere with it, safely stowed away in some pocket and held in a double bone tube that was corked on one end. To open the scroll, he'd hold one roller and let the other drop – let gravity do the work. On official business, Paplov would present it to gain entry at town gates or guarded meeting halls.

Nud's grandfather had never before parted with the scroll. Whatever came to pass, Nud figured he should be the one to hold onto it.

The first section proudly laid out his grandfather's diplomatic colors and those of Webfoot. Next were the emblems: a tree frog stamped into the upper right corner – the family emblem on his mother's side and a source of unbounded teasing from his Stout friends. Upper left was the town emblem – a bog scene, skillfully embroidered. Deep red circles for bog berries dangled from slender brown stems with tiny, oval leaves, and a silhouetted hill with huts on the horizon represented Webfoot. The branches crept along cushions of moss and wound their way down the left margin. Other sections of the document recorded Paplov's responsibilities, authorities and jurisdiction. Near the very bottom was an embroidered version of his personal seal and that of the mayor in the name of the Council, complete with signatures.

Nud rolled the scroll and popped it back into the bone tube lying around that it came in, then tucked the document away in his robe. He looked about the moonlit grove and took in the scene. Fyorn was up and about as usual, in the midst of hauling up his backpack. Holly had crouched down next to Kabor. The Flipside girl glanced over to Nud when he looked.

Nud averted his gaze, and to take his mind off things he got busy tending to a fire that didn't need tending and organizing a heap of chopped firewood and scavenged deadfall that didn't need organizing. Holly got up and approached him. She came and took his hand. It felt warm in his. He stopped stacking firewood and stood up. Nud looked past her to Kabor – the Stout seemed comfortable enough where she'd left him, wrapped in an old blanket. White as a ghost though, and Nud could see he was trembling.

"Just relax," Holly told Nud, tilting her head in an attempt to make eye contact. "We can talk about your grandfather, if you like. Or maybe tomorrow, once you've cleared your head.

And no worries about Bobbin and Gariff. I'm sure they're just in some cozy inn. Ya' think?"

Nud nodded, shifting his gaze down to his boots. "Yep. I wonder if they serve barkwood ale."

"Hope not," she said, "or we won't see either of them until noon if they get to arguing like last time." Holly didn't give her mission up so easily. Sporting a goofy smile, she ducked down to intercept Nud's gaze. She got in his face and giggled.

Nud smirked and shook his head at her foolishness. "I never heard Gariff talk so much as that night."

"Or so loud," Holly added, straightening up.

Nud met her gaze willingly. "Thanks," he said.

Holly shrugged. "They'll be so happy when they find out that you and Kabor are safe. Imagine the look on Gariff's face."

"I think he'll give his cousin a big bear hug."

"And Bobbin will be ecstatic. Guaranteed, he'll make some kind of silly song out of it all."

Fyorn ambled over to the fire with his pack and started tinkering with its contents behind Nud. Holly eyed what the woodsman was doing for a moment, prompting her to then look over Nud from head to toe. She grimaced at his many scrapes and bruises. "Your uncle's setting up to properly dress his wounds. You should see him about some of yours."

"Yeah," Nud responded.

She smiled. "Maybe you can tell me how you got some of them, later."

"Maybe."

She glanced over her shoulder to the pallid Stout. "I better get back to Kabor. I don't like the way he's breathing. He wheezes."

Nud nodded. Holly gave his hand a tight squeeze and then returned to her place at the Stout's side.

Her recommendation to "just relax" wasn't really an option for Nud, but Holly did set him on a task that actually did require immediate attention. It was time for him and Fyorn to lick their wounds, so to speak. Nud joined the woodsman, already well ahead on that aspect. His pack lay open beside the fire, contents spilling out onto the trampled grass. A small iron pot hung over the flames from a makeshift tripod, not far from a quarter-full whiskey bottle set on a flat stone.

"Nasty bite," Nud said.

Fyorn felt his wrapped-up wrist. "I'll live," he said. He gave Nud a measuring look. "Is there any part of your body that isn't beaten up?"

"I doubt it," Nud replied.

"I'll do yours first in a jiffy," Fyorn said.

"What about Kabor?"

The woodsman hesitated. "I'll get to him next for the surface wounds, but I have to say his condition is beyond my skill to heal." He gathered a spoon from his pack, squatted by the fire and stirred the pot.

"Did Kabor say what happened in the woods?" Nud asked.

"Paralyzed again," Fyorn said, "that much is certain. I fear there may be more to it though. Wraiths have dark ways about them. In some cases, their victims become as twisted and hateful as they are."

Nud felt rotten inside about leaving Kabor behind. "We should have stuck together."

The woodsman stopped stirring. "You can't second guess how everything went down. It could've been much worse." He turned his gaze to Kabor and smiled grimly. "Stouts are a resilient lot, aren't they? He may overcome this on his own."

"I hope so," Nud said. "But why weren't you affected? Those scratches on your neck look deep."

Fyorn gently rubbed the wounds and turned back to Nud. "I definitely felt something," he said. "Kith rangers gain certain resistances to poisoning, disease, and other ailments as part of our conditioning. The wraiths' poison is one of those accounted for. On a simpler level, I also weigh a lot more than you or Kabor, or one of those Glooms you talked about earlier."

Nud nodded his understanding.

When the contents of the pot were good and hot, Fyorn proceeded to bathe Nud's scratches and scrapes in the hot spirits. He mulled over one gash in particular, on Nud's thigh. Eventually he decided it needed stitches – a quick prick followed by a gentle tug and the thread glided through Nud's skin, almost softly. The Pip watched as the fire-sterilized needle zigzagged across the gash, each stitch measuring a careful finger's width distance from the last, to leave room for the wound to drain. The job took only a few minutes. When the deed was done, the woodsman applied a waxy healing salve and wrapped the area in a sticky, shimmering fabric – the same kind he'd used on his wrist. It luminesced with a patchy green glow.

"Spiderweave," he said while rolling up what remained.

Fyorn also checked the injuries that Nud'd sustained underground. When he seemed satisfied that every wound was set to heal as it should, and felt no broken bones under the skin, he told Nud that he'd end up with permanent scars on the back of his head and his lower back, plus the gash the woodsman had just stitched. Nothing serious though.

After sterilizing his needle again, Fyorn brought his medical kit to Kabor. Nud followed.

Fyorn shook his head at Kabor and Nud alike. "You two are rough'n tumble. He's as bad as you, Nud."

Kabor's breaths were short and shallow. "Except Leno's a delicate flower," he rasped. A self-indulgent smile crept across the Stout's face.

Despite all the visible scrapes, Kabor didn't require any stitches. Fyorn seemed most concerned about a pair of deep puncture wounds on the back of his neck. After taking care of them as best he could, he whispered his concerns to Holly – the same concerns he'd expressed to Nud earlier. The woodsman figured it was safe for Kabor to sleep, so long as someone checked on him regularly and made sure he drank water. Holly was a quick study. She dismissed Fyorn and got to work dressing Kabor's remaining wounds herself.

As Nud watched her work and the Stout rested his eyes, Nud contemplated the circumstances of everyone on the hilltop that night. They seemed an unlucky bunch, the four of them together. Apparently, Holly had dealt with more than her share of tragedy before the Numbits had taken her in – Nud didn't know the details. And then there was Kabor, taken in by his aunt and uncle after his parents were murdered. Fyorn was no stranger to hardship and loss, having fought against the Outlanders and Jhinyari slavers. And then there was Nud. *The world is a messed-up place when you piece it all together.*

Despite all that'd happened, at the first opportunity Holly stole some time from Fyorn to feed her curiosity – during which Nud kept watch on Kabor. For the Flipside girl, there always seemed to be some puzzle that required immediate resolution. *The busy mind of a know-it-all,* Nud thought, kindly. He was well within earshot of their conversation.

"What is this place?" Holly started, sounding sweetly naïve. She played that card when vying for attention or trying to pry out information, especially with older people.

Never fails, Nud thought.

Fyorn seemed happy to answer, in the midst of repacking his gear. "We are standing in a most hallowed place," he told her. "Important Kith ceremonies are held here." Hands busy, he flicked his chin at the monument. "That rune stone in the center is more than it appears. It's a symbol of our connection to nature."

Holly drew her eyebrows together. "Who do you mean by *our?*"

Fyorn paused. An innocent question, but it proved less than easy for the woodsman to answer. His eyes dropped as he searched for the right words, then tilted up to meet Holly's eager gaze.

"Those who take *and hold* the oath," he said at last – a vague answer at best. Nud settled in to eavesdrop on the long-winded explanation he expected would follow, but such an explanation was not forthcoming. Without pause the woodsman was up and away again, busy with a new task that Nud could only guess at. It was almost rude. Surprisingly, Holly didn't push for more.

That task of Fyorn's was a late dinner. And after a small, shared meal of dried meat and warm wine, cooked over a new and separate fire from the one disposing of wraiths, the two Pips and the Elderkin made final preparations for the night. Holly tried waking Kabor up to eat, but he'd have none of it.

Fyorn, at last, with weary, heavy eyes, asked Nud to keep the first watch for as long as he could stay awake, and then to wake him. He reminded the Pip not to let the cooking fire burn too low. He also called upon Holly to keep a close eye on Kabor during the same watch. "Let him sleep through the night if he can," Fyorn advised. "He may gain some strength by morning, but monitor his breathing and keep him bundled up."

To the hoot of owls and the lonely song of wolves in the dark reaches of the forest, Nud sat with Holly by the fire, huddled under her cloak, and chatted with her late into the night about all that'd happened. She fretted over Bobbin being in Harrow more than once, and Nud consoled her as best he could. In return, she offered her caring blend of polite consolation and advice about Paplov. Apart from a few suspicious branches cracking somewhere in the gloomy perimeter, nothing of concern interrupted them. Holly inched closer to Nud as the night wore on, gripping his arm or thigh at every snap in the woods, which the Pip didn't mind one bit.

She quizzed Nud in her usual manner about all things subterranean, until her eyes went heavy and her speech became choppy. Nud kept the fires burning steady until the Flipside hostess finally nodded off on his shoulder. Dreadfully tired himself, Nud tucked her in tight with her cloak and gently shook Fyorn awake, then claimed his own stretch of ground to sleep by the cooking fire. The night was cool. The soft, lumpy earth was far more comfortable than hard stone, and the fresh air cleansed his lungs. A sense of relief filled the Pip. And with it, openness. All in all, Nud had no qualms about being exactly where he was, protected and with the whole of the underground ordeal behind him, and with the bit about the wraiths settled. He was happy to be on the other side of things. Nud drifted off without another thought.

CHAPTER XIX

Interlude - The Hurlorns' stride

For the most part Hurlorns appear to be regular trees, at least at first glance. But to a discerning eye, a certain simplicity in form might be noticed. They tend to have fewer, thicker branches than their fully natural counterparts, and the leaves or needles tend to grow in rich clusters rather than spread out evenly. As long as a Hurlorn lives, it carries no dead wood on its limbs, and rarely have Hurlorns been observed to look sickly in any way. The noblest of the great Hurlorns – those with spirits from abroad instilled in them – have burl wood features somewhere up high in the trunk that, with a little imagination, resemble a face. Burls might be found in other areas of the tree as well, giving the appearance of shoulders or elbows or other vaguely human-like features. A precious few – one in a generation – from among the Spirit Hurlorns forgo even their predominantly tree-like forms to become a lumbering colossus such as myself, with scales of bark, a long, whipping tail like a giant vine, and a neck that stretches high above the treetops. They become what I am now, the *Green Dragon of Deepweald*.

Either way, Hurlorn roots must be contended with. In stride, they are long and whip-like, and do more than simply flail about during locomotion – they feel out the ground. And so, a Hurlorn has intimate knowledge of the terrain trodden upon. In particular, a former Pip transmuted to a Spirit Hurlorn would recall every detail.

In any case, it is best to steer clear of a Hurlorn's approach and give the creature plenty of room, or risk being lashed at, or worse, trampled upon. But when Hurlorns are still, as they nearly always are, their roots twist deep into the living soil. And at the base of their trunks, they tend to curl up in such a manner as to give the impression of toes on giant feet – a fitting signature for veritable trees that stroll through the woodlands. If you happen to come across roots that appear to be a pair of very large feet at the base of a very large tree, you may have just stumbled upon a dormant Hurlorn.

CHAPTER XX

Who's who

In the grey shades of early morning, the apparitions that haunted the grove in the night stood tall and silent. So proper in their place and so lasting in their presence, the advance of the hardwoods had seemed more the fabric of dreams than the substance of reality. Between their smooth, silvery trunks, Nud glimpsed a pale magenta light ascending over wooded hills and beneath blue-grey clouds.

"Good morning," Nud called to the Hurlorn sentinels in the grove. None responded. None were like Janhurl, or maybe they were still sleeping.

Nud rose, stretched, and then meandered to the edge of the bluff atop the Wild Elderkins' sacred hill. Facing southwest, a blanket of fog lay draped over the low-lying areas, punctured by the sharp skeletons of suffocated pine and spruce trees.

Holly was the next to wake up, groggy. She looked to the dead firepit and then to Nud. Her auburn hair was tousled, and the smile of acknowledgment she flashed Nud's way was soon conquered by a long-faced yawn. Fyorn was nowhere to be seen. Kabor slept soundly, but twitched violently every now and again. The other fire – the wraith fire – had been dug out and the foul ashes removed.

Holly regarded Nud. "What's for breakfast?"

The Pip replied with his best snobbish accent: "I have acquired a taste for vermin and blind fish of late. Allow me to serve you."

Holly graced the aspiring diplomat with a full view of her wide, flat tongue. She moaned and made an awful face before burying her head deep into a stuffed hood posing as a pillow. The Flipside girl sighed heavily, and then spoke into her pillow. "Where's Bobbin when you need him?" she complained, with a muffled voice.

Tagged with the responsibility to provide, Nud rummaged through Fyorn's pack and found some dried meat, some dried fruit and, yes, several rather large chunks of taffy – bone dry and hard as a rock. Anyone who knew Fyorn also knew he absolutely had to have sweets nearby.

After Nud and Holly consumed a fair portion of the meat and enough dried fruit, and were about to help themselves to the taffy, Fyorn stepped into the clearing. He stood sooty and sweaty, carrying a small shovel and a large, empty sack. It was no mystery what he'd been up to. Nor was it any mystery to the woodsman what the two Pips had been up to. His sudden entrance had caught them off guard and with their hands in the cookie jar, so to speak. Fyorn grinned widely as Nud shattered a chunk of taffy between two rocks and worked to divide it four ways.

"Would you like my axe?" he said, on his way to the monument.

Nud shook his head. "Not after last night."

Fyorn dropped his gear at the rock and then headed for the cooking fire. He gave Kabor a gentle shake along the way.

The Stout awoke and sat up. A shimmering line of drivel ran down from the corner of his mouth, which he promptly wiped with his sleeve.

Nud showed Kabor the candy morsels. "How about a bite?" he asked.

Kabor made a sick face and shook his head. Holly was quick to claim his portions. The Stout thirsted greatly though, and gulped downed the contents of a canteen that the woodsman had set beside him in the night.

Fyorn scooped up his bits before Holly got to them too. "We'll see rain by evening," he said. "Once we rendezvous with Bobbin and Gariff, you should all head for Webfoot together. Janhurl will guide you. Stay at the trapper's cabin if …" He glanced at Kabor. "… stay there the night if need be. Holly knows where the key is and Bobbin knows where the stores are. Lock up when you leave."

The woodsman rubbed his chin. "I won't be joining you. So as long as Kabor holds his own I'll be veering off to the Hidden City to report what I've seen and heard, and to seek council on recent events. I'll let them know everything that's been happening."

Fyorn fixed his eyes on Kabor and then Nud. "Harrow will have to answer for incarcerating the two of you, and the issue of slaves will cost them politically." He paused to drop the candy bits into his mouth. As he crunched away, he looked to each of them in turn, inviting questions. It was too early for questions though.

After swallowing, he brushed his hands together. "Good, now that that's settled, it's time for a *real* breakfast. We have a big day ahead. Holly, you're in charge." The woodsman held back a smirk, but Holly didn't notice.

She opened her mouth in protest. Her jaw moved, but she said nothing. She turned her head and it seemed she'd let it pass, but quickly turned back. "Okay, but just because I work in a tavern doesn't mean I know how to cook."

Fyorn egged her on, "You must've learned something."

She scoffed. "Yeah, like who's cheap and who's not, who'll try to cop a feel, who tries to pick a fight, and who'll stand up for you. Then there's who makes bad talk about their wife all the time, who cheats, who works hard all day, who tries to pick you up, who likes to have fun and who drowns their sorrows to forget. That's what I learned: who's who."

Fyorn jerked his head back at her response, then shot her an incredulous stare. "Knowing who's who is important."

Holly's own eyes went wide with enthusiasm. "Mmm … but it's fun though too," she said, "like on special occasions when everyone's celebrating. And out-of-towners are amazed when they order a big meal and I remember every tiny detail without writing anything down. Offerings are good sometimes."

She continued on about the Flipside and her patrons, delving into lively accounts of events and incidents. While she spoke, Fyorn began tidying up the campsite. When he came to packing the cooking gear, Holly interrupted his progress.

"You're not putting that away, are you? What about breakfast?"

Fyorn smiled thinly. "Of course not," he said. "Just getting to it." Nud could see the drawn expression on his face, but his uncle was nothing if not a good host. To Holly's delight, the woodsman stoked the fire, assembled his cooking gear and put his pan over the heat. Nud stuffed some fresh wood underneath.

The woodsman sent Nud off to a cold storage space that he maintained, down the hill in a glen. Nud found it easily enough, set beneath rocks deeply shaded by tall pines. Winter ice, doped with sawdust and pine needles, had persisted through spring and probably would into early summer. Under the rocks and the blocks of ice, Nud pulled out fresh crow eggs and a few black sausages spiced with garlic. Fyorn took it from there and whipped the teens up a quick and satisfying breakfast.

Holly served Kabor a small helping on a shallow wooden tray. She sat with him to eat her own, while Nud found himself nibbling at the fixings out of sheer pleasure – the Pip's shrunken stomach was already satisfied. All the while Fyorn minded a pot of tea of some unknown variety, tearing apart small, spiky leaves and dropping them in when the water came to a boil. The green-tinted brew came out pleasantly weak and sipping it imparted a tightening sensation that soothed the throat. Kabor, in his first gesture of non-grumpiness that morning, made his appreciation of the beverage known to all.

Cloud thunder rumbled in the sky as they finished up their meal. Fyorn doused the fire with the rest of the tea and then kicked dirt over the embers. While the Pips tidied up and the woodsman reorganized his pack so everything would fit neatly, Nud went over something he hadn't told them about yet, but that they needed to know – Nekenezitter's revelations about Taeglin's plans for the bog.

Fyorn, visibly irked at the mere mention of the Harrowian, spilled his taffy when he hoisted his pack up too fast. The pieces scattered into the firepit. He set the pack back down on the ground and huffed. "Taeglin is like a spoiled child," he gruffed, agitation showing through in his voice.

"But a *very* powerful one," Nud said. "Everyone knows he's the rightful King of Harrow."

The woodsman scowled. "The man seldom acts the part and few respect his rule while the First King still lingers beyond death. Did you know that the city master runs everything in Harrow? I'm not sure what Taeglin does, hidden away in that impenetrable tower of his all day. Drink wine, I hear. It's difficult to fathom that he came from the same stock as his proud forefather, Taradin." He crouched down and picked at the taffy.

Holly pieced together the implications of the woodsman's words. "Taradin is the *First* King – the one who led the First Men from Akeda?"

Fyorn responded with an iffy nod. "Taradin died a great hero long ago. He should have stayed that way. And he would have been far better off without all those abominations he surrounds himself with." The woodsman looked to Nud. "I speak of the wraiths, of course. They brought him back when they shouldn't have."

Nud took a long look at Kabor, wondering again what the wraiths might've done to him. The Stout raised his canteen and tipped it to his mouth. Only a few drops came out when he shook it. The woodsman tossed him a skin from his pack, which Kabor caught square against his chest.

Fyorn went back to his packing and scoffed. "Ingrate," he muttered under his breath, still hot under the collar.

Nud knew from experience the trouble that someone like Taeglin could cause, routinely overstepping the boundaries of his official jurisdiction to force his will on the surrounding territories. Fort Abandon tended to fall in line due to the strong influences of the Tor Lords in the bay area. The Tri-towns stubbornly resisted, but in reality, its districts were subject to Harrow's every whim unless Gan took issue. Lawless lands such as the Outlands or Scarsands were powerless to resist any incursion and not capable of organized defiance. Only the might of the Elderkin steadied the balance of power in the region.

Nud added, "I think Taeglin wants something in the bog that the Jhinyari lost from a battle long ago, or maybe he knows about the bog stones—"

"They're not his!" Holly cut in. "He can't just take them. That's *our* claim! *Our* bog!"

"No one said he was taking our claim," Nud responded.

"That's something we'll have to discuss," Fyorn said, hauling his pack to his shoulders. He gazed out over the bluff.

"So, is Taradin undying then?" Holly asked.

Fyorn hesitated for a long minute as he surveyed the landscape. "The answer is yes and no. Taradin is undying like the Elderkin, but the roots are different."

"What about the wraiths?" Nud said. "They look like they're half-dead, and the smell …" Nud crinkled his nose. "… and they most definitely are mad."

"Now the wraiths are different again," Fyorn explained. "They despise all life and especially those who are free to walk under the sun … but none more than the Elderkin. Even the touch of a wraith can be as cold as death itself. Taradin was never that way."

Holly shot Fyorn a quizzical look.

"The wraiths were that way *before* Taradin," the woodsman explained, "the results of initial experimentation with undeath through the Order of the Undying, led by Taradin himself. In gratitude, they serve the old king and only the old king. After losing him to the Jhinyari, and after many years of toil and struggle that went with that loss, the Order recovered Taradin's body and raised him from the bog. The wraiths were outcasts at the time, banished from civilization. With Taradin's reappearance, however dismal, they quickly re-established themselves."

Kabor grunted. "I'll vouch for the despising life part." He looked and sounded a little more like himself again. "If the wraiths hate surface dwellers even more than they hate the Glooms, I can only imagine what terror they have in store for us, if they ever gained control…"

"That's exactly right," Fyorn said. "They put themselves above everyone, but they still need others to achieve power they can wield – slaves of all kinds, in particular. That is their way. You catch on fast."

CHAPTER XXI

Strange attractor

Nud only noticed there'd been a breeze when it vanished. An eerie stillness took its place as he stood next to the Rune Stone. And such a fine rain fell, not a drop of it could be seen, yet it tingled the surface of his skin. A lone puff of wind sent a large elm leaf up the hill to circle around the Pip. Something in the hush and the agitated motion of the leaf set him on guard. Fyorn and Holly, still carrying on a spirited conversation about what it means to be undying in the style of Harrow versus what it means to be rejuvenated in the style of Gan, abruptly went silent. Fyorn tilted his gaze to the treetops. Nud's eyes followed.

Above the trees, debris swirled about. Nud heard the heavy gust before it came bearing down on them – branches snapped and leaves flapped violently. The rogue cushion of air that'd frolicked in their midst suddenly was overwhelmed. The leaf whisked away, out of sight. Nud raised his arm to shield against the onset of dirt, leaves and small twigs that blasted by.

The gustiness didn't last, and when it subsided, the strangest compulsion washed over Nud … *Go to Harrow.*

Was that a whisper? he wondered. Or maybe it was nothing but a gust of wind that triggered an urge. The Pip couldn't be sure.

"Why?" Nud muttered to the winds. *I just got out of there.* The winds gave no answer.

"Why what?" Fyorn tilted his head and made strong eye contact with Nud, a hint of suspicion in his gaze.

The Pip shrugged, not sure exactly what to say about what he'd just experienced.

Fyorn put the matter aside and addressed the three of them. "I want everyone ready to depart the instant Janhurl tells us the rendezvous time with Bobbin and Gariff, so if there's anything last minute …" He went off to check on Kabor again without finishing his sentence, then hurriedly exited the grove on some minor mission.

Nud scanned the hilltop to verify that everything in his charge was in order, then found a dry spot on the monument to sit. A break in the clouds released a sliver of morning sunshine into the clearing. The Pip closed his eyes for a moment's solace, soaking up the elusive rays. The heat washed over his face. He knew it wouldn't last long. Spots in his vision floated aimlessly about. For a few precious minutes, Nud put aside the Dim Sea and the demands of the leviathan. He put aside wraiths, Glooms, and whispers. Instead, he found himself longing for home, and Paplov. Holly came to join him. She sat an arm's length away.

"Want to see?" she said, dangling her pendant in front of his eyes, the one she'd found that disastrous day on the Mire Trail. Nud took it in his hands. She explained everything.

"It's brighter now than ever before," Holly said, when she was done. Her stone shone green.

"Really?" Nud let Holly's pendant spin on its chain as it dangled and sparked in the patchy sunlight. "It's a lot like mine, except the color, of course, and the grey rock mixed in. Mer would know for sure if it's the same stuff."

"Fyorn says the markings are from Harrow," she said.

Nud unsheathed his bog stone and took it off from around his neck. The familiar red glow was brighter than he'd expected. He put the two stones side-by-side: the green spark in Holly's gem faded in and out in a slow course while Nud's gem did the same, instead of its usual erratic flicker. "That's odd," he said.

"What?" Holly asked.

Nud smiled, placed Holly's stone into her small, cupped hand and slipped off the monument. She followed.

"Stay right there," Nud said, and made her wait until a cloud blocked the sun. It wasn't long. "Now back away – slowly, and hold your stone in front where I can see it." As Nud suspected, the sparks in the two stones grew slightly dimmer and out of synch the farther she went.

"Now walk towards me," Nud said. And as she approached, the lights brightened and the flickers synchronized.

"The creek..." she started, eyes dancing.

Nud nodded. "There might be more. And now we know how to find them."

"Closer," Nud said. She advanced a cautious step. They stood face to face. Nud set his stone against hers. Holly's eyes went wide as the two lights became one, shining bright and yellow and steady. In that moment, Nud felt that he touched her mind, her thoughts. Abruptly, she pulled away and broke eye contact, looking to the ground instead. Holly put her necklace back on, then swept her hair so that it draped over the chain. Out of the corner of his eye, Nud caught Kabor's quizzical, sideways look sizing them up from where he rested against a tree.

A mischievous smile crept across Holly's face. "Try to find me," she said. Playfully, Holly reversed her dark spotter's cloak and donned the camouflaged pattern, minus the hood. Her body shimmered like a blur as she dashed into the surrounding woods, blending into the scenery.

Holly pulled the hood over her head and closed it tight. "Find me!" she called again, wholly translucent. Nud closed his eyes and counted down from ten, out loud. Then he scanned the woods with a narrow, red beam. Nud caused the light to flash when he found her.

"That's cheating," she complained, completely hidden.

"You have to learn to throw your voice too," Kabor gruffed.

Nud put the stone away and she tried hiding again. At first, he couldn't find her. But after another few minutes of the game, he got better at figuring out where she was, especially if she kept sneaking about.

"You need to be really quiet," Nud said.

"I am quiet."

"And still," he added.

Fyorn returned, carrying a bundle of sturdy sticks in his arms. He took note of the Flipside girl's antics as he passed them by. Holly, gregarious as always, abandoned the game with a "humph" and took the opportunity to grab his attention. She flipped back her hood, and, as the woodsman walked on, spoke more to his broad shoulders and the back of his head than anything else.

"How do the Elderkin become undying?" she probed, carrying on their conversation from earlier.

The woodsman glanced back over his shoulder. He grinned and then winked at Holly. "Just like everyone else," he said, "and it all starts with the twinkle in a lady's eye."

Nud chuckled.

Holly smirked, rolled her eyes and shook her head. "Mine aren't twinkling." There was a long, easy silence, during which Fyorn strode over to Kabor and began sorting through the sticks that he'd gathered, gauging the size of each one against Kabor's build. Holly trailed behind him like an expectant puppy.

She crept close to the woodsman and peered around his shoulders. "Twinkle-twinkle."

Fyorn jerked back, caught himself, and then let out an airy laugh. "You're getting better," he told her, nodding. He turned and raised an eyebrow to her, like he knew something. "I think you've been practicing."

Holly just grinned back at him.

"A lot," he added.

Her eyes widened as she put on her "totally innocent" face.

Nud was about to call her out when Fyorn raised his hand and halted the Pip's words. Another gust began to rustle the leaves in the high branches.

"A whispering wind is blowing," he said.

As Nud's jaw hung half-open with the words still stuck there, Fyorn hastened to the edge of the bluff at the northwest section of the grove. He stared blankly down the rocky path to the lowlands. "News from Janhurl," he started, as the wind ruffled his hair. The woodsman hesitated. He didn't look right – his expression tightened. The sticks fell from his arms.

"What is it?" Holly said.

Nud dreaded the answer. His heartbeat quickened. *Paplov?*

Fyorn rubbed his forehead. "Bobbin and Gariff have been

taken prisoner," he stated bluntly. His tone suddenly turned accusing. "Apparently, there was a generous reward out for the capture of a *certain escaped Pip* and his *Stout companion,* caught thieving in the Iron Tower." He swung his gaze to Kabor and then Nud. "Ring any bells?"

Nud felt his ears flatten with the way Fyorn said the words. *Thief?* His chest tightened, and his lips trembled as he tried to shape a response. Fyorn's eyes drilled into him. The Pip muddled several consonants. "I dit … it's shust … Nekenezitter … what bad luck," he sputtered.

Fyorn huffed, irritation rising in his voice. "Nud, it isn't luck." The woodsman stooped over and scooped up the discarded sticks in his arms, then huffed again. "I'm not mad at *you,*" he said. "This just … complicates things. You don't know how much it complicates things."

Holly confronted Fyorn. She placed her hands on her waist. "You said it would be safe."

The woodsman pressed his lips together and shook his head. "I never imagined … I mean … no one could have predicted something like this would happen."

Except maybe Hurlorns, Nud thought. He kept the notion to himself.

The Flipside hostess stepped aside and shot Nud an odd look.

Fyorn tossed one of the sticks to Kabor, who caught it in one hand. "Try that one." He turned to Holly. "I can't even go to Harrow to put a stop to this. Sending word to Gan is hopeless – they'll debate for days and then decide to act after the consequences have already played out." He looked to Nud next. "Paplov can't go; Mrello's a joke; and …" He trailed off.

"Webfoot is obligated to negotiate," Holly said. She addressed Fyorn directly, her tone now accusing. "Did you talk to Mayor Undle about sending diplomats before you left, like you said you would?"

"I did," Fyorn replied. "We'll need to have a word with them, if we can catch them before they enter the valley. But if it's just Councilor Mrello, the effort will be wasted."

Kabor chimed in, trying out the walking stick. "The Webfoot Council will be either too slow or too accommodating – can't be counted on either way."

Holly nodded, and the notion seemed to make her worry even more. She swung her gaze back to Nud. "Leno, *you* have to go. You have to get them out. They're on the chopping block because of you, y'know."

Nud wanted to volunteer and make things right. He wanted to impress Holly. Bobbin and Gariff were imprisoned because they were trying to help him and Kabor. Yet, he couldn't just abandon Paplov.

Nud sighed heavily. He lowered his eyes to his boots. "But then I might never get to see Paplov again." His chest seized and his stomach tensed at the words. He looked to the others to see what they thought.

Fyorn grimaced. "Not good. Not good at all. They could be put to work in the mines, or worse."

"What about the ritual?" Holly asked.

Fyorn took a deep breath, but didn't reply.

"Ritual?" Nud said.

Holly sighed, and then explained the details as though he should've known them. "A ritual where they sacrifice people, Leno," she said. "What if they sacrifice Bobbin or Gariff? You have to get them out!"

"They do that in Harrow?" Nud said.

"That's not going to happen," Fyorn responded. "That so-called 'honor' is traditionally reserved for intellects and high achievers – the best of the best among the city populace, excluding the ruling class, of course."

Kabor scowled in the background.

"Leno," Holly said, "you have your grandfather's colors now. Isn't it your obligation to negotiate? You're the closest representative from Webfoot, and the colors—"

Nud shook his head. "As long as Paplov is gravely ill I *must* go home, *that* is my obligation." He paused. "The Council is better equipped to handle this sort of thing anyway. We just have to make sure they send someone other than Mrello."

Holly gasped in disbelief. "Yeah right, the Council," she said. "There's more who are crooked than just Mrello. Gariff and Bobbin came here to get *you*, Leno. You and Kabor. We all did." Holly stormed off.

"What about the Bearded Hills or Turnsby councils?" Nud said.

"How do we know they're not just as crooked?" Kabor asked, examining another walking stick the woodsman had tossed him. "There are problems in the Bearded Hills, for sure." He cocked his head at the piece and raised an eyebrow to it.

"Kabor's right," Fyorn said. "If what Holly says is true – and I believe her – there's no trusting ANY liaison to Harrow from ANY of the councils."

"Then there's no other option," Holly called to them, insisting. "Leno has to go straighten this out."

The woodsman sighed and scanned the grove, studying the treetops. A light, swirling breeze blew up. He grabbed Nud's shoulder and spoke in a hushed tone. "More news is on the way. Nud, come with me this time – I know the best spot to listen. This one is out of Webfoot." He glanced at the bog

stone around Nud's neck. "I gather it has much to do with you
– everything hangs in the balance for you right now."

The two of them returned to the summit's edge and faced
the steady southwesterly rising up the hill slope.

Holly called after them. "I'm coming too."

With the woodsman's back turned, Kabor whipped both
sticks Fyorn had given him over the edge of the hill. He hun-
kered down and rummaged through the discarded pile and
chose another one instead. Grunting with the effort, the Stout
pushed himself to his feet with his new walking stick. Slowly,
he hobbled after them.

The Pip wasn't sure what to expect. The woodsman went
completely still. "I hear it," he whispered. He crouched slightly
and addressed Nud at eye level, the way he used to whenever
he was trying to teach the Pip something important. "Nud,
you have to be open to the whisper. Relax your eyes like there's
nothing to focus on. Then relax your ears the same way. Relax
all of your senses. Let them go. Let them go and your mind
will follow."

"What about me?" Holly said.

"You can try the same thing," Fyorn told her. "No guaran-
tees. Hush now."

The wind rose up and the leaves began to rustle more
urgently. If the whisper was not in the wind, it sure sounded
like it could be. And so very faint, Nud had to strain his ears.
There were many whispering noises it seemed, streaming in
and out and softly padding over one another. Nud tried to
focus on one among them, but there were too many layers.
He closed his eyes, inhaled deep, and let out a calming sigh.
Then something came to him. He heard his second whisper, or maybe it was his first, but either way it was definitely
a whisper.

It came as a quiet rhythm of syllables, fully immersed in the other gentle sounds of morning. It was not smooth, like the whisper of a secret from one to another, but rather as grainy a sound as the rustling of leaves. The words formed imparted a good feeling, or *sense*. "Better. All better," is what Nud made of it. He turned to Fyorn.

"Did you hear that?"

The woodsman smiled and nodded. "It sounds like your papa is going to be fine."

Holly gasped. "I heard something too," she said. "I don't know what it was, but it *felt* good."

By all accounts, the whisper was positive. Paplov seemed to be on the road to recovery.

"That's odd … truly remarkable really, considering his condition when I last saw him." Fyorn looked introspective for a moment, and then snapped out of it. "Did you hear that part about the old gaffer being spotted up and about early this morning, tending to his garden?"

Evidently, Nud still had much to learn about whispers. "No," he said. "That sounds like him, though." Holly shook her head.

Fyorn added, "How about the fact that no one from Council has been sent to Harrow yet?"

"Nope," Nud said. "But ask me if I'm surprised."

Nud waited for Kabor to say something, like "it figures," but the Stout held his tongue. He'd only made it as far as the dug-out firepit.

"There's a lesson here," Fyorn said, looking to Nud. "The whisper also picks up something of what it finds along the way, between sender and receiver. Don't think you've heard it all just because you picked out one intended message. The whispers collect as they propagate, and the sources multiply."

Holly looked to Nud. Her eyes lit up with anticipation. "Leno, that means you can go to Harrow and get Bobbin and Gariff out. You're free to negotiate."

The good news about Paplov and Holly's pleading eyes were enough to seal Nud's decision: he'd go to Harrow. Webfoot was lagging, Gan ineffective, the need was desperate, Paplov was fine, and Nud had full diplomatic authority as long as the Webfoot Council didn't oppose – and they wouldn't. They couldn't. And with the authority granted, Nud could negotiate for everyone's release – even his parents, assuming they were actually prisoners. *Paplov would be ecstatic.*

It gets better. Holly would see him as a hero if he saved their friends – doubly so if he put a stop to Taeglin's plans to mine the bog. Nud might even challenge the Iron Tower on treaty matters, for Fyorn's sake. The woodsman would appreciate that. Paplov, of course, would be proud of him. The Hurlorns might even be proud of him. People would gossip, and when they spoke his name, Nud imagined they'd say something like: "Nud Lenokin the wraith slayer, defender of the wrongfully accused, and protector of the bog."

Kabor kept silent on the matter. He caught Nud glancing over to him and seemed annoyed, or in pain, or some combination of the two. Nud swung his gaze to Holly.

"You're right," he said to her, then regarded Fyorn. "I have to go back to Harrow, it's the only way to make things right. Bobbin and Gariff are there because of me. And I think the Hurlorns want me to go as well. I think they whispered it."

Fyorn raised his eyebrows and tilted his head sideways. "The Hurlorns are not sending you back."

Nud knew that the woodsman was wrong though. "Bobbin and Gariff need me," he went on, "Webfoot needs me – I can convince Harrow that they don't need to drain the whole bog to find what they want. And I need to know ... I need to know what happened to my parents. I think a whisper wanted me to go back. It happened when the wind came, before any of this. Did you hear it?"

"No," Fyorn said. "I heard nothing of the sort. And you don't know if you can accomplish anything on your list."

Nud didn't argue the woodsman's point. *Maybe he's right.*

"And this business about the bog is nonsense." Fyorn scoffed. "They can't mine it."

"What about what Janhurl said?" responded Holly-miss-know-it-all. "You said there was a loophole about mineral rights, and that for some reason it *must* be important. Well..."

"Neither Harrow nor Gan are permitted to occupy the Tri-towns," Fyorn said. "It's a veritable no-man's land according to the Non-aggression Treaty – Pips and Stouts exempt, of course."

"Yes, that's true," Nud said. "Turnsby had similar clauses in their dealings with Fort Abandon concerning the Flats – a rich agricultural borderland. There, a complicated land lease agreement has been in effect for decades."

Nud paused. "But mineral rights are different," he went on. "If we can't deny them somehow, then Harrow might be permitted to initiate and maintain a strong, practical presence in the bog that includes 'protection' of their assets."

Kabor interjected. "That matches up with those HME claim posts we found along Blackmuk. Right, Leno?"

"HME ... Harrow Mineral and Exploration," Nud explained to Fyorn, "is state-owned and run by the Tor Lords. I know because it was in one of the legal documents for the deal with Turnsby."

A quizzical look came across Fyorn's face. "So," he said, piecing it together, "you're saying that if a Dim Lake company staked claims all over the place and then started mining them out, then Harrow might try to justify large troop deployments to protect their assets?"

"Something like that," Nud replied. "HME already has several claims in the bog lands and around Turnsby."

Fyorn added, "They can't just send in troops like that. Harrow would need a strong basis to do such a thing."

Holly cut in, excited. "Well, get this: to justify the added security, all they have to do is make the bog lands a more dangerous place to conduct business."

"Whoa." The idea hit Nud like a ton of bricks. "That explains the raiders on the Outland Trail, and worse things that've been happening. It used to be safe, but now everyone in the Tri-towns worries about the dangers of traveling."

"That's dirty," Kabor remarked. "Really, really dirty."

"You can't say that for sure," Fyorn argued.

"Harrow takes what Harrow wants," Nud replied. The woodsman said nothing to deny that common saying – a fact, really.

"They certainly have their ways," Fyorn admitted. "But this?" He hesitated, one hand rubbing his chin. "Then again, Janhurl did find it important enough to whisper … hmm."

Holly turned her gaze to Nud. "I'm going with you," she stated, flatly. Nud smiled at her. She smiled back.

Clearly frustrated, Fyorn shook his head at Holly. "You're not going anywhere."

Holly ignored his words, which only served to frustrate the woodsman more. "I can help," she told him. "He needs a diplomatic aide. My presence will add legitimacy."

Fyorn crossed his arms. "Oh? And what exactly will *you* do when you get there?"

"They'll kill you both," Kabor rasped. He'd taken to

stirring up dirt with his stick where the wraith's ashes had been. "The wraiths will kill you and feast on your flesh."

"Not if I can get to the gate first, with my diplomatic colors in hand," Nud said. "I'll have diplomatic immunity."

"True enough ... *in theory*." A complex look washed over Fyorn. He regarded Kabor. "Nud and any aides of his would be protected by code of law. Harrow goes by the book on that, at least. Wraiths don't come out in the light of day and they don't eat diplomats. Thieves maybe..."

It was the Stout's turn to scoff. Nud knew what he was thinking. Kabor had seen what Nud had seen.

The aspiring diplomat hadn't thought everything through, but he couldn't back down now, not with Holly behind him all the way and Fyorn warming up to the idea. "Maybe Taeglin can't be reasoned with," Nud conceded.

"He couldn't be bothered to meet with you anyway," Fyorn said. "He'd just send you to Garond, the city master, who'd give you the run-around."

"But there's another I can meet with – the First King. If I can just convince him to listen—"

"Well, that's a big 'IF.' He's demented. Do you think you can reason with a madman? Plus, there are rules and procedures for that kind of visit." The woodsman closed his eyes and let out a heavy sigh. Nud could see he was deliberating internally. And Nud believed Fyorn understood what it meant to be chosen by fate for a task specially suited to one person and only one person. It was about being in the right place at the right time, with the right means and the right plan. And the fact that Holly and Nud were in that place together, both with stones that tapped into the Hurlorn consciousness, was no small happenstance. Nud believed that Fyorn also knew what it meant to put his trust in fate, when backed by the

Hurlorns. The Pip had made it through the underworld virtually unscathed, after all.

And so, it was settled. The woodsman grinned and shook
his head one last time in a gentle "no" that actually meant
"yes." And Holly was going with Nud.

"It's nearly an hour's hike, as the Hurlorn strides, just to
get to the eastern shores of Dim Lake," the woodsman started.
"It would be best to get there bright and early."

From there on, the woodsman explained how Holly and
Nud could make their way past the docks, through the outer
gate and the market square beyond, and then to the area that
held the administrative buildings, the bethel named *Karna's
Vessel*, and of course the Iron Tower.

"Don't mention the wrongful capture of Bobbin and
Gariff to the tower guards," Fyorn said. "They confuse easily
and it might prompt them to incarcerate the two of you on
orders long stale."

"If someone gives us trouble," Holly said, "I'll just say 'too
late, the search is off 'cause they've already been found – ask
anyone.' And that I'm a girl; they're not looking for a girl."

"You're not even a Stout," Kabor added.

Fyorn smiled and nodded. "They can be really odd, trust
me." He went on to insist that Janhurl return and carry them
to the edge of the woods. After that, Holly and Nud would be
on their own, but not unwatched. The woodsman rhymed off
a long to-do list for himself. In the meantime, he'd see Kabor
to Webfoot, check up on Paplov, wait for word from Janhurl,
gather news, and act accordingly when the time came. Above
all that, he wondered openly about slipping in a quick trip to
Gan, like he'd originally intended.

The thing about plans is they never quite seem to work out
exactly as anticipated, especially when Hurlorns are involved.

CHAPTER XXII

Words to deeds

Janhurl arrived at the sacred grove, leaves still dripping wet from the morning dew. Nud had only a few minutes to tidy himself up before departing. The robe from Nekenezitter, shabby as it was, would have to pass for diplomatic attire. He straightened the makeshift vestment as best he could, tightened the rope belt, and then swung his gaze over to Holly. Her head was tilted down and she had a barrette clenched in her mouth.

"You look good," Nud told her. He wasn't lying, and if her attire wasn't a perfect match for the role – form-fitting clothes beneath her shimmery cloak – he knew from experience that aides rarely received more than a passing glance. On top of that, Pips are known for their casual dress. "All you need to do now is carry yourself with an air of politeness and formality. You know – a bit uppity, but not too uppity."

Holly's eyebrows shot up and she tilted her head at his remark. Then she gave him a slight nod and spoke between her teeth. "I'm sure I can handle it." The Flipside girl gathered her hair, drew it back and applied the clip.

The time had come to embark on their well-intentioned journey. Holly and Nud quickly said their goodbyes. The young diplomat smiled when he saw Kabor up and about, drinking tea and complaining that none of them knew what they were getting themselves into. In the end, he wished he could join them, and thanked the two Pips profusely for going after Bobbin and his cousin. Following the usual handshake ritual with Fyorn, they parted ways. The woodsman stood watching them as they descended the slope and entered the deep shade of the forest, where they climbed upon Janhurl.

The morning sun disappeared behind dark grey clouds as the Spirit Hurlorn strode through the trees, tendrils whipping in her wake like animated vines. Riding their perches upon her high branches, the Pips soon crested a hill overlooking their destination. The vale that cradled Dim Lake opened up beneath them. The Iron Tower loomed in the distance with the city of Harrow sprawled out beneath it. Behind the tower, the lake's blue waters drained into the wide and deep Dim River. Beyond that lay the rugged Western Tor.

Janhurl could take them no farther. She fluted an incomprehensible farewell and gently set the two Pips down on solid ground. In response, Nud wished her well and repeated Fyorn's parting words: "By sun, wind, rain and earth."

Nud turned his gaze to the lakeside town. The closest structures were the shipyard's floating workhouses. As the two Pips made their descent, snippets of song, quick and clever rhymes, and shouts of frustration billowed up the hillside. Harrowians cut and hammered at planks in dry docks carved into the lakeshore, while gulls cried out from the nearby pilings, screaming for entitlements. A scattering of oar-driven dories glided across the calm, grey-lit waters amidst sparse puffs of thin morning mist. Farther west along the lakeshore were moored scores of small fishing vessels, a handful of black schooners all in a row, plus one larger sailing ship. Dim Lake was a fair size, but not big enough to justify the presence of the galley – it could only be intended for eventual sea voyages.

On nearing the outer curtain wall, the aroma of smoked fish saturated the still air, accompanied by the music of a lively fiddler sawing out a whaling tune. The guards at the east gate let the diplomat and his aide pass easily enough, once Nud showed them his colors.

A guard called after Nud, "Here for the festival or for business?" A simple question.

The young diplomat's stomach twisted in knots at the asking. If he replied "business" they might ask for details, and if he replied "festival" they might see he was lying. Nud peered over his shoulder and nodded, rather nervously, while Holly kept pace along the cobblestone path without looking back. Their confusing responses didn't seem to raise any suspicions.

Nud and Holly soon made their way into the open square that defined the marketplace, filled with colorful, open-air tents and spritely banners that painted a festive atmosphere. Children ran across a wooden stage that'd been constructed in the middle of the action. Business was already picking up for the shopkeepers. Holly's eyes darted about the grounds as she took in the sights. She'd never been to such a grand place. For once, she seemed at a loss for words, and she stuck close to Nud's side as they strode casually across the square to the next curtain wall, encircling the royal grounds.

Nud could hardly believe that he was actually going through with the plan. The words of defiance he'd uttered in the grove had taken on a life of their own, and were now converging to consequence. He hadn't really imagined himself at the gatehouse to the Iron Tower, being scrutinized by intimidating tower guards and begging his way into the hall of a dead king. But that is exactly where Nud was heading, and by his own volition. Nud had said the words, and they came to be. He wondered exactly how he'd call upon the laws of inter-state diplomacy, should the need arise…

CHAPTER XXIII

Interlude - Youth immortal

Time is pressing. Urgency is everything. Now that I am sheltered from the weather in this deep grotto, I write with a pen fixed to every spare claw and branch. Masterful creatures Hurlorns are, slow and lumbering in the bulk, but quick-minded and coordinated in twig and bough. The papers strewn about cover every flat surface beneath my leafy crown. Inkbottles sit upright and lie overturned about this secret chamber. I hear the wind howling above. If it ever reaches down this far, there will be quite the mess to clean up … quite the mess indeed! I'll leave that to the young ranger. Words come in a flurry now.

You have to understand that I was fifteen and girl stupid at the time. More than that, I was naïve about the dangers of the world – especially the familiar world, which I insisted I knew. Clearly, from everything I could put together at the time and the state I was in, the return mission to Harrow never should have happened. And Fyorn never should have allowed it. The political engines of the Tri-towns and Gan were far better equipped to handle such delicate negotiations than two teens ever could be.

And I cannot say with certainty why Holly and I supported one another with such willful determination in the cause. Pheromones, testosterone and adrenalin, perhaps, bringing on some measure of uninhibited irrationality. Or perhaps it was something more. But what is risk to an immortal teenager? – not to say that I was really immortal; it's more like I did not fully appreciate the harm that could come my way, or the harm that could be put on others as a result of my actions. Consequences.

As I said, Fyorn should never have allowed it – the mystical notion of encouragement by his bark-skinned advisors must have clouded his good judgment. Who could expect a pair of Pips to divert the will of the Iron Tower? Harrow takes what Harrow wants. Indeed.

Ahh … to be girl stupid, young and fearless again. Those were truly the glory days of youth immortal.

I feel nostalgia coming on. And as the end nears, I just want to enjoy everyone in my sphere, in being and in memory, and sip from the fine wine of life one last time.

CHAPTER XXIV

The Iron Tower of Harrow

The Iron Tower loomed over the displaced ocean-side town of Harrow, a pale reminder of more glorious days when the forefathers of the townsfolk thrived on the shores of former Fortune Bay. They thrived and conquered, lived and loved, died and were raised. Some say giants forged the iron blocks of the monolith out of meteoric ore from Gabber's Bowl in the Western Tor. Others say the tower was raised by Karna herself to guard the entrance to another world that knows no death. None could argue the landmark's practical construction. Besides being a royal house and a hub of political activity for the town, it also served as a lighthouse, built in the extravagant manner of old Akeda with a royal beacon that cut through foul weather like a scimitar of light.

As Nud and Holly approached, like typical out-of-towners they tilted their eyes upwards to gawk at the Iron Tower's impressive height. At the top, six pillars supported an iron crows' nest over the lantern room, some four-hundred feet above the courtyard. Standing within was a statue of the First

King himself, raising his staff to the sky. His stony gaze kept watch over town and lake.

The inner curtain wall was of black stone and it protected the courtyard surrounding the tower. Sentries armed with crossbows patrolled the wall walk, above. Intricate depictions of leviathans graced the barrier's four corner towers: in the foreground and to the left, a white whale with actual smoke billowing out of its blowhole, and then a kraken to the right. In the background, a giant mollusk to the left and a sea dragon to the right. Bursts of fire routinely flared from the dragon's nostrils.

A guard manning the iron-bar gate bellowed out to Nud and Holly on approach: "Who goes there? What is your purpose? State your names and state your business with Taeglin, Rejuvenator of this Iron Tower and Protector of the Lake." The man came off as abrupt and professional. He was the shorter of the two guards stationed there, by a head and a half. Behind him, two tower shields served as wall mounts and several more hung along the interior of the dim passageway that tunneled through the wall. Each depicted the sigil of old Fortune Bay and now Harrow – a frothing wave gliding across ocean waters by night. One of the stars that shone in the backdrop was actually a lighthouse lamp, to guide wayward ships home again.

Using Paplov's most polite diplomatic voice, Nud cleared his throat. He answered loud and clear, doing his best to sound authoritative.

"I request an audience with Taradin, the Old King of Fortune Bay," Nud began. He halted in front of the two guards and fumbled through his pack. "Allow me to introduce myself," he checked the front pocket, "I am Nud Lenokin of Webfoot, here on official business … ah, there they are – my colors." The Pip retrieved Paplov's rolled-up leather from its bone tube and handed it to the shorter guard. The man unfurled it, gave it a quick glance, and then handed it back. He gestured to Holly.

Nud introduced her. "And this is my aide—"

"Holly Hopkins of Webfoot," she broke in, with as much of a curtsy as a girl wearing pants can pull off. The smaller guard nodded to her, and then addressed Nud.

"I haven't seen you two before. You must be new at this. You mean Taeglin, right? Everyone gets the two confused. Go see Garond, the city master across the way, he deals with the little Tri-town folkish issues." The guard pointed to a building diagonally across the square, built into the side of a flat hill. All of the buildings in that quadrant had an administrative look to them.

"No," Nud insisted, "I actually do mean Taradin. The city master won't do." *Little folks? What an oaf.*

The guard crossed his arms. "No one asks for Taradin. You are mistaken." Then he flicked his wrist at them. "Now run off."

Nud firmed up his tone. "I am asking for Taradin, the former King of Fortune Bay."

The taller guard spoke. "What would Taradin want with a couple o'toads like yous? He doesn't see anyone. Go see Garond or git back to yer lily pads." He was plainly stupid – toads don't sit on lily pads, frogs do. Who doesn't know that?

Nud stepped forward and looked straight up at the burly guard, eyes glaring daggers. Putting his agitation on display, he turned to the shorter guard and pointed to the tower. With an even, serious tone – the same voice Paplov used when he felt he was being disrespected – Nud verbally blasted the man. "Get in there and tell your superior that I'm wasting valuable time waiting here for you to do your job. Taradin himself requested this meeting."

The man stared back.

"What's your name?" Nud demanded.

"Clandt, sir," was all he said.

"Now, if you can fit a second thought in that thick head of yours, tell him that I'm here to discuss artifacts from the bog lands – you might want to add the words *unique* and *valuable*, and how about *last chance*." Nud raised his voice and enunciated the important parts: "U-NIQUE AND VAL-UABLE, LAST CHANCE … GOT IT?" The larger guard snickered at the scolding of his comrade.

Nud threw his arms up in the air. "And why not mention your belligerence towards his invited guests while you're at it … it will save me the trouble, Clandt."

Clandt looked to his half-giant companion, who, with a smirk, nodded his head and waved his hand to the guards in the gatehouse. The tall guard barked a command their way, "Just put'em up for the day."

He swung his gaze to the shorter guard. "Now, Clandt…"

"Woe-woe-woe," Clandt interjected, shaking his head. "I'm not going down there."

Down? Nud wondered. *Why down?*

A loud clang initiated the rising of the two portcullis gates – one on either side of the passageway under the wall – followed by a metallic grinding as they lifted off the ground. The larger guard raised his voice over the racket.

"What? 'Fraid of a little spooks, Clandt? Git goe'n."

"But—"

With a slice of his hand through mid-air, the half-giant cut him off. "GIT GOE'N!" he boomed, drawing the attention of a guard on the walkway above.

"Everything all right down there?" asked the crossbowman.

"Just Clandt," replied the half-giant. "He's a'scared to see ole' Taradin."

The crossbowman laughed. "He won't bite," he said, then went on his way. After a few steps he muttered back. "Better you than me."

"I'm not afraid," Clandt said. He huffed a protest, but once the gate was fully raised, he started off for the tower at a quickened pace.

The half-giant took on a kind and apologetic demeanor towards the two Pips. "Terribly sorry, sir, ma'am," he said. "Clandt don't know better. Grew up in the Tor wrestlen' giants just for a bit'o rabbit 'n such. I think one'o'em picked'im up 'n dropped'im on his noggin. He was always the runt'o dem…"

Nothing the guard said made much sense to Nud, but the Pip nodded in acknowledgement just the same and offered a gracious, yet pitying smile. Nud caught Holly smirking.

In the intervening time, the guard asked about what was in Nud's pack. The Pip told him only some rare wood: "Bog wood," Nud said, assuming he wouldn't know any better. The man rummaged through and didn't make a fuss about the contents. "It don't look like much to me," was all he said. Indeed, only a few pieces of deepwood remained. Nud felt a little safer knowing that *Shatters* was in there. He never did recover *Sliver*.

Clandt certainly took his time executing his errand. While they waited, Nud couldn't help but to re-evaluate the rationale behind his decision to meet with the undying former King. Holly was on his side, at least. Back in Deepweald, her confrontational spirit had prodded him on, full of fire and fury about retrieving their friends and protecting the bog ecosystem. *Where is that fire now, though?* Nud wondered. Ever since entering Harrow, she'd acted timid. *This is all new to her,* he conceded. *Maybe she feels intimidated or has second thoughts…*

As for Nud's own doubts about the mission, he put them aside. If the Hurlorns really did whisper to him, then he should treat the words as a benediction. They had their reasons and he needed to trust in them.

The guard finally returned with a reply in the affirmative. He looked a bit gaunt for the asking. With a slight shake in his voice, he also offered a polite apology from the First King himself, for neglecting to instruct his gatemen to be on the lookout for anyone offering something "unique and valuable, especially from a bog." The response came off like a slight, and his words triggered a sour feeling in the pit of Nud's stomach.

Reluctance heavy in his footsteps, Clandt proceeded to escort them through the entrance passage. Midway, Nud noted a third portcullis, fully raised and easily overlooked. It could come crashing down at unawares on unsuspecting visitors.

Once through to the other side, Clandt led them along a slate path to the tower doors. Landscaped gardens, ornate statues, elaborate fountains, and private groves filled the yard, so visually pleasing and elegant that it put Turnsby to shame. In stark contrast to the artful greenery, the black metal of the tower rose high above, bleak and imposing against the backdrop of overcast skies, not a single pit or streak of rust to mar its surface.

A wide, black hall lay beyond the iron-rimmed doors of heavy oak. Although lacking in direct, natural sunlight, wall-mounted lanterns kept the hall bright. Their stroll through it was pleasantly hot and smelled of incense. The walls showcased storm-driven ocean scenes on canvas. Wind swirled and water frothed as oared sailing ships tossed about like toys on giant waves. In one turbulent depiction, the massiveness of the sea and the fierceness of the weather contrasted the frailty of a lone vessel, vulnerable to open water.

Nud tilted his gaze up. The arched ceiling hosted a nest of murder holes and a series of trap doors, cleverly worked into the artful decor. At the far end of the corridor a gated archway, with the gate raised, led into the next chamber.

"Are those originals?" Nud said to Clandt, gesturing to the paintings.

"Huh?" he replied, scanning the walls. He shrugged. "What else?"

Clandt took them through the arch and then swung to the left. The lighting beyond was far dimmer, and it smelled of torch smoke. Nud bumped into the wall once, before his eyes adjusted, and Holly stepped on his heels. They rounded another corner and came upon a long, red hall lined with torches, a single red door at its end. Two female guardesses of the half-giant variety stood watch there, gripping tall, black halberds and garbed entirely in deep red suits of padded armor.

"Red Maidens," whispered Clandt, on approach. "The King's Guard. Don't be fooled by their good looks. They'll slice your heart out if you step out of line."

The wall guard raised his voice on approach. "I present Taradin's honored guests ... a diplomat and his aide."

"Did you search them?" one asked.

"I did, m'lady," Clandt said.

"Did you inspect their passes," the same woman asked.

"I did, m'lady," Clandt said.

She called upon her comrade. "Khotahri," she said.

The one named Khotahri took over from there. "Raise your arms," she told the Pips.

Holly and Nud raised their arms as the Red Maiden patted them down. The other guardess picked through Nud's supplies.

"Asthana," said the one named Khotahri, "They have nothing." She turned back to Nud. "May I see your colors?"

Nud handed Khotahri his document. She scrutinized every letter before rolling the leather up and passing it back. Satisfied, she nodded to Asthana.

"You may pass," Asthana said. She returned Nud's pack.

The young diplomat squirreled away his colors while Khotahri opened the door for them. Clandt ushered them down the shadowy stairwell that lay beyond. A sudden chill came in the air.

Nud leaned over to Holly. "Strange," he whispered, "to be entering the lower levels. A former king should have a high chamber in the tower, don't you think?"

Holly nodded her agreement.

A single flight of stairs brought them down to a sloping corridor. Like the tower's exterior, the walls were constructed of heavy blocks, predominantly dull black but in this case tinged with multicolored streaks and swirls, mostly shades of red.

"Into the belly of the beast," Nud muttered under his breath.

Torches lit the way, held in smooth, translucent sconces, each made to resemble a mask of sorts. As Holly and Nud struggled to keep up to the wall guard's long-legged pace, Nud noted the chiseled-out face of one shining mask grinning at him from its roost, as though it knew some terrible secret. Another looked wickedly amused as it clenched a torch in its eye socket, and yet another seemed surprised that it had somehow swallowed a torch … whole. Its cheeks, nostrils and crystalline eyes glowed red with the light cast. A set of two opposing fixtures appeared to be enjoying some forbidden pleasure with their torches, not spoken of in polite company. Even with an abundance of fiery lights to guide their way, Nud could still smell dankness in the heavy air.

"The walls!" Holly exclaimed, pointing. They both halted.

"What is it?" Nud said, taken aback by the urgency in her voice.

"They're moving!"

Subtle but true, Holly was right – the muted pattern was not entirely still. The walls seemed alive with a slow, sickly motion, fluid and churning like chaos. Shapeless forms danced and swayed amidst the mess of colors. Swirls of blood red, mustardy yellow, foul green and deep purple faded in and out, hypnotic and upheaving to the stomach, if stared at too long.

Clandt placed a firm hand on Nud's shoulder. "Just keep going," he said, eyes fixed straight ahead. "And try not to look."

"Unreal," Holly whispered, almost to herself as they resumed their pace.

The down-sloped passageway curved around several turns before straightening, where it also widened. The way never did quite level out though. Three stone doors lined one side of the sloping hallway. Mask sconces lit the way to the third door, but beyond that, the corridor was lost in inky darkness.

Clandt led them all the way to the third door. He used the brass knocker three times and waited. The door and the wall shifted in color to a translucent aquamarine. Fiery light filtered through from the blurred interior, giving a vague sense of what lay within the chamber. The swirling motion faded to the point of being barely visible, and wavering splashes of red marked blazing fires on the other side.

Nud heard a click. The door swung inwards, half-open. Clandt alone stepped in, leaving them unaccompanied. The door shut firmly behind him. Silence filled the hallway.

Nud turned his gaze to Holly. She stood hunched, glancing at the stone and rubbing her arms to fend off the chill. Her face looked pale.

"Look to me," Nud said, trying to get her mind off the walls.

Holly offered him a nervous smile. Nud took her nervous smile and sent back a reassuring one. It wasn't real though. Nud didn't know what undeath really meant, or what to expect of Taradin, or what to expect of this strange place he'd brought her to.

As they stood waiting for Clandt to return, the translucency in the wall turned dark and murky. Deranged notions darted through Nud's mind about what they might find on the other side of the door: limp bodies hanging from the ceiling by nooses, or half-opened iron maidens propped up, with ghastly corpses staring out blankly. Or perhaps they'd find a huge iron pot over a cooking fire, filled with gruesome stew and an arm dangling out.

A minute later, Clandt emerged, closing the door behind him only partially. The warm, red glow of the chamber radiated into the hallway.

"Taradin will see you soon." The guard read their wan expressions and gave them both a pitying look. "Don't be afraid. He wanted me to tell you, 'He knows the Way. He can get you what you Want.'"

The words of the leviathan, Nud recalled. The Pip knew exactly what he wanted. All he really needed now was the way.

CHAPTER XXV

Hall of the undying

"Honorable guests of the Illustrious Bog," a young girl's voice began, filtering into the passage from the chamber beyond. Proper, soothing and fully nasal, it carried the faultless accent of high society. "Vicegerent Taradin, the once and mighty King of Fortune Bay, will see you now. Enter and be seated at his table, if you would be so bold."

Holly and Nud exchanged glances.

"Bold?" Holly said. "What's that supposed to mean?"

Nud shrugged.

Feet planted, Clandt pushed the door and held it open with a stiff arm. He inclined his head to the two Pips. "Get going," he said, out of the side of his mouth.

The young diplomat was the first to step through the doorway. A kind of sweet rot hit him on the other side. The reek of death was new to Nud, but even so he recognized its lingering presence for what it was. The terrible smell interlaced with hints of a tangy aroma that carried on thin trails of smoky incense, disguising all but the slightest trace of cadaver.

The guard, holding his breath and holding his expression to the limits of composure, nodded to Holly, prompting her to follow. By the look on her face, she was already struggling.

Nud pushed forward despite the smell, hiding his disgust as best he could. Holly entered and stood next to him. She coughed and put one hand to her chest, then dry-heaved uncontrollably. The door slammed shut behind them.

Two Red Maidens stood tall and motionless, one to either side of the doorway's elaborate trim, their faces placid and their eyes unblinking.

I need to breathe, Nud thought. *Breathe.* He raised his arm to his mouth and drew a breath through his sleeve. Nud's eyes darted about the chamber. The young diplomat and his aide had stepped into a great hall with a high, domed ceiling supported by four intricate pillars of carved stone, depicting life-sized mermaids peering out of dense kelp with bright green eyes. A ring of large braziers burned in the center, suspended by thick chains. The fiery light cast long shadows over the stone floor, polished to a mirror-like smoothness with red veins streaking through it. Beyond the ring of fire hung the cured hide of a great, battle-scarred leviathan, hauled up from unimaginable ocean depths. Other than the Red Maidens, the chamber appeared unoccupied.

Holly's eyes danced across the room as she took in the sights as well. Stunning in a freakish way, the scene was lush and captivating – an opulent suite abound with priceless artwork, elegant decor, and lavish furnishings. The glow of metal was fluid and writhing in the wavering firelight, and the sheen of gold entered every quarter: woven into fabrics, inlaid into earthenware and spiraling up the mermaid columns in thin ribbons. Set on marble tables were gold vases, silver flagons and cups, candelabra, and intricate, aquatic-themed treasures. The heads of gem-encrusted corals served as bookends on shelves of ebony, where many old tomes had been laid to rest. Large shells of unusual shape and vivid colors mixed with the books.

Textures were plentiful and pleasing to the eye; a rich wash of blood red and velvety purple fabrics with gold accents covered chair frames and wall hangings. Elegant tapestries depicted seafaring scenes, with details barely discernible in the dimness. The walls themselves conveyed the active turbulence of grey weather on the rise. Nud could almost smell the salty air. He relaxed his arm with the sleeve filtering his breaths. The terrible odor had largely subsided – that or he'd just gotten used to it. He no longer wondered why the royal chamber was "stuck" below ground. Indeed, in all ways it seemed fit for a king.

Holly seemed to have gotten past the stench as well, and now bore a starry-eyed expression on her face. She whispered into Nud's ear, "It's true, isn't it? He really *is* a king." She had every reason to be excited as they prepared to meet a celebrated character out of myth, and a hero at that.

Nud mouthed the words just loud enough for Holly to hear. "Red and gold for death and glory, purple for royalty." She smiled. It was a line from *First King's Silver Thread*, spoken in the Great Hall of the story, where the Orbweaver is deceived by none other than Taradin.

Could this be the Great Hall? Nud wondered. He shook off the notion – even if the story were true, the events would've happened in the old world before Akeda even existed, never mind Harrow.

There was no sign of their host. The voice had told them

to "be seated." Nonetheless, the two Pips casually wandered about, admiring the various display pieces. Holly commented on a prominent portrait of a stately noble, adorned in jewels and wearing the finest linens. Piercing blue eyes shone from under a silvery crown. Desiring to sit, she patted a pillow on the chair beneath the portrait. A cloud of dust flew up. A closer look at the fabric revealed its age: old and decayed.

Holly wandered back near the exit. After careful prodding, she discovered that the guardesses at the door were actually statues, so lifelike they'd passed for real at first glance.

Nud, on the other hand, approached one of the bookshelves. The leather bindings of its holdings were tattered and smelled of mildew. The furniture was in poor condition as well – especially the chair cushions, split and frayed. Not all of it though. Near the far wall stood an intricate table with six plush chairs, all well-kept. Nud moved closer for a better look. Cups for wine and a freshly filled decanter had been set. The stone-slab tabletop glimmered aquamarine in the dim firelight, supported from underneath by a single pedestal carved in the likeness of a sea serpent, finely sculptured. A shallow depression appeared in the center of the tabletop, rounded like a bowl. Holly joined him.

"This must be where we're supposed to sit," Holly said.

"Of course," Nud replied. "Shall we?" He pulled a plush chair out for Holly.

She paused, staring at the wall behind the table, which began to shift, slowly, depicting the swirling charcoal haze of cloud cover in the night. Briefly, a shrouded moon shone through and then a patch of starlit sky, before the clouds folded over the break in the haze.

A click sounded to Nud's left, followed by a voice. But the words spoken were gargled and incomprehensible. The young diplomat and his aide turned to see a statuesque figure step out of a dark corner, thinly veiled in a long purple robe. He stepped out of the shadows against the backdrop of a storm passing. The robe was torn and the man deathly gaunt. By the crown he wore, he could only be the First King. His slow and fluid approach seemed both elegant and unnatural for his critically-ill appearance. The tattered remnants of what might have been considered fine apparel at one time hung ragged upon his imposing frame. As if the sight of the figure wasn't ghastly enough, an equally ghastly smell preceded him, increasingly vile as he drifted closer. Taradin's presence saturated the air with aromas of bile, urine, mildew, and some underlying flowery scent – perhaps to mask the others. It was more than enough to turn anyone's nose. Nud glanced to Holly. By her pale demeanor he thought she might pass out. The man reached the corner of the table, cleared his throat and then addressed them again, rasping his words.

"Do you care for wine?" he said, before even introducing himself. "I hold all the best Doncaster vintages. Fine little brewers, they are." His long teeth flashed when he grinned, like daggers of worn enamel. Only a scant bit of gummy flesh held them in.

"No thank you," Nud said, fighting the urge to run away screaming. He tried not to think of the man that stood before him as decayed or deathly ill. He tried to think of him as a normal person with an unfortunate condition.

"We had our fill this morning," Nud said. The thought of eating or drinking anything at that moment was repugnant.

"Yes, I'll have what you're having," Holly said, to Nud's surprise.

"Spectacular," he slurred. "Please, join me little ones … my *great* guests of honor." Taradin's outstretched arm gestured to the ornate table. The limb hung in the air, frail and emaciated.

Holly finally took her seat, her back to the entrance door. While their host grasped the flagon of wine, Nud took the head chair closest to Holly and carefully laid his pack at his feet, mouth breathing in shallow breaths all the while to deal with the awful pungency in the air.

Arm quivering, the grim figure poured a cup of red wine, raised it, and steadied himself with a quick swig. He paused for a long moment to ponder the flavor of the liquid as it swished and sloshed in his mouth. At the same time, his pale eyes studied their expressions. Finally, he made a satisfied nod, swallowed, and poured a fresh cup. With a thin-lipped grin, made crooked by a patch of stiff flesh, he passed the cup to Holly and promptly refilled his own.

"It is quite good," he said. "You have to be careful with the Seawind Flats label; oft times it is vinegary. But elsewise, it is masterful."

Holly couldn't stop rubbing her arms. *Nerves*, Nud surmised, but the withered figure had a different impression. He produced a metallic scepter from the confines of his robe, then reached out and tapped the wall. Seconds later, it came alive, set ablaze with images of a leaping fire, except they were more than just images – Nud could feel the heat radiating.

"I had told the servants I wanted a strong fire in the braziers," he complained. "Good help is hard to find, these days."

The sound of blood rushing thudded in Nud's ears. *How is this possible?* He was at a loss for words.

Nud mustered his resolve and composed himself. *Now is not the time to ask,* he thought. *Now is the time to get to the business of this visit.*

Their host gazed upon the two Pips, the grotesqueness of

his face in plain view. Remnants of dry and hardened flesh clung to his ghastly visage, and sunken-in eye sockets cupped exposed eyeballs with blue irises – a slash of fiery light across each one. His whole left side appeared rough and ragged. Rusty orange and yellow patches of lichens – as cover rocks, old wood and tombstones – had taken hold to skin and exposed bone. In a few places, beneath tight skin, the glint of metal shone through. Revolting to behold, yet too remarkable to look away from, the First King appeared as though he belonged in a cemetery, or the rubble of ancient ruins. A "Crypt King," perhaps, given the jeweled rings of gold and platinum that decorated his boney fingers, and the matching platinum crown and necklace that completed the set.

Is this Dim Lake's blend of rejuvenation that Fyorn spoke of? – hardly rejuvenating at all!

With the grace of a bodiless spirit, their host took the expected seat across from Nud and formally introduced himself. He addressed them in a hushed tone that adult's normally reserve for polite conversations with children.

"I am Taradin," began the gruesome spectacle, "former King of Fortune Bay and now Vicegerent of Harrow, an honor bequeathed to me by the rightful heir and ruler from the Iron Tower. I speak in his name and also in the name of Karna's Vessel – *He Who Seeks Beneath the Waves.*"

Nud mouthed the words – "I speak in his name." That was exactly what Nud wanted to hear. The young diplomat introduced himself. "I am Nud Lenokin, Councilor of Webfoot. I speak in the name of the lord mayor in this dealing. My views and opinions also reflect those of the Tri-town Council."

"Reflect," Taradin repeated, before nodding to Holly. The crown he wore caught the light in that moment. At the slight bow of his head, it sparkled with tiny diamonds encrusted in the froth of a wave, as appears on the sigil of Harrow. Front and center, beneath the frothing wave, the crown bore a large aquamarine gemstone, light blue and teardrop-shaped. Arcs of black pearls curved along each side.

Holly blurted out her introduction. "Hopkins," she said with a nervous tone, "Holly, of Webfoot also. I'm here to assist Leno ... ah ... Mr. Lenokin ... Councilor Nud ... Lenokin." She covered her mouth with her hand.

The First King let out an airy laugh. "Well cheers to you both, Councilor Nud and Hopkins Holly." He lifted his cup in salute.

Holly followed. "And cheers to you, Vicegerent Taradin."

Cupless, Nud offered a nod and an awkward smile.

Following the salute, Taradin set his cup down and placed his palms flat on the table. He leaned his meager physique forward, and in so doing, his arms spread wide, like wings. The First King stared at Holly. By all appearances, he seemed awfully concerned about her.

"Before we begin – Hopkins, are you ill-prepared? Do you require quill and paper? There is a writing desk near the archives..." Holly and Nud made passing glances to one another with raised brows and wide eyes. *He doesn't know.*

"That will not be necessary, Your Highness," Hopkins replied, "Pips have perfect memory."

Taradin rubbed his boney chin. "Really?" His eyes rolled up and to the left, contemplating. "All Pips?"

"Yep." Holly covered her mouth. "I mean, *yes Your Vicegerentship*, pretty much."

Taradin nodded. "That explains a few things ... yes ... from what I've heard of ... *Pips* as you say. Intriguing, very intriguing. Ah then, to what do I owe the pleasure of your company? A lesson in history, perhaps, connected to something you found in your bog?"

"I love history," Holly said.

"Shall I start from the beginning?" Taradin asked.

The prospect was tempting. And Holly finally appeared to be in her comfort zone. But Nud was not in line with her pleasant approach. She'd try to put them on friendly terms with Harrow and win cooperation through kindness and reciprocation. But Nud knew better. Not only would Holly's strategy fail, it would serve to raise the ire of their Tri-town partners who were already struggling to deal with Harrow's unreasonable demands. This negotiation required firm action.

"Perhaps another time," Nud interjected. "That would be wonderful, really, but it will have to wait."

Nud raised his fist and slammed it onto the tabletop. Not a hard slam; not one like Mayor Otis might've done back in Turnsby, but forceful enough to make a strong impression. A pause followed. All eyes turned to Nud. The Pip raised his voice and sharpened his tone.

"I am here, Taradin, because you have wrongfully incarcerated two citizens of the Tri-towns: a Pip by the name of Bobbin Numbit and a Stout by the name of Gariff Ram. Further, I have been made aware of evidence to suggest that you are holding political prisoners."

"Do you represent the Tri-towns?" Taradin said, contention in his voice.

"I represent their views."

"Legally?" he enquired.

"No," Nud admitted, "Legally, just Webfoot." *And even that's shaky.*

"May I see your colors?"

Reluctantly, Nud reached down and pulled the bone tube

from his pack. He extracted the leather document and handed it over. While Taradin examined it thoroughly, the Pip began to make his demands.

"Webfoot respectfully requests that the two forenamed individuals and any political prisoners you might have in custody be released immediately, and that all charges and allegations against them be dropped. Secondly, we know about your plans to mine the bog, and we recognize that there is some legitimacy to your claim of mineral rights. I am also here to discuss possible alternatives to that course of action."

"You are well informed, are you not?" The question was rhetorical. With a kind bow of his head, the First King handed back the leather and continued to speak. "I am at your mercy then, and your service."

The negotiations were going well. This Taradin could be a bit short at times, but all in all he seemed polite and cooperative enough, and, more importantly, legal-minded to the letter of the law. *He must be very different from Taeglin,* Nud thought. The man came off as ... honorable, although in a kind of twisted way. And how could he not be somehow twisted, being what he is?

"I hope to be at your service as well," Nud replied, returning the head bow, "but first, we must find resolution. Webfoot, the Bearded Hills and the whole of the Tri-towns will not stand for injustice – the Pip and the Stout must be released."

Taradin gestured to the scroll. "Remember, you speak only for Webfoot."

"Indeed," Nud said, and tucked the leather away. "But the Tri-towns will concur. Send a raven if you doubt it. Furthermore, the Stout is residing in Webfoot, currently. That puts him under my charge."

Taradin nodded in acknowledgement.

"With regard to the bog," Nud continued, "the entire Tri-town region has a vested interest in the area. And I know my people – no amount of riches can replace our way of life or detach us from our forefathers. The bog waters course through our veins the same way seawater flows through the blood of your people. Mining the bog will destroy our livelihood, our life-blood."

"And yet we persist, separated from that which we long for," he said. "In many ways, the struggle has made us stronger."

Taradin grinned a secret thought. "Do not fret, little one, Harrow will restore the land back to its original condition after the extraction – as per the Treaty. And Webfoot promptly shall receive the agreed upon tax – a full tenth of the value after expenses. You will never know the operation was even there. It is only temporary."

"What do we do in the meantime?" Nud said. "You might be there for ten years … twenty even. During that time, the bog ecosystem will collapse. There will be open pits, drainage, tailings, destruction of habitat…"

Holly interjected, "There are other solutions. We can section off one area at a time to excavate, and build a solid road to it without ruining the town or the greater habitat."

She was out of place, of course. Diplomatic aides were to remain quiet until spoken to, apart from the occasional whisper into one's ear.

Taradin, being a man of formality, shot her an annoyed look. Nud acted annoyed for show, before extending Holly's line of thinking.

"I apologize," Nud said, then looked to Holly. "It is not your place to interrupt." He turned his gaze back to Taradin. "She's new."

Taradin nodded with a forced smile and repeated a phrase

he'd said earlier. "I gathered that," he said. "Indeed, good help is hard to find these days."

"She's quite good, actually," Nud said, "and what she says is true. Harrow could simply guarantee a higher duty for use of the land while excavating, sort of like the deal we have going with Turnsby. Webfoot would handle inspections, approvals and would also provide advice."

"My son of sons, Taeglin, already has a plan in place, and your suggestions would complicate it unnecessarily."

"Taeglin's plan dismisses Webfoot entirely. What I am suggesting is honest and forthright – and everyone benefits. You *must* convince him."

"Must I, now?" remarked Taradin snidely. If he'd had eyebrows, Nud was sure one of them would have risen while he spoke. "Humph." A grim smile crept across his face. "To ease your strife, Taeglin is proposing to relocate your little bog people to more fertile grounds south of Harrow's Gate, between the two rivers. And at his own expense, for the entire duration of the operation."

Nud shook his head. *And what of Bobbin and Gariff?* Taradin was avoiding the issue of Nud's imprisoned friends, not to mention the political prisoners ... his parents. Nud's arguments were passionate and sound. The only thing lacking was the fact that he was making them to a walking corpse.

There was more to the First King's proposal though. "If you, Councilor Lenokin, act as our emissary and convince the Webfoot Council to relocate without a fuss – lobbying the promise of great reward for those personally involved in the decision – I am prepared to negotiate bonuses to make you all wealthy Pips. This offer would elevate you even beyond the dreams of your Everdeep clan, whom I have dealt with in the past."

Mrello. I knew it.

"As a gesture of goodwill," their host went on, "I will personally arrange to send you home in a chariot loaded with precious artwork, jewelry, metal bars and other gifts to distribute as you see fit, along with your little friends who are currently … shall we say, enjoying our hospitality."

"What of the political prisoners," Nud said.

Taradin hesitated. "Simple. There are none. Harrow put an end to that sort of thing years ago."

Nud didn't fully believe him. The words spoken sounded more like Taeglin's now than his own. From everything Nud had heard of the man, Taeglin was the type to take the easiest route to get what he wanted and would tell them anything they wanted to hear. Nud imagined he'd follow through only long enough to suit his purposes: fickle, capricious and plainly unreliable.

On the other hand, the thought of rolling into town in a chariot laden with expensive gifts gave Nud pause. And Bobbin and Gariff would be free. Holly gave him such a sharp look though, that he shook off the notion immediately. But there was more.

The First King had lapsed into an internal state, swaying back and forth ever so slightly – a pendulum corpse, it seemed, heavy with the weight of indecision. Taradin's jaw dropped slightly and his eyeballs shifted up, signs of deep thought. He stopped swaying, and then his gaze met the young diplomat's. "There is one other thing I can offer you, Councilor Lenokin; a great thing. In return for your loyal service, I am willing to put you on the path of rejuvenation. And your aide as well, if you fancy her." Taradin looked Holly up and down.

No, thank you, Nud thought straightaway. He wouldn't dare say it though.

Under the table, Holly's hand lashed out and grasped Nud's wrist, ice cold.

As the young diplomat pondered how he should respond to the words of enticement, the repetitive motion of the man's lichen-covered hand kept the Pip distracted. Repeatedly, Taradin stroked the amulet around his neck and the chain holding it, as one might comfort a loved one or a favored pet. Nud came to realize it was his habit. At first, he thought the worst part to be the weak yet nagging scraping sound he made while doing so, until he saw that the chain disappeared into the flesh where his fingers ran across it – a groove down to the very bone.

"What about Web footers?" Holly said, speaking out of turn again. "They will have nothing."

Taradin flashed her an annoyed look and then turned to Nud for action. "You must learn to control your aide," he said, his voice a harsh rasp. "She lacks the proper respect."

Nud nodded to express agreement, then sent Holly a scolding glance. "Enough," he told her, "or it's back to the Red Rooms for you!"

Holly glared daggers at Nud momentarily, then lowered her eyes and made a good show of being shamed into obedience.

"Without me," Taradin remarked, "Harrow would be naught but a simple fishing village with a powerless fool at the ship's wheel. But under my careful guidance, this humble country is on a most glorious path, and soon Harrow will become the hub of civilization as we know it, and the envy of all. You can be part of that."

Evidently, "His Excellency" liked the sound of his own voice. *What about my proposal? What about Holly's idea? Had he even heard them?* Maybe not: Nud took notice that his ears presented little more than shredded scraps of flesh.

The lichen-covered king faced the Pip directly. "Nud, you look a little pale. Are you well?" The fire reflecting in his eyes seemed to flicker and swirl, and there was a kind of inquisitiveness in his voice that made Nud believe he might be searching for something; something wedged in between the words the Pip might say, or written in the expression on his face, or hidden in his eyes.

That moment, Nud realized that the fiend was only toying with him. "I'm just fine, but thank you for asking. You look a little gaunt yourself."

There was just enough flesh on Taradin's lips to form a broken smile. Then a change came over him. He took on a more serious composure, cold and purposeful. The fiery scene on the wall snuffed out, replaced by a churning storm. The room darkened.

Taradin raised his scratchy voice. "As you said, you are here to get down to business." He cleared his throat. "You are in a position to ease Harrow's exercising of agreed-upon rights under the Treaty to obtain something desperately needed by its good people, but you choose to put up barriers instead." He leaned back in his chair; chin raised. Elbows on the armrests, he folded his hands together upon his sunken chest.

"I fear we are at an impasse," he went on, "for I agree with my son of sons. It is much easier to simply move the Pips out, bribes or otherwise, and drain the bog. And prisoners are wonderful for exchanges. I can tell you this much: those who would aid Harrow to achieve its goals will be richly rewarded." Taradin gripped one hand into a boney fist. "Any and all who dare to stand in the way of the Iron Tower will be crushed."

The vicegerent cleared his throat again, coughed and

sputtered. Raw muscles in his chest contracted as he heaved. He'd worked himself up, it seemed, beyond what his bodily facilities could withstand. After a long moment, he regained his composure.

Nud glanced to Holly. She raised her eyebrows and shrugged.

"I wish for you to be the one that helps us, Councilor Lenokin," Taradin continued, "I really do. I am rather fond of your bluntness and adventurous spirit. The earth holds many secrets, young Pip, and each secret tells part of the story of a larger design, and each design is part of one higher, and derives from one lower, and joins many others across, and influences more that we haven't even dreamed of, and is driven by others we cannot even perceive or know to perceive …" Taradin trailed off, introspectively.

"I will aid you in the negotiations and help find a viable solution," Nud responded. "Just send us on our way with the Pip and the Stout that you—"

Taradin leaned forward and slammed his own fist on the table. "You have to be my 'Man on Council,'" he insisted.

"Don't you have one already?" Nud responded.

"He is a fool," Taradin said. "I want a better one."

Nud glanced to Holly. Wide-eyed, she returned a slight nod.

"I'll do it," Nud said.

"And inform me who my opponents are?"

The young diplomat hesitated, then sighed heavily. "Agreed." He'd say anything to get out of there alive, with his friends.

Taradin stroked the chain around his neck yet again. "Too late," he said, at last. "I retract the offer."

Nud felt like pelting him. Taradin's boasting about the

First King's great people and great kingdom persisted after that, until the words grew faint to the Pip's ears. Instead, the sound of his voice penetrated Nud's chest and gripped his beating heart. Then it hit him. This man was terribly cursed and terribly mad, with little more than curses and madness to offer. Fyorn had been right: he should've died a hero, long ago.

"What is it you want?" Nud said, finally. "What exactly are you looking for?"

Taradin leaned back again, raising his chin. "I admire that you have come here to save your friends and preserve your village," he said. "Noble causes, indeed they are … very noble causes and I commend you for taking them on. I did much the same once, long ago. But I made a decision to further my own line above all others. Family comes first. You plan to have a family one day, don't you?"

The lichen-covered king was rambling, and he wasn't answering Nud's question. The Pip prodded on. "What is it that Harrow needs so much from the bog lands?"

Taradin sharpened his tone. "You will find that out when the bog is drained," he stated flatly. "There is new knowledge hidden beneath your mud flats – perhaps even directly beneath your makeshift village – and the way to begin excavating a bog is to drain it. Your precious wetland sits high compared to the lands south. All that needs be done is to dig a few channels whilst damming or diverting any inflows."

Nud was desperate. "I know what you really seek," he said at last. "I have seen *IT*. I'm sure I can tell you exactly where *IT* lies. Release my … the persons you have wrongfully detained, and I will prove it."

What exactly is IT? Nud was bluffing … sort of. His best guess was that the Iron Tower was searching for the Jhinyari battleground, of course, but perhaps there was something more: the "mother lode" of sparking stones similar to the one Nud found, or the "Spears of the Gods" cave for all he knew, or the Hanging City, or Dromeron Odoon, or Isotopia, or perhaps something special within the Hanging City – devices. Whatever it might be, Nud was treading into dangerous territory.

"You have professional informers then, don't you? Very well then. Prove what you say. Where is that which I seek most?"

"If I tell you, I will have nothing to bargain with."

"Just tell me 'what' then."

Nud blurted it out. "The location of the Jhinyari batt—"

"Scoundrels, I say," Taradin broke in, "Let them rot! You are getting warmer. So, what of it?"

Taradin had the young diplomat cornered, for Nud could only speculate on the specifics of the Iron Tower's interests and intentions.

Nud fumbled his words. "I don't know … I mean, I can't explain because we were lost underground for so long."

"Lost?"

Nud turned to Holly. Her expression tightened. He shifted his gaze to her necklace, tucked under her shirt, then raised an eyebrow to her. She glanced down, then her eyes met Nud's. Holly reached to her neck, grasped the black iron chain, and paused. Nud nodded, and so she retrieved the light-bearing crystal gained from the hags. She pulled it out from under her shirt, peeled off the cloth she'd wrapped it in, and then dangled the pendant in front of their host.

It was a desperate move to keep the negotiations on track.

Taradin stared at the piece in stunned silence. The light danced and sparked in rapid bursts. There was no doubting the vicegerent's sense of intrigue; he couldn't look away.

"Jhinyari ... yes," Taradin said, as though recalling a distant memory. "I remember now ... this dancing light ... the warlords ... all of it." He closed his eyes and winced in pain, then shivered. "I will never forget the 'silver swords' that cut us down from afar."

He's taken the bait. I have that corpse right where I want him.

Nud continued with his plea. "And in my travels, I have beheld the Hanging City, and nearby, mammoth crystals I call the Spears of the Gods, and a dancing pool. I can lead you to all of these wondrous places. There are secret ways underground that can bring a crew to the bog without disturbing it or even revealing their presence. What you seek is underground, yes, but you don't need to dig out the bog to get to it. You can start somewhere below this very room ... the entrance is literally beneath your feet!"

Taradin stroked his jeweled amulet hard and the chain holding it. The intensified scraping of raw bone on metal sent a shiver through Nud's spine. The Pip tried not to flinch at the sound, nor at the sight of the spectre's fibrous neck muscles, exposed and contracting as he tensed.

"Compelling ... and quite ironic, to say the least," Taradin said, finally. "I call for a game of Pirates' Dice to settle this matter. As you well know, it is within my rights to name the deciding game of chance. As I said already, we are at an impasse. Your trinket changes nothing."

There was no such "right" and Nud could see plainly that the mad king was bluffing. He could see it in the man's preoccupation with the stone, and he could see it written on the walking corpse's rotting face.

CHAPTER XXVI

Gambler's ruin

The lich king grinned a wide grin and pointed his metal scepter at a narrow desk, set along the wall. There, amidst ornate paintings and statues, two sets of dice and two shakers – one white set and one red set – began to wobble. Shivers ran up Nud's spine as they rose from the desk and drifted to the table. Next, in the same fashion, he retrieved an ink well and a white feather quill, and set them at the Pip's end of the table. His chore complete, Taradin tucked his scepter away again. His boney hand scooped the two white dice in front of him into their matching cup. He rattled them as he spoke.

"The dice will reveal your integrity," he explained. "They always do. If you roll true and wager well, you will be vindicated by the will of Karna, as I once was. I have six rings to wager and a coin, all quite valuable. You have your stone. The coin represents the bog, so I own the bog for starters."

That hardly seems decent, Nud thought.

Taradin locked eyes with the young diplomat: "My child,

on top of your stone you have your life and the lives of your sweet companions. That only sums to three though – I'm counting all three friends as one. Trust me; it's better for you that way. There are no political prisoners to add."

Taradin knocked the dice cup onto the table. "I will start the game by fronting you two of my rings," he went on. "Now we are even at five a piece. The game continues until one of us has lost all five wagers or we both agree to call it quits."

"That's not fair!" Holly snapped. "You would have us lay down our lives against your stupid rings? Forget it. Leno … Councilor … we're leaving." She stood up. "Let's get out of here."

"I have no life to bargain with," said the lichen-covered one, "and if you abandon me now, neither will you, nor will your friends." He leaned back in his chair, hands motioning for her to reclaim her seat.

Holly hesitated, glanced to Nud, then did as Taradin bade her.

A confident smirk crept across their host's face. "So," he said, with a slight snarl forming on his lips, "sit back and take in the game, and when your life hangs in the balance by little more than a silver thread, relish it! That is what it means to truly live … you must look Death in the eye, again and again, and dare it. You must do so until you can bear its gaze no longer, until you are sick to death of seeing Death. And then, you must look Death in the eye one last time."

As his words faded into soft echoes, Nud gazed into the eyes of the undying one. *Staring down Death couldn't be much worse,* he decided. Nud had witnessed Death already – in his dreams – and that fiend had turned out to be nothing more than a destructible wraith.

If life did not sustain the thing that sat across from Nud,

then what did? This spectre counted himself not among the living, yet he was more than simply dead. Dead ... alive ... he seemed to be neither, or both. Perhaps he lay somewhere in between.

At least for the moment, Nud owned the lives of his friends. "I suppose you will not agree to end the game at this time?" he opened with.

Taradin's smirk disappeared and he gave the Pip a vile look. He sighed and shook his head.

Nud agreed to his terms in full realization of their dire circumstances. Holly nodded to signify her compliance as well. They had no real choice in the matter. They had to play, or die. They had to win, or die. They had to save their friends – and maybe save the bog – or die.

Nud understood the game: a simple two-player contest, and each must start with an equal number of tokens and two six-sided dice. One player acts as the "attacker" and the other the "defender." Each turn, the players agree on what to wager, then roll their dice in any order. Whoever rolls the highest die, or rolls a pair (the higher of both pairs if each rolled a pair) wins the toss, the tokens wagered, and defends next turn. In the event of a tie, the defender wins the toss. The game commences with a "roll-off" to determine who defends first. In the event of a tie in this case, the roll-off is repeated until a win occurs. The game ends when one of the players has nothing left to wager. There is no "honor" for a player in Pirates' Dice. The game is infamous for escalating during play – desperate players down to one token, with odds stacked against them, often plead with their opponent to add new and valuable tokens to the game, at the discretion of said opponent.

Taradin drew a deck of blank cards from his robe and

passed two of them over. Holly took them. Nud picked up the feather quill, dipped it in ink, and passed it to Holly.

"You write," he told her. "Mine is too messy."

Taradin watched as Holly scribed in neat cursive: "Councilor" on one card and "Holly, Bobbin and Gariff" on a second. She had a particular way of writing "Holly," with a curvy "H" and an extra big loop under the "y" that underlined the entire name. When she was finished, Taradin handed Nud the two white dice together with the matching shaker, and kept the remaining red pair and shaker for himself. Nud took the shaker, emptied the dice into his hand, and weighed the bringers of fate. They were heavy and metallic.

"Ready to roll?" Taradin asked.

"Ready," Nud replied.

"Ready," Holly said.

The diplomat and his grim opponent threw dice into the bowl, carved into the middle of the slab tabletop. It was flat at the very bottom. A slightly curled lip at the top deflected any high rolling dice back down.

Taradin won the first toss for defender. Nud then rolled a "1" and a "2" on the attack, while Taradin rolled a "4" and a "5" as defender to win the toss. Nud gave the lich king a ring, of course.

For the next turn, Nud passed the dice to Holly to roll on their behalf. She rolled a "6" and a "1", and smiled confidently at her luck. The dice, unfortunately, were not kind to her either. Taradin rolled double sixes, winning the toss again. A wry smile crept across his face. Nud added another ring to his kitty. If they lost the next round, Holly would have to put in her light-giving stone. They gathered their dice for the next roll.

Nud rolled "6" high and Taradin a "5" high. The diplomat

was now the defender. Taradin returned one ring. Then Holly rolled a "4" high and he a "6" high, winning the turn for their opponent and making him the defender. The next turn was devastating. Holly rolled a "5" and a "4" – not bad, except for the fact that Taradin rolled double sixes – again! The Pips had no choice but to hand over Holly's stone.

Holly leaned forward, palms rubbing her knees. "We would like to quit the game now," she said, pleading with her eyes as much as her voice. She turned her gaze to Nud.

Nud nodded. "This game has gone on long enough." He met Taradin's stare. "You have the stone and the bog. Do you accept our offer to terminate?"

Taradin took a long moment to mull over the decision, or at least he pretended to do so for dramatic effect. While waiting for his response, Nud contemplated a passage from the legend of the First King: "He rigged the game so that no matter what the roll, the Orbweaver could devour everything *except* the First King and his followers ..." *Could Taradin have rigged this game too? A game rigger is a game rigger*, Nud decided.

Finally, the lichen-covered fiend offered a way out. "You may quit now, if you like, for the price of one life."

Holly grabbed Nud's wrist. "Quit," she whispered. "I will do it."

Nud shook his head and stared Taradin right in the eye.

"Next roll, winner takes all," Nud said.

Holly and Nud were in this together. Together they'd seal their fates and the fates of their two good friends. The game had so quickly come down to their lives. Nud's only hope lay in chance, and the notion that the dice might be loaded.

There was no response from Taradin as he weighed his options. It was his way of torturing his guests. To accommodate

Nud's request would be courteous, but nothing bound him to do so.

"Winner takes all," Nud stated again.

Repeatedly, Taradin ran his fingers down the chain around his neck. Nud could hear the bone scraping against the links … louder … faster. Slowly, Taradin nodded his head. "Very well."

"And we switch dice," Nud added.

What little flesh that still clung to one of the vicegerent's eyebrows sprung upwards. He sneered when he spoke. "What is wrong with your dice?"

Holly answered. "Can't you see, Vicegerent? They're bad luck."

Taradin leaned forward, once again resting his palms flat on the table. He had the most serious look in his eyes. "You must know that I once rolled dice to save the whole of mankind, and won! Do you really think it is possible that I could lose to the likes of you?"

Nud didn't know what to say.

"Well … do you?"

Rather than nod or shake his head, Nud simply returned the man's stare, blankly.

"You're short," their ghastly opponent spat. Part of a tooth flew out of his mouth and clattered as it bounced along the tabletop and onto the floor. He'd gotten himself all worked up again and was falling apart, it seemed. Taradin wiped his lip with the sleeve of his tattered robe.

"You have only two wagers remaining to my eight," he said, anger rising in his voice. "To keep the game balanced, you both have to offer something extra. A service perhaps … a small price to pay for all that might be gained, judging from your current predicament."

Holly tugged on Nud's sleeve. She shook her head at him. But how much could it possibly matter? Whatever Holly's reservations might be, they'd have no choice but to accept once again.

"What are your terms?" Nud asked.

"In addition to providing me with the location of the stones …" Their opponent tilted his head and paused to ponder the offer he was about to make. His boney jaw hung half-open. "… you must seek out the leaders of your own community in the bog and convince them to join our league. Name it 'The Rejuvenation League.' Webfoot will fall under the protection of Harrow, and your village will share in our wealth and knowledge of longevity. A gracious and respectful associate of mine, who is attentive to the needs of Pips, will be assigned to your village council and will aid in all decision making henceforth. All your council need do is accept our generous offer, and a new and wondrous age will enlighten your people."

What possible influence could I have over the council? Nud wondered. He was barely of age and wholly new to his position; they wouldn't pay heed to his words at all. Nud's contemplating must have been written all over his face, for Taradin gave him the answer to his internal question.

"I will outfit you for the task as though you were a high lord. You will have our finest coach drawn by the noblest of steeds in all of Harrow, a most esteemed entourage, plentiful gifts of goodwill as I said earlier, and City Master Garond will accompany you to draw up the contracting arrangements. Your council will have to take you seriously. Tell them there is a great sage in Harrow who will guide them all to riches and immortality. And be sure to tell them this of Karna's Vessel, for whom I speak…"

By the way the next words rolled off his rotten tongue, you'd think they were sacred.

"He knows the Way. He can get you what you Want."

Again – the words of the leviathan. The two had to be connected somehow.

Taradin sneered. "I will hold your lives to ensure that you do your utmost to fulfill the task agreed to. Holly, you would do well to help him. If you succeed, I will give you back your lives and the lives of those you seek to rescue."

"And if I am not successful?" Nud asked.

"Hmmm … then I would have to say that your life's work would become mine," Taradin responded, "to do with as I see fit … perhaps you would make a good serving boy, or maybe an acrobatic fool. You seem clever enough though, so the laboratory may serve you best – if you could learn to click with the Gropers. You are a good reader, I presume? The Gropers can do most anything BUT read. How are you at *story time?*"

Nud offered a blank look in return.

The lich king swung his gaze to Holly. "As for you, my dear, I have other uses in mind. Perhaps Harrow could use a Red Room." He laughed a sinister laugh.

Nud didn't like the idea of leading the council down this path, nor did he like becoming a slave. An impulse jolted in his mind. *Just get out…*

"If I do not succeed," Nud pleaded, "but if I knew of a stone like Holly's except brighter, could I trade that for one life back?"

"Have you seen such a stone?"

"I'm not sure, but I have an idea where to look."

"Agreed," he said, all too quickly.

Taradin and Nud swapped dice. The Pips knees went weak and he felt sour in the pit of his stomach. The next words to hit his ears sounded alien to him: "Then I agree to your terms as well," the voice said. The words were Nud's.

In a moment of clarity, Nud realized it was stupid of him to have listened to a forest of trees in the first place. And why Holly had insisted on accompanying him to pursue this folly, he could not fathom. She had her sense about her by then though, it seemed, signifying her disapproval with flared nostrils, pursed lips and a shaking head. She was scared too. Really, really scared. The young diplomat wondered if Holly truly realized that Nud had no real choice in the matter. He had to keep the game going at all costs … *I have to give luck a chance.*

Taradin handed Nud two more cards from the stack. On one of them, Nud wrote: "Convince the council or be a slave – Nud."

Holly reached for the quill to write on her card. She knocked the inkbottle over, jerked her arm back, and in the process knocked her wine cup off the table. The pewter clanged several times before rolling underneath a chair. Taradin rolled his eyes. His patience with her was up. With a quick apology, Holly ducked down to retrieve the cup.

Nud's hands trembled as he poured the red dice into the shaker. He rattled them for a good long time, and then rolled their fates. Taradin tossed his dice into the bowl simultaneously. All four dice, red and white, bounced and jittered up and down the gentle slope. They clattered and they skidded. One die from each collided, stuck together, and began to slide down the arc of the bowl towards the bottom. Nud's die was on "6" and his opponent's on "1". The Pip gasped in anticipation. The other two dice were still in play.

The fact that Nud hadn't revealed that the stone was on

his person gave him solace, as did the knowledge that the toss was showing to be his. *Win ... WIN!*

But just as the final two dice were about to settle, Nud toppled. The Pip didn't even see the numbers, for his chair suddenly tipped over and he tumbled onto the floor. He heard dice clatter in the bowl above him one last time, before coming to rest.

Two sixes for me, Nud bet.

Nud believed his roll whole-heartedly, but it wouldn't matter. Only Taradin was privy to how the dice landed. A condition of diplomacy is that a witness must attest to the events that transpire during a negotiation and what is agreed upon, or it simply does not count. As far as Nud was concerned, that last roll had become null and void, and the game forever spoiled.

CHAPTER XXVII

Into the gloom

Lying flat on his back on the polished floor, the young diplomat met the steady gaze of the sea serpent. Its painted eyes shone bright and yellow, while its sinuous tail wound up and around the pedestal base of the ornate dice table. The Flipside girl pulled Nud in close and draped the wild elderkin cloak over the two of them. To the outside world, they suddenly vanished.

Nud started, "What the—"

Holly slapped her cold, clammy hand over his mouth. She delivered him a harsh whisper, "This negotiation is over, Leno."

A "tap tap tap" sounded from above, metal on stone. *Taradin's scepter.*

Nud quietly slipped his backpack onto his shoulders. Still sharing the cloak with Holly, he rose with her to a crouched position for a quick getaway.

The tapping stopped.

"What is going on down there?" Taradin asked, impatience building in his voice.

"Ahhh," Nud called out, faking his pain. He dragged his leg back and forth over the floor tiles, as a sound effect. "Half a moment, if you will."

"He'll be fine in a second," Holly added. "Is your knee all right, Mr. Lenokin, Sir?"

The two Pips used the distraction to steal away from the table towards the door, unseen and unheard.

"Come now!" Taradin complained. His voice rose a notch on the grandiose scale. "Rise now, and behold your fate, Webfooters! Rise! Feast your eyes on the treachery and glory of Pirates' Dice! Oh, how wonderful it is to behold!"

When they gave no response, Taradin slapped the table. "Come now, this is absurd! Get back up here. What are you two doing down there, anyway?"

Nud and Holly crept with small, quiet steps, practically invisible. The spectre's chair scraped across the floor as their host stood up.

"Do I need to haul you up myself?" he rasped. "No farewell kisses under the table ... Whaaa?"

Surprise, surprise.

The First King burst out at them. "Get back here!" he growled. "Where are you hiding?" Suddenly, his voice became hoarse and monstrous. "Come out!"

They'd almost made it to freedom when Nud bumped into one of the Red Maiden statues beside the door. It was a hard knock, a full check. The statue toppled over, grazing the other Red Maiden on its way down, which began to wobble. The two Pips scrambled back as the stone figures smashed to the floor one after the other, crisscrossing in front of the door. Bits of red stone exploded out. Holly let out a squeak.

"STOP!" commanded the lich king.

Holly leapt up over the fragments to the door and found the handle. She pulled and pulled but the door wouldn't budge. The cloak slipped off as she gave it a hard yank.

Taradin bellowed on, "The game is not over until you behold your fate!"

To hell with that. Nud braced his back against the wall and kicked with full force at the broken chunks of statue blocking the way. Holly kept pulling at the door; it scraped open a crack.

"More," Holly cried, pulling with all her might.

Nud grunted with effort as Holly pulled and Taradin came for them. A grinding noise sounded as the biggest piece slid. Holly forced the door open just enough for her to squeeze by. She reached back through the opening and grabbed her cloak. Nud scrambled to his feet and followed her through to the other side. But the wall guard was ready and waiting.

Although not the brightest conversationalist, Clandt proved to be quick-minded when it came to, well, being a guard. Before Nud even realized what was happening, Clandt had hauled Holly up off her feet, and using a swift kick he sent the young diplomat stumbling backwards. With a sickening thud, Nud's head slammed against the edge of the doorframe. Clandt grabbed hold of Holly's cloak and flung it away, down the passage.

Realizing the lich king himself soon would be upon them, Nud darted away from the door to the middle of the passage. The maneuver was just in time.

Taradin's boney arm swiped through the doorway. The morbid figure became stuck trying to force his way through, lacking the strength needed. Scepter in hand, he shouted commands. "GUARDS! ... GUARDS!" His voice was a frustrated gargle. He tapped the wall with his scepter and the stonework turned translucent.

Nud charged at Clandt. In one fluid motion, the guard extended his foot and, with a shove, effortlessly redirected the Pip's momentum. Nud tripped, stumbled, and smacked the floor. As he struggled to his feet, a metallic "schwing" sounded behind him. He glimpsed the glint of steel. Nud glanced back. Clandt had adopted the middle-guard stance of a swordsman, short sword drawn and brandished. He had Holly in a headlock.

"That's enough," said the guard. There was no tolerance in his voice. Holly gave Clandt a handful to mind, but he rough-handled her into submission.

Daring the sword, Nud hazarded a step towards Clandt. The wall guard waved his weapon at the Pip in warning. The Pip didn't believe Clandt wanted to hurt him, but he saw in the man's eyes that he'd do his duty.

"You can come with us," Nud offered.

Clandt shook his head. "Stay right where you are," he commanded, waving his sword dangerously.

At that moment, remarkably, the door to Taradin's chamber warped to let him pass. The solid stone slab bowed like a lithe young twig. Nud gasped. His mind scrambled to understand. Half a moment later, the corpse-like figure stood in front of the doorway.

"Honor your deal," he scolded, pointing his scepter at Nud. "You have lost everything … the both of you are mine."

"Never!" Nud shouted, unsheathing his bog stone. He sent forth a burst of blinding light. Clandt shielded his eyes and Nud dashed towards him. The Pip snatched Holly's hand, but the wall guard wouldn't let go. Nud pulled hard and Holly squirmed to free herself.

"No!" she cried out, clawing and kicking. Clandt yanked her back and waved his sword blindly. Holly's hand slipped out of Nud's and the young diplomat fell backwards.

Holly grunted. "Let me go!" With a swift elbow to the groin, she broke free from Clandt. Also blinded by the flash, she tripped herself up on the sloped floor and toppled.

"Holly," Nud called out. "This way!" He leapt to his feet.

Holly rose, waving her arms in front of her as she stumbled towards Nud. "Leno?"

Taradin spoke: "Very well then, Councilor Lenokin."

Nud sensed something awfully foul in the tone of Taradin's voice. He swung his gaze to the First King. The grim figure was manipulating his scepter.

The floor beneath Nud's feet suddenly became slippery – as slippery as oil, but dry instead of wet. He lost his footing, fell hard, and entered into a backwards slide. Arms flailing and trying to grip something, he glided away from the door and down the hallway.

Clandt latched on to Holly and held her firm. Beneath them, the floor hadn't changed.

Nud tried to dig his heels in, but it only made him spin. He slid and spun into the discarded cloak, which bunched up around him. Down he went into the unlit portions of the corridor.

"Holly!" Nud yelled. She grunted in frustration at her captor.

"Take the girl to the holding cells," Taradin barked at Clandt, "and send someone to retrieve the body from 'The Catcher.'"

Body? Catcher?

Gripping the cloak, Nud steadied his slide and brightened his stone. He beamed it ahead. A huge gaping maw appeared at the end of the hallway – the skull of some great beast with fiery eyes. *A trap.* Directly to the right of the maw, he glimpsed an open passage.

With quick hands, Nud unraveled the cloak. Then he balanced himself to a crouched position as he accelerated towards the maw. At the last possible instant, he whipped the hooded end of the cloak towards an unlit wall sconce around the corner. It caught and, to the sound of fabric tearing, Nud whirled into the side tunnel and smashed against the back wall. He felt out the ground beneath him. It was firm. He breathed a sigh of relief.

Faint voices echoed down the sloped passage.

Clandt called out, "He hooked into the tunnel."

Nud got up and flashed a beam of light into the maw. Through the opening, he spotted rows of deadly spikes that lined the bottom of a shallow pit, thin and razor-sharp. *It was a trap.*

"I see him," Clandt called. "There!"

Nud stepped to the other wall of the tunnel, out of view. Palms pressed against the cold stone, he peered around the corner and up the sloped corridor. Clandt still had a firm grip on Holly and appeared to be tying her hands, while two Red Maidens rushed down the stairs. Nud could hear other voices behind the guardesses. Men's voices.

Holly screamed out, "Run, Leno, RUN!" She still struggled to free herself, but with no real hope of escape. And Nud had no hope of reaching her – it was too slick and he'd just slide into the maw.

"I'll come back for you," Nud yelled back. "The Tri-towns, Gan, even Fort Abandon … none of them will stand for this!"

"Go!" she yelled, just before a Red Maiden gagged her. "Hurry!" came next, muffled.

A pang of guilt hit Nud as he unhooked Holly's cloak from the wall. The face on the sconce it'd been snagged on bore a horrified look, with an unlit torch set like a spike through its skull. *I can't believe that helped,* he thought.

The walls suddenly morphed – a thousand eyes stared from all around. They all focused on Nud.

And a terrible, yet familiar sound arose from up the slope … a wheezing voice. Nud sheathed the stone and looked around the corner to confirm his suspicions. Clandt still had hold of Holly. She was terrified. And yes, others had arrived. Nud jerked back and flattened himself against the wall.

Damn! Wraiths! At least two of the foul creatures were present, maybe more. He felt terrible for Holly. *They better not hurt her.*

The next words Nud heard were faint and echoey. "He's long gone by now," said someone – it didn't sound like Clandt. "Pips are fast little creatures…"

Nud couldn't hear all of the conversation.

"He won't get far," another seemed to say.

Nud peered around the corner again. The wall across from Taradin lit up. The lich king pointed his scepter at it.

"No, fools," he told them. "Behold! Lenokin is watching us!"

In the distance, Nud saw images of himself from many angles, projected onto the wall in front of them.

The eyes … of course!

The Pip pulled back and wrapped Holly's cloak over him, torn and stretched out of shape as it was. He donned the hood and glanced back again. Nud saw that he'd completely vanished from their imagery. He rekindled the bog stone and turned his attention to the new passage. When satisfied he'd memorized the course ahead to the limits of vision, he sheathed the stone. With a heavy feeling in his chest, the Pip started on his way down the corridor. Bleary eyed, Nud forced himself to focus on his escape route.

When he reached the limits of what he'd seen and memorized, he flashed the stone again, just for a moment, to memorize what lay next. Every time he repeated the procedure, he noted the wall's searching eyes honing in on his position.

Nud scolded himself as he went. *It was stupid to come here, and it was stupid to bring Holly. We should be safe right now, far away. We should be in Webfoot. And someone else — other than me — should be planning Bobbin's and Gariff's rescue right now, and saving the bog for that matter.*

The young diplomat didn't want to think about the consequences. *Why can't that walking corpse just die already?*

"You'll wish you'd stayed dead by the time I'm done with you," Nud said aloud, his final words in the dark before going silent. He actually hoped that the walls had ears as well as eyes, so that Taradin could hear him say it.

*

Padding softly, Nud kept to the main tunnels and avoided the lesser ones where possible, navigating several divides in the hallways and passing many closed doors. Despite his maneuvering, every so often he could hear faint voices from behind, or footsteps, or clanging metal echoing down the hallway.

I'm being tracked.

The Pip began to take alternative paths and to walk longer stretches without lighting the way, and he made efforts to navigate in total darkness by the feel of the air sighing through the passageways. Every so often, Nud would stop to feel along a wall for a door or a wall sconce he'd glimpsed previously from a quick flash, to verify his position. He heard clicking noises here and there and small animals scurrying across the floor, but not a soul was met wandering through the catacombs.

One of the doors he felt out happened to be open. When he paused there, he heard a trill from beyond it.

"Nud?" called a voice in the dark.

"Who's there?" Nud replied.

Soft clicks and hushed chirrs filtered into the passage, along with clinking sounds of metal on metal. Nud generated a quick flash of light, revealing a metal door and a room full of Glooms, busy at work. He recognized one of them from the group he'd met near the Spears of the Gods cave – the one with the bald, spotted head that reminded Nud of an over-sized raven's egg.

Of course! he thought. *Glooms just 'see' me as normal in the dark.* Quickly, Nud stepped inside. He gently shut the door, then brightened his stone. He quickly checked the walls. *Good.* They were "eyeless."

"I'm so glad to see you," Nud said to the Gloom, who stood at a metal table with a half-dozen others of his kind crowded around it. Occupied with some task, the Gloom swiveled his head Nud's way. Stringy, grey hair fell in long strands over his face; a thin veil to obscure the empty eye sockets and all but the tip of one ear. The other ear was either malformed or missing altogether. He angled those ears and homed in on Nud's presence.

"Busy <click>. Must wait," he said.

The Gloom with the spotted head turned back to his duties. Another half-dozen or so chittered away as they worked at another table nearby. Their hands were all busy with small implements and they wore the same drab robes as their brethren in the mine. The room had an infirmary's sterile air to it, as well as that same sense of operational efficiency. Nud glimpsed an unmoving body on each tabletop, but couldn't quite see what the workers were up to.

Voices sounded in the hallway. *They're gaining.* Nud set the bar lock down on the door and then sized-up the room for hiding places. Compartments along the side walls appeared to hold the most promise for concealment, opening at about table height, with doors hinged from above. Only two doors were up at the moment, held in place by red, rusty chains fixed to iron rings in the ceiling. They opened into empty cavities conveniently sized to fit a very large person, lying flat.

Quarters for the deceased, Nud surmised.

The Bound Ones, pre-occupied as they were, didn't pay much heed to Nud's entering and snooping about. They worked together flawlessly as one extended body, exchanging tools and coordinating tasks with the utmost speed and grace.

The Pip scanned the rest of the chamber. The space was cramped for all of the equipment present and activity within. Liquids and powders occupied a short table near to the door, held in glass containers with embossed markings, while a workbench displayed metallic cutting and hooking tools, carefully laid out over a white cloth. In one corner stood a washbasin.

Nud closed in on the Gloom he knew. "Please help," he pleaded. "Wraiths are coming. You know what they'll do to me." Like crickets disturbed in the night, the Gloom chatter suddenly ceased. The slaves stopped what they were doing.

After some incomprehensible arguing amongst the Glooms and heated exchanges of razor-sharp trills about "Isotopia," the majority agreed to stow Nud away. Soon after, someone pounded hard on the door to the room. A harsh voice called out. "Open up!" A long pause followed, then some shuffling. The bar latch scraped open.

And when the wraiths and guards entered, they trashed the room and terrorized its occupants. They pulled out the cadavers, then poked and prodded the compartments. Despite their efforts, they were unable to locate the small Pip tucked away with the dead, blending into the stone and dodging every move. After much cursing, searching and interrogating, the wraiths and the guards simply gave up.

"We've looked everywhere," said a tower guard. "He must not have come in."

"Perhaps the Gropers created the flash without knowing it," offered a Red Maiden. "They cannot see a thing."

"Could be," said her cohort. "A false alarm. We see it happen from time to time when they work the burners."

Taradin's guards stood waiting, silent, while the wraith leader – the one whose eye Nud had shot out – made her final threats to the terrified Glooms. In her rabid voice, she lashed out.

"You filthy Gropers are hiding that pitiful thing, aren't you?" she hissed. "I'll tear out your tongues and trim the ears off of your ugly heads if you lie to me."

In a show of the utmost bravery and conviction, the Bound Ones held their tongues.

The wraiths departed cursing; the guards left in silence.

Later that day, dogs barked in the distance. The door to the compartment remained shut. Stuffed into a corner and bundled in his cloak, the young diplomat dealt as best he could with the heavy air and the pungent reek of death all around him in the confined space. It was even worse than the smell of Taradin himself. Lucky for Nud, no one else entered the chamber.

A place like Heaven, to those underground dwellers who call themselves the Il'kinik, is purely metallic and situated somewhere beyond the reachable depths. In the beginning, flames ignited the surface world and the protection of the rock ceiling was absent. Fire from above burned down through thin air.

It is said that long ago, the fire in the sky grew so terribly hot that it burned off the fifth sense of the original Earth Born, and would have charred their bodies wholly had Kech not built chambers of rock for them to withdraw to, set with cool waters to quench the flames.

And so, the Arch and the Pillar became the greatest holy symbols of Il'kinik theology, and spiritual deliverance was granted by a water-deity. The Arch, the Pillar and the Dim Sea are The Protectors, bestowed upon the eyeless people ages ago by the self-proclaimed god they worship, named "Kech," who is none other than the White Whale of many legends. A false god, no less — a living leviathan composed of a thousand minds writhing in agony.

- The Diviner, On the Beliefs of the Eyeless of Everdark

CHAPTER XXVIII

Raven

After at least a day spent mostly in hiding and no further visits from guards or wraiths, the compartment door creaked open. Nud sparked up the bog stone. A Gloom stood facing the opening in a watchful way, dried blood smeared from one cheek to the bristled eye socket above it. He hooked the chain dangling above his head to the door handle and let the metal slab relax, suspended. His voice was coarse and he seemed to struggle with every syllable.

"Out <click> Out now. Go <chirr>."

The Gloom's words were a welcome change from those that'd kept Nud huddled in darkness, his only companion a stuffy, stinking corpse: "Guards. Hall <click>. Stay," the Gloom had said many times.

The young diplomat peeled off the hood of Holly's cloak and dispensed with the scrap of scented cloth that he'd been given to breathe through – a thin barrier for the deathly odor in the confined space. The Pip crawled past the fallen Harrowian and slid out of her compartment, onto the floor.

His head ached with the motion and his legs felt nearly as rigid as those of his bunkmate. Nud gave each leg a shake to get the blood flowing, then walked off the stiffness. The room had been put to order again, fully restored since the ransacking and the infighting.

While in hiding, Nud had heard the Gloom occupants squabbling over something unknown to him. Now that he was out of the cavity, they all bunched together, nearly nose to nose, muttering clicks and clacks punctuated with excitable chirrs and trills. No doubt, his presence had much to do with it. Nud stood aside to let them sort it out, whatever it was, and to stretch his tight muscles and make himself limber again. When the argument was over, they split up and got busy on a new task. The room, so neat and tidy, quickly began to come undone again, as each seemed bent on fouling the majority of the substances and implements in their stores.

"Are you sure you want to do this?" Nud asked the one who'd set him free. They'd spent hours setting the room right after the searches.

"Now <click> is time <chirr>," he said. And so, Nud helped with the destruction. It was liberating.

They scattered powders onto the floor, poured liquids down a central drain, and pulled up the floor grating to drop metal instruments down the hole it covered. The cadavers, they left untouched.

A small collection of dusty old books lined a shelf built into the back wall – books none of the Bound Ones could ever hope to read. Even so, when an angry looking fellow began tearing out pages, another stayed his hand and delivered to him an earful of sharp and piercing ticks. Instead of destroying the volumes, the intervening Gloom loaded them into a carrying bag and slung them over his shoulder.

As the demolition continued, Nud was drawn to one of the bodies laid out on a table, the only one uncovered and ready to be worked on. She wasn't much beyond a girl by the shape of her face and the youth still showing in her skin. Her long dark hair contrasted the palest complexion. She didn't look as dead as she did asleep. *A sleeping giantess*, Nud thought, for her length surpassed that of normal old-worlders and Outlanders. She slept with her eyes open though. *And a noblewoman*, he gathered, by the refined features of her face and the gentleness in her hands. The native blood of the Dim Lake Tor Lords once coursed through her veins, to be sure. Just to convince himself she was not alive, Nud reached out and touched her peaceful arm – it was not warm, yet the skin felt soft and supple. The Pip wondered what had brought her to such a place and what procedure had been in store for her.

By the end of the endeavor, the Bound Ones had smashed or otherwise rendered useless all of their holdings, and packed up those items deemed worthy and transportable – a serious act of defiance. If caught, the wraiths surely would slaughter them. Satisfied, one by one they exited into the hallway. Before leaving, Nud checked the spotter's cloak top to bottom, as carefully as he could in a hurry. The lasso maneuver had done a number on the garment, and several areas appeared to warp the background. *It'll have to do though*, he decided. Nud adjusted the cloak as best he could and donned the hood. *It got me this far.*

On his way out, Nud gently closed the giantess' eyes, then left her behind. In the hallway outside the chamber, the wall sconces were lit and the walls had resumed their familiar pattern of ominous shapeshifting – no eyes. Nud checked both ways – all clear. Before departing, one of his companions addressed him.

"Isotopia … go," said the Gloom.

Nud believed this one to be a "she," but the conclusion was not obvious. The Gloom was a little taller and thinner than the others, or maybe just stood straighter, and was also fine featured. Thick white hair stuck up in tufts on the top of her head. She motioned with her hand for Nud to lead the way.

"Raven," Nud said, gesturing to the first Gloom that he'd spoken to earlier, the one with the spotted head. The Gloom stepped forward, clicking softly with ears angling – scanning the Pip over, it seemed.

"I don't know the way," Nud said. "But if you help me out of here, I will find your Isotopia. I promise. I just need to get to the surface."

Raven stepped back with a flurry of protesting chirrs, shaking his head and waving his arms at Nud. The Pip stood there for a long moment, puzzled. But then he remembered his conversation with Nekenezitter. The Gloom with eyes had alluded to the answer; the source of Raven's unease. The world above was nothing short of a burning hell to these people. And so why would Isotopia – the "Land Promised" – have anything to do with the source of all evil? They weren't even half-wrong. The young diplomat tried to put the Gloom at ease.

"There might be clues about Isotopia in books, or in stories passed from one generation to the next, or in other records," Nud said.

Raven motioned to his companion's book bag, then patted it. Nod nodded.

"Lots of information is in books," Nud explained, "and there are rooms full of books on the surface. Books are not bad, are they? Maybe that's why the answer is so hard to find – no one thought to look for Isotopia in a book."

Raven went still. "<click> Hidden <click> knowledge <click>," he said, "on Surface?"

"Yes," Nud said. "But it doesn't have to be hidden. And there are books you can read by feeling the words. Maybe one day …" He trailed off with the thought.

"<chirr> Bring <click> feelking books <pop> down to <Il'kinik> – Gropers?" he said, pointing to himself and then motioning to the others.

"Yes," Nud said, "… for Il'kinik."

The Gloom raised his index finger to one side of his chin, snapped two rapid and sharp high-pitched clicks, and then followed with a low, popping sound. "I get it," was Nud's guess. The Pip started back the way he'd come.

"Not <click> that way <chirr>." Raven adjusted the hold on his sack and started down the hall in the opposite direction. Nud couldn't have asked for a better guide or friend in all of the catacombs.

Marching on through the torch-lit passages, the company of Glooms proved to be less than gloomy company. Their spirits had risen, and had done so despite their trials with terrible wraiths, the dissention among them, and the danger looming over them by helping Nud. The Il'kinik clung to a kind of persevering hope – hope that their troubles might someday fade into the distant echoes of some long-forgotten cave; hope that the future would give way to a sweet resonance of freedom and prosperity.

They met other groups of Il'kinik in the halls going about their business, and came upon two tower guards that didn't take much notice. Without issue, everyone passed them by.

And as they made their way deeper into the heart of the tunnel system, the usual clicks and clacks of Gloom conversation matured into something more entertaining. The chatter took on a life of its own as streams of chirps and pops and other sharp sounds began to coalesce into a rhythm, picking up the pace of their march and bringing out the spring in their steps. Despite wanting to pass without notice, Nud couldn't help but to join them. The Pip's companions turned their heads to him one by one, quizzically. Nud figured they were wondering exactly what to make of his nonsense. Slowly though, he began to decipher bits and pieces of their language. Perfect memory is a great help in that regard.

After a drawn out stretch that lacked any features worth mention, the path began to slope downwards, eventually coming to a three-way branch where they veered left.

Without warning, the walls turned to eyes again. Nud stooped and kept to the middle of the group, walking silent, shrouded. Carefully, he drew the cowl of his hood as tight as it would go. He didn't even breathe. The Il'kinik simply carried on as usual, at unawares. The wall eyes searched for a long minute, and then faded away into the swirling backdrop.

At last, the crew came to an iron door, double locked by bar and key. Raven produced the key, wrestled the bar up and held the door open as the rest of them stepped through. On the other side, the stonework transitioned from well-ordered blocks to roughly hewn rock. The floor became uneven and slick in places, with no shortage of small stones to stumble over, while the ceiling dropped to almost zero headroom.

"<click> Old workings," Raven said.

Nud nodded.

Wispy strands of long abandoned spiderwebs matted the sides and ceiling of the passage, and straddled every nook and crevice. There were no torches within and the walls did not bear the swirling patterns of Taradin's catacombs. Nud let out a giant sigh of relief. *No more eyes.*

Feeling hot and sticky, he took a minute to discard the robe Nekenezitter had provided – stuffing it into a cranny. The group pushed through, past the many fissures and cramped cave openings, grimy and vermin infested. Small animals made scurrying sounds around them.

Nud used the bog stone to light the way ahead, but only sparingly, sparking it up in slow, regular pulses – each one just enough to process a glimpse of the coming passage. It just so happened that, as they trudged on, the pattern of Nud's flashes came to match the rhythm of clicks emitted by his companions.

Eventually, they reached an opening under construction for widening. Raven stopped and bit his upper lip, then shook his head in disappointment. Discarded chisels and hammers lay strewn about for half a dozen workers, along with open sacks spewing moldy contents. It seemed they'd left in a rush, until Nud noticed a charred heap tucked away in a hidden nook. He felt sick to his stomach.

Carrying on no less, Raven made his way through the opening and beckoned the rest to follow. Hesitant at first, with heads turning nervously, the other Glooms gave in after a series of encouraging clicks from their leader.

The inside was less a cave and more the bottom of a tall and narrow fissure in the rock. Sparse rays of natural light filtered in from high above. Dripping wet walls, unscalable, glistened red as Raven led them along the rubble-strewn path. They struggled to keep their footing. At length, they arrived at a sharp divide in the passage – a meeting of two fissures. The new one pinched in at the top. Before entering the new branch, Raven motioned with his hand for all to stop. On the other side was a chamber, glowing red with torchlight. Nud sheathed his stone. The Glooms went silent.

With slow and careful steps, Raven moved ahead, skillfully disguising his soft clicks in the plopping sounds of trickling water from above. Then he stopped, "peered" in with a short burst of chitters, and waited. A few moments later, he motioned the others forward.

The coast clear, they entered a large, oval cavern with a high ceiling. It appeared to be unoccupied. Burning torches lit the way, supported by sconces of a familiar design – the same twisted faces of anguish witnessed in the hallway outside of Taradin's chamber. Jagged pinnacles of rock spiked out of the floor like the grey fangs of some great beast. The largest seven had flat tops and served as pedestals for statues.

Again, ocean themes dominated the decor. Each statue possessed a basin of some kind to catch the drips of the cave icicle hanging above it. Some held clam or cone shaped basins, filled with colorful stones and glistening coral skeletons. One statue featured a pool inside the gaping maw of a sharply inclined white whale carved with smooth, elegant curves, mathematically precise – a common feature of Harrowian artwork.

"<click> Nexus <trill> Chamber," Raven said.

Indeed, that is exactly what it was. Offshoot tunnels, seven in all including the nearly hidden one they'd entered from, fed into the cavern at varying angles, sizes and heights along the craggy wall. The Nexus Chamber's tunnels branched out in all directions: there were stairwells leading up, some smooth and some roughly hewn, together with a passage leading down, and some level to the polished floor.

On the far side of the chamber, a grand, gold-rimmed doorway stood at floor level as the main attraction. Runoff water flowed down hewn channels on either side into clamshell basins, each bearing in its waters the likeness of a shiny black pearl the size and shape of a person's heart. The doors themselves were plated with a golden whale motif and fastened shut with a short bar latch. Elegant script along the arch spelled out, in golden letters, four words of a phrase Nud had heard many times on his journey.

He knows the Way.

One of the seven passages – the main throughway by the size of it – stood out as being skillfully worked and lavishly decorated. A curved set of ornately carved stairs led up.

Nud turned his gaze to Raven and pointed to those stairs. "Is that the way out?"

"Up," he replied. "<click> Surface <chirr>." The Gloom lowered his head.

Nud reassured him. "It's not that bad. You can come with me. You wouldn't be the first." The Pip stopped himself from saying more, remembering the veil of secrecy under which Nekenezitter had traveled. Raven gave Nud a quizzical, head-tilting look.

"You go?" Nud said, pointing to the stairs.

"No <click>. You go to Surface," Raven replied.

Nud gently grasped the Gloom's wrist and tugged at Raven to join him, for his own good. But Raven jerked free, threw his arms up and shot out an ear-piercing buzz with a razor-sharp edge to it. The sound struck Nud as an emphatic "No way! I'm not crazy! Go to Hell by yourself!" The Pip was getting rather confident about deciphering Gloom talk.

CHAPTER XXIX

Song and trance

The Gloom stood hunched, still as stone. With his blank, grown over eye sockets he could've passed as a grey statue. Had he been bent over a little more, maybe a gargoyle. Nud had one more thing to say to him.

"Raven," he said, gently.

"Yes," the Gloom clicked.

"I'll get you out of here."

Raven tilted his head, quizzically. "Isotopia?"

"Of course," Nud said, "Isotopia." He knew the answer he gave wasn't completely true, but how hard could it be to find them a place better than what they had?

Raven let out a soft chirr.

Nud sighed, walked to the stairwell and lightly grasped the metal rail. Then he donned his hood and adjusted it to fit snug. Holly's scent lingered in the fabric, warm and reaching, woven in with the freshness of crushed pine needles early in spring and the slightest hint of a smoky seasoning underneath.

As the soft material brushed over his face, he could almost taste her companionship.

He turned back to Raven. The Gloom was still in place, watching the way he watches. "Can you keep an eye – I mean an ear – out for a special friend of mine while I'm gone?" Nud asked. "Her name is Holly. She's been imprisoned, unjustly."

"Bound <click> ... like us <chirr>?" he said.

Nud nodded slowly, conscious of Raven's measured tempo of ticks. "Yes."

"She's about my height, with a sweet voice. Say my name to her, if you can. Please tell her Nud is coming for her and that he won't be long."

"Holky?" he said.

"That's right," Nud said, "Holly. Tell her that Nud will not rest until she is free."

"<click> No go back <click>," he said. "Words ... send <chirr>."

That would have to do. Nud nodded three times, slowly.

Raven nodded back, slowly just as Nud had, and then tapped his own head. "You know the way," he said, perfectly. The young diplomat bade his new friend farewell and began his climb. There were many, many stairs.

*

With soft steps, Nud crept up the helical stairwell, continually peering around the next bend as he went. Nearing the end of his climb, he stopped short. From what he could see, the room at the top of the stairs was grand and stately, shining bright with natural light.

Nud peeked over the top stair for a more revealing look. Two pairs of warning black eyes stared back, right at the Pip. A throaty growl cut through the air. About twenty feet in, two black dogs with thick heads gawked at his position, ears perked. Several guards in formal dress stood nearby. Nud's heart raced and, for a moment, he doubted the cloak. One of the canines scanned a little to the left and then a little to the right, licked its lips and sniffed the air.

"There's nothing there," said a man's voice, annoyed and authoritative. But the dogs were not convinced.

Nud ducked down. *Maybe I should just take this cloak off,* he thought. *If I just walked up the stairs like anyone else would they might not suspect anything...* But then he might have to show the guards his diplomatic colors. *They must've been alerted.* Nud needed to know if the guards were checking people as they came and went. He chanced another look over the stairs.

In a sudden rush, one of the dogs bolted straight at him, barking ferociously. The other chased after. Nud gasped and scrambled down a flight of stairs as fast as he could. The two brutes skidded to a halt at the top of the staircase, barking down at him, paws shuffling and nails scraping on the smooth floor. Heart thumping, Nud glanced back to see them snarling and barring their teeth.

"What's gotten into them," said another voice from the room.

As Nud fled farther down the stairs, he heard choking yelps from the dogs as their master hauled them back by their collars.

There's no getting around those guard dogs, Nud decided, *not without a distraction or an entirely different way out.* In silence, he withdrew to the bottom of the staircase.

His energy drained and his limbs feeling heavy, Nud hid in the shadows of the Nexus Chamber trying to decide what to do next. He clutched his hands and rubbed them together as a group of three men wearing robes and speaking in hushed tones passed through. *It's hopeless,* he thought. *I'll never get out of here.* When their footsteps faded, the Pip called out softly: "Raven."

A little louder: "Raven!"

The name echoed back through the offshoot tunnels. The walls gave no answer. Nothing stirred or sounded save drips from the ceiling and wavering shadows that swayed with the torchlight.

Damn, Nud thought. *Why didn't I ask him to wait, in case things didn't work out?* He scanned the cave for some sign of where the Glooms might've exited. The bar latch on the heavy golden doors had been lifted, so he stepped softly to the arch and pushed hard at one of the doors. It glided open easily.

Nud entered the empty hallway and cast off his hood. A salty current of air swept over him. The passage was elaborate, its floor blood red and polished granite. Hanging lanterns cast an orange glow over rich depictions of old Akeda, done in fresco along the walls. The ceiling was arched and richly gilded, end to end. The Pip walked on through to the other side, passing two stairways leading up.

The other end of the hallway opened into a domed coliseum. The cavern was massive, with seating for thousands, complete with its own cove and a half-circle at center-stage that bulged into its placid waters. Two small circular pools appeared closer to him, on the stage itself. Nud stepped into the coliseum and felt the airiness of the structure's volume. Immensely open and lavish to the extreme, it had to be the most fantastic underground chamber ever known.

Pole-mounted torches and bright lanterns along the walls glazed the interior with a fiery glow. Bright red banners decorated the stands. Stretching over the inlet to the cove, a fantastic archway framed a watery view of twilit shores – the sunless sea of the leviathan. There, the waterway pinched to a narrow channel that met open water.

The emptiness and solitude of the place seemed altogether off. Even the water didn't seem quite right, so clear and still and reflective of fire. Over the haunting silence, Nud could almost hear the resonating roar of a thousand voices.

Once his eyes met the wall decor, there was no turning away. A kind of morbid curiosity set in. Violent scenes erupted out of the stonework, some large and lifelike, chiseled out of the natural rock of the cavern, others miniature and painted on flat surfaces of varying proportions. The scenes were arranged in panels, each separated from the next by a mast-like column, crows' nest and all. Above was the domed ceiling, intricately carved and decorated, with a squat, inverted rendering of the Iron Tower at its apex. Bright light shone through crystalline facets mounted on the miniature battlement.

"What is this place?" Nud said aloud. Unexpectedly, he received an answer – a familiar trill erupted from the stands. Raven popped up out of hiding, followed by his hesitant cohorts. "Back? <click><chirr>" he said.

"Guards, dogs, top of stairs," Nud replied, mimicking Raven's manner of speaking, then he made a barking sound.

"Oh," said the Bound One.

Before Nud could elaborate, Raven raised one hand and shook his head. He had something to say to the others, and consulted them with a flurry of quick beats. They chittered back and forth for some time while the Pip waited. Finally, he turned Nud's way again.

"No <click><click> problem," he said. "<chirr> Free Bound <click> Ones." He began nodding his head as he spoke. "<click> Bound Ones run everywhere <chirr>. Guards come; <clack> dogs chase; round up. Nud leave when guards gone <trill>." He stopped nodding and waited for the young diplomat's reaction.

"But the wraiths—"

"<chirr> No wraiths. We say ground shake, <click> rocks crack <clack>." Raven nodded his head again, and actually smiled. "Happens. <click-click> Wraiths never come <tick> for that."

Nud was out of options and the Gloom seemed to know what he was doing, so he put his trust in Raven's plan. *They must really want me to find this Isotopia for them.*

"Do I just wait here then?" Nud asked.

Raven lifted one hand to eye level, four fingers showing. "Four hours <click-click-click-click>. Highest cave <click> Nexus Chamber <clack> … be there. Guards, dogs <click> go down. <click> Nud <tick> go up <chirr>."

Nud reiterated the plan. "Yes. Nud waits in high tunnel. Dogs, guards go down other tunnel. Nud leaves, up the stairs."

Raven nodded.

"No guards up there."

He nodded again.

"How will I know four hours have passed?" Nud said.

"You <click> not count? <clack>"

"No."

"Eight <click> guard patrols. <trill> Leave by <clack> seventh to be sure. <tick>"

"Okay," Nud said. "That makes sense."

"Soon go," Raven went on. "First, <click> honor <click-click> Bound Ones. <click><clack> Lost." He gestured to the sea.

"Here?" Nud said. "The stadium?"

"Ritual," Raven replied.

From what Nud could gather of the choppy explanation that followed, Dromeron Odoon entertains its own version of the same brutal practice. The Gloom rulers follow the Harrowian leadership: they honor the very best workers, slaves and scholars by sacrificing them. Yet they don't deem themselves or their kin worthy of such an honor, except in a few isolated cases having more to do with rivalry or politics than honor. Sadly, the Bound Ones must endure sacrifice both in Harrow and in Dromeron Odoon.

Raven and the others congregated at the central platform and stood facing the Dim Sea. As they exchanged hushed clicks at a slow tempo, Nud stepped past them along the water's edge and marveled at the massive columns supporting the arch, and then at the arch itself. A white whale, jutting out in high relief, formed its keystone. Something was off about the whale though. On closer examination, he could see that the creature had many sets of eyes, extending diagonally from just above the crease of the mouth halfway to the blowhole. Writhing tentacles lashed out in a flailing pattern from the forebody, clutching a woman who looked to be at peace.

Nud gasped. *The leviathan?*

Finally, it struck him. *But it can't be ... why would Harrow offer up sacrifices to the White Whale?* The notion didn't make any sense. The leviathan that he'd met was helpful and wise, and would never lower himself to such a level – accepting sacrifices. The beast Nud knew would much rather exchange news and stories with someone than witness that person sacrificed in his name, wasted, and the knowledge he or she possessed lost to the world, forever.

His mind raced. Kech was the name the Glooms gave to the White Whale. Karna was the Orbweaver in stories and the one Harrow took to be a goddess worthy of sacrificing their own citizens to. None of it made sense. *I'm missing something.*

Nud turned to the arch and gazed upon the waters of the leviathan. A few stretched fingers of ambient light reflected off the rippled surface to the greater blackness beyond. Rushing water sounded somewhere in the far-off distance. The soft noise seemed to filter in from all directions.

His chest heaved. He felt heavy.

And in that heavy moment, gently swelling over the rush of the far-off falls and the rhythmic train of caressing wavelets, the most beautiful music filled his ears and prickled into his spine. It was nothing like anything he'd ever heard before. Entranced, Nud turned to face his gloomy-no-more rescuers. They stood together on the central platform, united in voice and mind, blank eyes riveted on the open sea. Their voices, if indeed so plain a word as "voices" could describe the sounds they crafted, were purely ethereal. And as they wove crescendos, the uplifting joy of life and the brilliance of being awakened inside of him, like a fire rekindled. And as their tones deepened, his heart and soul fell through the hard stony earth, to touch loss unbearable and longing unfathomable … and the overwhelming desire to call back the dead from dark waves.

And there was no chorus. A chorus would bring you back, but this song marched ever forward, unrelenting. And when the song reached its climax, anyone listening would know it had to end that way, and that the only road to absolution was to complete the song right then and there, lest it linger and be diminished, never to rise again to such fantastic heights and such profound glory. In the final bar, the hymn released the living to life and sealed the dead in their watery tombs, forever submerged.

CHAPTER XXX

The sunless bay

Two uniformed guards poked their noses into the stadium every half hour, just as Raven had indicated. The first time, that was all they did. The second time, they sauntered across the stage and then walked through the stands, surveying as they went with firm expressions on their faces. Even though Gloom workers were present and making casual glances to a particular blank space along the story wall – blank, but not unoccupied – the guards never noticed the quiet Pip standing in plain view, admiring the artwork.

Activity was picking up in the chamber. Gloom workers hobbled in and out frequently, running errands for their Harrowian masters. Some pushed sack barrows, others bore dishes and cups or carted maintenance gear. A small group began to set up a booth of sorts near the entrance, and another what appeared to be a food stall in an area of the stands that offered prime seating. That section of the stadium had private booths and small, lavish rooms – luxury meant for the highborn, no doubt. And the wall scene above was the most dreadful of all. Nud had to stand back to fully appreciate it. *They must revel in gore,* he thought, wincing at the sight of it.

At first glance, the foreground was similar in style to most of the other flat story panels – an ocean scene with sailing vessels and wild water, painted in graduated hues of blue and grey. But something about the piece stood out: the presence of the color red, for one, streaking along the swirling contours of an all-consuming whirlpool that dominated the seascape.

Nud's eyes couldn't resist but to follow the helical trail of panicked swimmers and severed body parts, set adrift in a messy red wash that rippled as it twisted downward. In the violent waters near the rotating rim, a fountain of pink spray shot up, laced with white frothing. Blood and guts drew towards the depths of the whirlpool, red water gradually darkening to a central black hole. There were no sharks, as one might expect of such a dark scene. Instead, the White Whale swam amongst the carnage, torn flesh streaming from its jagged teeth. In the background, grey ships with black sails kept a safe distance. The true-to-life detail extended to the innermost confines of the whirlpool, down to the minute figure of half a woman rapidly descending into the tightest swirls of perspective distance. Nud moved in close to examine that part. No more than a thumbnail in size, the workmanship was complete in every feature, even the dazed stare and misplaced grin etched upon her terrified face.

Nud sighed and looked about the stadium. He was getting restless. Having had his fill of artful slaughter, he abandoned the ocean scene and descended to the stage. Before the next patrol was due to arrive, the quiet Pip crossed over to the boardwalk and passed under the arch. Ambient light from the stadium revealed a small island not far off shore, little more than sheer cliffs set against a backdrop of gloomy, honey-combed rock walls, thin and frail and shadowy.

Straightaway, he discovered another raised walkway behind some large, jagged rocks that he hadn't seen before. It started at the water's edge and curved to his right along the shoreline, hugging the rock wall out of sight. Emanating from that direction, he could see other sources of light reflecting out onto the water. The sounds of faint voices and activity drew him closer.

Another way out? Nud was determined to explore his options.

Around the first bend and after a short hike, the wood-plank walkway brought him to a small, rocky bay, full of lights. Teams of old-worlders and half-giants tended to their vessels, ropes, and cargo, to the sounds of crates scraping on the piers and ship hulls gently bumping into pylons. Small rowing watercrafts heaved and swayed gently alongside their berths, tie lines creaking. Landward, the yellow blaze of post lanterns and the glowing windows of small, wooden shacks lit up the shoreline. A few dozen people went about their daily business. The shabby dwellings seemed to have sprung up out of the rock, anywhere and everywhere, without regard for order or planning. From the pipe chimney of some, thin trails of smoke streamed out over the bay, while others looked aban-doned and completely dilapidated. A small but bustling mar-ket was situated near the docks, spread out over the only flat piece of rock anywhere.

Two larger vessels equipped with sail and oars were also present, everything about them sleek and dark but one much longer than the other. They sat lonely and unoccupied, and the three slips beside them were empty.

Treading softly and keeping to the edge of the walkway

where the boards never creaked, the Pip continued to slink along the shore, unseen and unheard, while he made his way to the wharf. He drew near to the smaller of the two – a whaleboat by its live harpoons – and glided his hand along the gunwale as he paced alongside it. End-to-end she must have spanned nearly thirty feet, close to six in breadth. Next, Nud ran his fingers across the overlapping hull strakes. The wood was dark and dull. Scribed across her hull in elegantly scripted, dull gold letters were the words "Karna's Whim." The second boat – a longship – was of similar construction, but twice the length and with the name "Black Sliver" embossed on her bow in the same gold lettering.

From his new vantage point on the pier, Nud took in the greater view of the village. His gaze was immediately drawn to the wide cave opening on the far side of the bay that he hadn't seen before, with occasional mariner-types passing through. The wayfarers wore packs and carried ropes, tackle and other such gear. Echoes of their voices from the throat of the passage revealed talk of fish, winds, shoals, and even leviathan sightings out in the open water. Nud watched as one man led a mule hauling a fully loaded cart down to the wharf.

The Pip snuck across the bay to the cave entrance. Burning braziers stood to either side of the opening, while lanterns lined the tunnel. Nud waited for the next group to pass, then quietly slipped inside. Keeping to the wall and flattening himself to dodge the occasional passerby, Nud eventually came to a three-way split. Straight ahead was the main throughway. Well-traveled, he could see, by its trampled ground. From that direction, murmuring voices and clanging tool work sounded in the distance, and a variety of odors seemed to be circulating. The leftmost branch was dark and smelled strongly of smoke and fish, which only made him hungry. The rightmost branch had an airy feel to it. In silence, Nud explored the middle tunnel. It led to a wide hall littered with carts, barrels, and crates. Space for workshops, storage, and even a small stable for beasts of burden branched off to either side. Again, old-worlders and half-giants labored – no Glooms that he could see. The hall itself ended in a ramp that sloped upwards to a set of metal doors, wide and chain-locked.

That could be another way out. Nud lingered in a quiet corner, waiting for someone to unlock the doors. But after an hour with no results, he backtracked to the split and took the rightmost branch instead. As suspected, the passage wound its way back to the original Nexus Chamber. By Nud's reckoning, it wouldn't be long before the Glooms began their diversion. The time had come to head for the high cave.

Activity had picked up in the Nexus since his previous visit through. A steady stream of Harrowians now sauntered down the curved stairwell from the surface. They passed through the chamber and on through the golden doors to the stadium. People from all walks of life, it seemed, sporting their best attire, came to partake in some special event. Anticipation reveled in the air. *A play,* Nud surmised, from the snippets of conversation he overheard, *something about mariners battling sea monsters.*

"… never seen a leviathan before …" said one lady in a fine dress as she passed. That comment disturbed him. The woman was small for a Harrowian and slim, and her accent put her from the coast.

At the next lull in people traffic, Nud cupped a drink from one of the basins and then hastened across the room to the foot of the passage Raven had chosen. He climbed the narrow flight of hewn stairs to the opening. After slipping inside, he found a convenient cranny masked in shadows, and backed into it. His position offered an ideal vantage point overlooking the Nexus.

To quell his rumbling stomach, the Pip had himself a quick bite to eat. He rummaged through his pack and dug out half a loaf of bread and some heavily salted fish that Fyorn had given him before setting off to Harrow.

A loud horn blasted through the tunnels. Nud jolted and nearly choked on his meal.

The alarm.

Eyes watering, he coughed up a chunk of fish, swallowed, and then gulped down his last piece. The Pip set his eyes on the chamber below, watching for the guards and their dogs. Some people halted and looked about, others ducked down or scuttled to cover. Heads tilted and shoulders shrugged as they exchanged confused looks.

At that moment, a small, disproportionate man uniformed in blue with gold trim strolled into the Nexus Chamber from the stadium. The middle-aged old-worlder had white, wispy hair sticking out sideways from beneath his cap. He positioned himself to one side of the golden doors, eyes darting about the disrupted crowd as the blast sounded again.

The doorman removed his cap and waved it high above his head. "Carry on," he bellowed out. "Nothing to be concerned about. A little trouble in the mines, is all." He spread his arms wide and added grandeur to his voice. "Carry on to witness the Miracle of Rejuvenation! Come one, come all!"

The dwarf held the doors wide open as the crowd began to move again. He flashed courteous smiles and extended warm greetings to the showgoers as they strolled on by. With quiet thank yous, he graciously accepted gratuities dropped into his outstretched cap.

Dogs started barking upstairs. *It's time.* "Clear the way,

coming through," a voice boomed from the same direction. The doorman unleashed an animated look of surprise when two dogs bounded into the chamber, their masters in tow. The crowd parted to let them through as they dashed to the down-tunnel, just as Raven had expected. Two additional guards hurried after.

Now's my chance.

Nud drew a deep breath, adjusted the fit of his cloak, and prepared to descend and cross the chamber. *I can do this*, he told himself. *I just have to keep quiet and weave through everybody.* About to take his first step, the Pip thought he heard something – half a whisper, maybe, from behind him in the tunnel. Nud turned to look. He saw nothing, but then he heard it again.

"Leno, are ya there?"

The young diplomat didn't answer. He heard sniffing.

"Leno," the voice whispered again; closer, louder. "I can smell the fish. Bobbin cooked'em up the other night."

Sure enough, a Stout with a lantern emerged from the depths of the high cave, rounding the bend and carrying a pick over one shoulder. Behind him, a Gloom followed.

It can't be… Nud didn't move, unable to trust what he was seeing.

The pair stopped before they got to the cranny. The next whisper was a loud one.

"Leno, are you there?" Gariff turned to Raven. "What if he's already gone?"

"What <click> do you mean <clack>?" Raven pointed at Nud. "He's right there <chirr>."

Nud threw his hood back. "Gariff! What are you doing here?"

"Leno!" Gariff put his gear down, rushed to the Pip and

grabbed his shoulders. He shook Nud firmly. "Glad to see yer okay." He gestured to Raven. "I met this feller here who thought I was Kabor, for a second."

"Shshsh," Raven said, holding a finger to his lips. "<click> Too loud <chirr>. Sound carries from here."

Nud kept his voice low. "Thank you, Raven." He regarded the Stout. "C'mon Gariff, we can get out of here. Now's our chance." The Pip stood on the tips of his toes to peer behind them. "Wait a minute … where's Bobbin?"

Gariff shook his head. He spoke quietly. "Hear me out."

Nud glanced over his shoulder to the stairs, and then back to Gariff. His chance to escape was evaporating. "There isn't much t—"

"Your friend here told me all about your plan," Gariff cut in, "and what you said about Holly, so I asked him to bring me to ya. Then that loud horn goes off – you must've heard it. These little fellas started running all over the place like blind mice. We have to talk, Leno."

"Who's up there?" called the dwarf by the door. Were it not for a well-timed gratuity and the accompanying obligatory acknowledgement, their presence might've been investigated. Gariff dimmed the lantern and the trio shuffled deeper into the high cave tunnel, well out of sight and out of earshot.

"Kabor's okay," Nud assured him.

The Stout nodded. "I know. Off to Webfoot."

"How d—"

"I'll git to it," Gariff cut in, "but first, listen."

"Can't it wait? Tell me later."

Gariff stood firm. He crossed his arms.

"This whole crisis is a fake," Nud pleaded, "it's just a distraction to get me out – us out. But we have to get moving." He paused, wondering how to work Gariff into his plans. "Just head up the busy stairwell patting your pockets and acting like you forgot something."

"What about Holly and Bobbin?" Gariff asked.

"Holky <click>," repeated Raven.

Nud nodded. "I'm coming back for them." He grasped Gariff's arm and gave it a pull. "I can't get them out without help from the Council and help from Gan. Fyorn will know what to do … and whom to raise the issue with. I just need to get outside."

Gariff wouldn't budge. "Whom to raise the issue with?" he repeated. The burly Stout shot Nud a blank look, then shook his head. "Not until you hear me out."

Nud bit his lip and glanced to the curved stairwell. They were empty for the first time in a long time. He swung his gaze back to his best friend.

"Gariff!" he implored.

"First off," the Stout began, dismissing Nud's urgency entirely, "Bobbin and I went lookin' fer ya's in town here and got into some trouble. That Numbit – he'll strike up a conversation with just about anyone. I blame everything on his flapping lips. He just doesn't know when to shut up sometimes."

"Gariff!" Nud repeated, "later." The Pip tugged on him harder, but moving Gariff was like trying to move a tree stump. He wasn't going anywhere.

The Stout talked on, "Anyways, while waiting for the parade to come by, we spot this humongous off-duty guard sittin' on a pile of logs just outside the Harrow Inn. Well, Bobbin drags me over and starts yappin' in his ear."

"La-ter," Nud urged. "We can both hide in Holly's cloak once we get to the top, if we need to. The stairs…"

Gariff pursed his lips. A pained expression came over his

face. "There isn't gonna be a *la-ter* if we don't fix this *now*, Leno. You need to hear me out."

Nud felt his insides quiver. By the tone in his friend's voice and the defiance in his stance, whatever the Stout was trying to tell Nud, it was serious. A sudden awful feeling washed over the Pip. The worried expression on Gariff's face only amplified Nud's worst fears. The young diplomat let out a heavy sigh, then lowered his head.

"Don't tell me," Nud said, meaning exactly the opposite.

Gariff filled him in. "So, the big lug asks Bobbin, 'Is you a Pip?' And Bobbin says, 'Yep, pippy as they git.' Then Bobbin sneaks me a smirk, and this guy stands up and blocks out the sky – not just the sun, the whole sky, clouds and all. The guard says to him, point'n his giant finger at me, 'Is this oaf a Stout?' I didn't fancy being called an oaf."

Gariff shook his head. "'Yep', says Bobbin, 'as stoutly as they git.' Well, Bigfoot cracked a big'ol half-toothless grin from up there in the clouds. 'Well, it's me lucky day,' he says like he's some kind o'half-ass pirate. 'Looks like yer comin' with me, maties, yous them two the tower guards been after.'"

"Unbelievable," Nud said, bringing to mind the moment Fyorn had conveyed the whisper. He shook his head.

"Well, we protested that we was not 'them two,' whatever two he was talking about. Turns out half the city was on the lookout for you and Kabor, and it just so happens we fit the description perfectly – a froggy Pip and … err … a stumpy Stout."

"I know all about it," Nud said. "Fyorn warned me. That's why I'm here – to get you out."

Gariff grunted. "Well, fine job at that yer doin'."

Nud gestured to the curved stairwell across the chamber.

"You're free to go, aren't you?" But the Pip knew by then there'd be no quick escape up the grand stairwell after all.

The Stout shot Nud a grimacing look and then continued with his story. He started by shaking his head, in genuine disbelief. "That there hairy mountain just yanked us up one at a time – Bobbin by the scruff of his neck, no less – and slung us over his wide shoulders like sacks of potatoes. Then he brought us to a room in the tower. The guard in there just sits around guarding keys, by the looks of it."

Loud giggling filtered up from the Nexus Chamber as a group of young girls raced through on their way to the stadium. A few seconds later, an older-sounding man laughed and commented to someone, "I still think they're too young for this sort of thing."

Gariff kept talking. "That giant got a reward, the lousy lug – the guard flipped him a few coppers. And he smelled awful too – the giant, not the guard. Bobbin said right to'im on the way over that he smelled like old beer and farts. Now *that* earned him a solid thump on the giant's shoulder. Knocked the wind clear out of the poor hopper!"

"How did you get here then, if you were jailed?" Nud asked.

"Before we even get thrown in the slammer, this pompous sort strolls in with a glass of red wine in his hand, acting like he's King Prissy. He says to the key guard, 'These are not the right thieves – one is too round and the other is too stocky. But thank you for your excellent service.' Then he flips him a silver. Imagine that! Just fer sitting there look'n at keys!"

"Gariff, that sounds like Taeglin, the rightful ruler of Harrow."

"Well, he didn't *seem* so grand to me. Whatever ... 'Let

us go then!' I says, but the bugger just waves his hand like we don't matter and then leaves."

"And how did you get here?" Nud repeated.

"Oh ya. It gets really bad, Leno, really bad." Gariff shook his head again, bit his lip and stomped one foot hard to the ground. "It's like Bobbin joked, but worse – oh ya, you weren't there."

"Where's Bobbin?" Nud said.

"I'm gettin to it," the Stout replied. "We weren't in the clink long before some crazy bag'o bones with two red guards comes to visit."

"You mean Taradin," Nud interjected. "The First King and his Red Maidens."

"Whatever," Gariff said. "I don't know all the political mumbo-jumbo. Anyhow, first Bag'o Bones looks at me and says 'This one won't do.' Then he takes one look at my pipes …" Gariff patted his biceps. Nud had to admit, they were impressive. "So, he sends me down to the mining level with an old pick and a bunch of eyeless freaks that just never shut up." Gariff glanced to Raven, "No offence intended."

Raven just stood there, blank.

Gariff regarded Nud again. "But before I go, Bag'o Bones looks at Bobbin and says to the guard, 'Find out more about what this one knows. I suspect he has a keen memory.'" The Stout paused. "After he sent me away, I pick'n hammered all day and slept back at my cell at night. Bobbin was right across from me. One night I came back and Holly was there right next to'im. At least we got to talk some when the guard dozed off. Bobbin told me a tall, thin man with spectacles visited him three times and asked all sorts of questions about his past, and then wrote it all down. Holly too."

Gariff drew in a deep breath and let it out slowly. He put his pick down to lean against the wall.

"But that's not the worst of it, Leno," he continued, shaking his head, "That's not the worst of it."

"So, Raven freed you with the other slaves?" Nud said.

"Raven? Oh … this fella? Yep, but there's something you gotta know." Gariff steadied his gaze on Nud's for a long moment, but then lowered his eyes. He shuffled his feet and kicked some dirt around.

"What?" Nud said.

"Leno," he started, staring at his boots.

That strange feeling worsened in the pit of Nud's stomach. Slowly, the Stout tilted his gaze back up. His eyes were glistening.

"Bag'o Bones has Holly pegged for some kind of wicked ceremony. Bobbin too. No one said what it was, exactly. But it don't sound good, Leno. It don't sound good at all. I have my suspicions … you know about the sacrifices, right?"

Nud felt sick. "We have to do something."

Gariff nodded, visibly choked up.

Then Nud thought of his promise to Raven and he felt even more sick. He looked to the Gloom. *I made a deal.* Raven's hopes hung on the young diplomat's shoulders – all the Bound Ones hopes did. "I'm so sorry," Nud said to him, "but Isotopia has to wait."

Raven shrugged. "Plans change," was all he said.

The Gloom's response took Nud by complete surprise. So easily had Raven accepted the collapse of their grand scheme. Nud thanked him profusely for his patience.

"Time <click> short," Raven interjected. "Burning arch <chirr>. Kech take <click> knowledge <chirr>."

"What does that mean?" Gariff responded. He turned his

gaze to Nud. "I hope it isn't … y'know … Leno, what does he mean by that? He's just sounding a little choppy."

Nud had a very bad feeling about what Raven meant, from all the legends and from what Holly had told him. It finally occurred to him that the central platform in the stadium was not just for shows. It was an altar, with stairs descending into the waters of the leviathan. And through the act of devouring, knowledge lost by the prey would be gained by the predator.

Nud placed a hand on Gariff's shoulder. "Devour and archive is what he means, dear Gariff. Devour and archive."

CHAPTER XXXI

Clear as mud, Nud

A new plan was needed.

If Nud escaped now, his good friends would be long dead by the time help arrived. But all he had to work with was his bog stone, an obstinate Stout, and a blind but friendly Gloom with underworld connections.

Gariff was fidgety. His hands seemed to have minds of their own, acting as though they could do something about the situation just by pulling at one another or waving about. He kept staring at his boots as he shuffled back and forth.

"Leno," he said, "can't you just call a meeting or something in that stadium and spring them with fancy talk? Yer diplomatic mumbo jumbo? Agreements, treaties … that's what yer good at, isn't it?"

Nud shook his head. "I thought I was good … until now. I can't reason with the leadership here. They don't listen. They don't care. They just do what they want to do, even if it ruins everything. And I have nothing to hold over them to make them listen."

Gariff shook his head. He looked pale.

"Dealing with Taradin is out of the question," Nud continued. "He's just mad. Maybe Taeglin, if I could meet with him. But I really doubt it from everything Paplov told me. Even if he agreed to see me, what do I have to offer that might compel him to go against his own flesh and blood?"

"There's barely any flesh and blood on that bag'o bones," Gariff said. "There has to be something you can do, Leno. Something. Anything."

Nud's mind was still humming with all the bad news.

Gariff kept on, "Maybe we can just rush in, grab'em, and rush out."

"There's no way that would work," Nud said. "How could we get them past all the guards. And there might be wraiths." He turned to the Gloom. Raven tilted his head at Nud, and his ears seemed to home in on the Pip.

"Raven," Nud said. "I need to speak with Gariff alone for a short while. We need to make an important decision."

"Ar-lone?" he replied.

"Yes, alone," Nud said.

Raven nodded politely and disappeared down the high tunnel passage. If he was offended, he didn't show it. The Stout leaned against the wall of the tunnel and put his hands in his pockets. Nud gathered his resolve.

"Gariff," he started, "I need you to go with Raven."

The Stout guffawed. "What am I gonna do with the likes of him while all this is going down? No way, Leno. I'm stick'n with you."

The young diplomat chose his next words carefully. "I need you to go with Raven to convince him and the other Bound Ones that if they help to rescue Holly and Bobbin, we can show them the way to Isotopia."

"Isotopia?" Gariff repeated.

"Yes. It's a place like heaven to them. They'll do anything to get there – the slaves will, not the slave masters. They'll need to be convinced though … and fast."

Gariff squeezed his eyes shut and rubbed his forehead. "What makes you think they'll believe we can bring 'em there?"

"They have a prophecy, that someone with 'The Fifth' – who can see – will lead them to Isotopia."

Gariff scoffed, then regarded Nud. "That could be just about anyone, 'cept them."

"But they've only ever known wicked Harrowians here in the catacombs. That's why they keep asking about Isotopia. We're the first they've met that don't treat them that way, and I'm sure the fact we're more their size doesn't hurt either."

"So, ya think they really believe in such a place?"

"Yes, I do. And we can deliver. You know the Bearded Hills will make room for them."

Gariff nodded. "It won't be Isotopia."

"They can call it that, if they want to. Tell them about the mines you admire the most. Tell them about the vein of gold that runs like a river. They'll like that."

"I sort of made that one up."

"Tell them anyway."

"Why me? Why not just send Raven?"

"You have to find the one named 'Clickety-clack' or something or other – Kabor got to know him. He flies … giant beasts – cloakers. Kabor calls them 'stone ghosts.'"

Gariff's eyes went wide. "Stone ghosts are real?"

"Sure as I'm standing here," Nud said. "And tell him you're Kabor's brother."

"But he's my cuz—"

"You two are practically brothers."

Nud gave Gariff some time to sort through the proposition. In the minute that followed, the Stout measured his worth. Brow furrowed, he pressed his lips together in a slight grimace and held that expression as he tilted his head in a side-to-side rhythm. The Pip could almost see the indecision churning inside his skull, weights balancing on a scale. In the end, and without another word to the contrary, he sighed an airy sigh and then nodded.

"I'll do it," he said.

Nud smiled at his nervousness. "It's the only way."

Gariff grabbed his pick by the handle and scooped up the lantern. "Let's get Raven."

Nud and Gariff caught up with spotted Gloom. The Pip tried to repeat the pilot's name to Raven as Kabor had pronounced it, but the words "Clickity-clack" only resulted in a wrinkled-nose kind of expression.

"<click> I will ask around <clack>," he said, finally.

Nud's new plan, as crazy as it sounded, was for Clickity-clack – or whatever his real name was – to swoop in from the open water on his flying mount, drop out of the dark heights and whisk Holly and Bobbin away the moment they appeared on stage. Basically, a repeat of how Kabor had rescued Nud from the slavers outside of Dromeron Odoon. Unprepared, the young diplomat wagered that few Harrowians, if any, would dare tangle with such a frightful beast as a full-grown cloaker. And it would happen fast – a quick "grab and go." Nud explained everything to Gariff and Raven. When he was done, he regarded his Gloom friend.

"Watch out for the guards," he said to Raven.

"<click> I will," the Gloom chirred in response.

Nud didn't realize until later that he'd used the word "watch."

Gariff winked at Nud. "Catch ya at the Flipside then, after this one."

"I owe you a barkwood," Nud replied.

With those parting words, the two unlikely companions went on their way.

*

Until their return, Nud's role was to do the only thing he could think to do: keep tabs on events in the stadium and be prepared to act when the time came, with or without help from the cloaker riders. He had no idea exactly what he might try to do in the event things didn't go as planned. Something would have to be done though, no matter what. Nud had to try, for Holly's sake, and Bobbin's … and for the Glooms.

CHAPTER XXXII

Interlude – Time reveals

I'd like to say I had a plan. And I'd like to say that plan included a clever diversion, a coordinated break out, and a daring escape, all orchestrated by yours truly. But there was no *real* plan.

A *real* plan does not hinge on an off chance, in this case, an uprising of disgruntled cloaker riders. That might be called "hope" or "desperation." Most certainly, it does not constitute a well-defined course of action.

That is what I needed – a well-defined course of action. No, the odds did not look good, but there was still *time*. And a little time can reveal its own mysterious value, in equally mysterious ways.

CHAPTER XXXIII

Diversion

Certain undeniables about escaping kept gnawing at Nud. By the time the ritual started, the guards and their dogs would be back at their posts, so a quick escape up the stairs was out of the question. If Nud and his friends fled to the back tunnels, the wraiths would swiftly hunt them down. As for those huge metal doors near the underground workshops in the stadium area, they seemed impassable. *But maybe, in a pinch.*

No matter how Nud played the scene out in his mind, a proper rescue ended seaward – a getaway across the open water before a pursuit could be organized. Nud and his friends would disappear amidst the maze of honeycombed rock walls. With the cloaker riders on hand, that task could be trivial. Without them, a break out seemed undoable. They could still head for the waters, but the leviathan would be waiting, unless *… Maybe I can convince the White Whale to let us pass?*

Either way, Nud knew what he had to do. He had to prepare for every contingency in case his plan fell through. That meant coming up with options. *The wharf is the best place to start,* he told himself. *There's a lot of stuff I could use there: a boat, maybe, rope … something to cause a distraction…*

The flow of people into the Nexus Chamber was at its greatest and the line to get into the stadium was bunching up at the golden door. Wrapped in Holly's elderkin cloak and keeping close to the wall where the shadows pooled, Nud snuck between the naturally formed ground spikes to the other side. Then he began retracing his steps to the sunless bay. The wide passage made it easy to avoid bumping into anyone, and those he met along the way were far too caught up in conversations about sacrifices to notice the quiet Pip's passing, concealed in his cloak.

"Who will it be this time?" was the most common question Nud heard amongst passersby, complete with all manner of speculations – the Harrowian architect of a new bridge, yet another Gloom engineer, an archivist from Gan, a clever town official … the list went on. One elderly woman commented: "My favorite part is the thrashing, with the body still in its mouth." The young diplomat wondered what these same people might end up talking about after the day's festivities came to a close: "Did you see that crazy Pip dash in and try to save the girl, and then get eaten?" Nud sighed heavily. *Hope not.*

At the wharf, activity had dropped off to only a few scattered hands lingering about. A salty breeze carried the smell of fish on a frying pan. Nud set his sights on an abandoned-looking shack set atop a high rocky outcrop. It leaned heavily to one side and the door to it hung half open, crooked and splintered. A few rows over, smoke billowed out of the pipe chimney of a slightly less dilapidated shack – the source of the cooked-fish smell. The rest of the village seemed quiet and empty. *They must be at the stadium,* he surmised.

Nud made his way over to the leaning shack and slipped inside. He rummaged about for something useful – anything. The place was a wreck, but he did manage to find a rusty old fisherman's knife and some lamp oil in a collapsed cupboard. The rope he discovered was rotten and useless. He slipped the knife into his pocket and the oil flask into his pack. By the time he hazarded a peek out through a broken window, the remaining dockworkers were all heading for the smoking shack, and soon disappeared inside of it. Scanning the empty wharf, Nud spotted a sturdy dory in a rather shadowy place, near the walkway that led to the stadium.

Perfect.

Keeping low and using the terrain for cover, Nud worked his way down to the waterline. He unhitched the dory and climbed in. With quiet dips and slow, steady strokes, he began rowing out of the bay. A dog popped its head up from under the smoking shack and barked at the Pip, but no one took notice except to shush it.

Keeping close to the raised walkway, the Pip paddled along the coast to the mouth of the great stadium's inlet. When he neared the arch, he brought the dory in closer still, using the large rocks along the shore to keep out of sight from those within the chamber. The chattering voices of the building crowd spilled out over the dark waters. Nud coasted to shore into the perfect hiding place, where the water ran under the walkway. He nosed the boat in, dragged it ashore, and con-templated what to do next.

Nud still only had half a plan. His head started racing as he went over his options. If the Bound Ones didn't show up, he'd have to create a distraction – such as a fire – to draw people's attention away from Holly and Bobbin. Then, Nud would have little choice but to attempt a rescue of his own.

Use the cloak to slip past the guards, cut my friends loose and make them disappear with me. Holly and Bobbin would vanish right out from under their noses.

That was definitely a Kabor move, so bold and unthinkable it just might work. Nud only hoped they could all squeeze together tight enough to fit huddled under the cloak. *Where would we go then?* he wondered. There were only two options he could think of – the boat and the metal doors. But the only way to avoid the leviathan was the second option. He'd have to bring Holly and Bobbin to those metal doors and lie hidden in carts or barrels for when they finally opened. Where they led, he could only guess.

It'll have to do. Now, what can I use for a distraction?

The only real distraction he could think of was to set the rowboat on fire and, with a firm push, launch it across the mouth of the cove. With all eyes on the burning boat, he could attempt his disappearing act.

That was all he had – the young diplomat's plan in a nutshell. Nothing else sensible even came to mind. Sure, Nud thought along the lines of Gariff's suggestion to come up with some kind of a legal argument that would halt the heinous ritual, something he could just state that would bring the weight of official process down on it. But Nud knew the Harrowians gathered there would just blurt out fifty reasons to justify the sacrifice of two harmless Pips to a hungry whale. Why? – because that's what they came to see. Blood and gore. *And look what happened when I tried to reason with that walking corpse.* Nud shook his head to himself. *Never again.*

The Pip double checked his pockets to make sure he still had some of Nekenezitter's matches, then counted them. *One-two-three.* Next, he wrenched open the flask of lamp oil he'd acquired from the shack and doused the boat's interior with it.

There was nothing left to do but wait. Wait and watch as the masses poured into the stadium to claim their seats. The event was shaping up to be standing room only. It wouldn't be long before the stadium filled to capacity. Indeed, as the Pip sat and watched, with a loud clang the golden doors soon slammed shut.

Serving men and women, showing exceptional poise and grace, kept everyone of status comfortable. Beer, wine, and steaming appetizers were made available to all of the affluent. The masses, on the other hand, formed long lines around small serving booths that'd sprung into existence throughout the common stands.

When the ceiling torches finally dimmed and the last of the highborn took to their seats, the drone of casual conversations escalated to a dull cheer. Musicians were the first to spill out onto the stage, dressed in sharp black and bright white, attended to by an entourage of chair- and instrument-bearing Glooms to help them set up.

As the musicians took their seats and warmed their instruments, the crowd murmured on. Nud crept a little closer through the rocks to get a better view, and found good cover just back of the arch. Finally, the conductor stood in front of his band. He raised his hand high; a hush came over the crowd. And when he lowered his hand, the air resonated with the beginnings of a lively mariner tune.

The crowd "oohed" and "awed" later on when acrobatic dancers tumbled onto the scene, rolling and throwing themselves about the stage. They topped off their performance with a series of springing dives into the two round pools, from which they never emerged. All in all, they were nearly as talented as the Flipside performers.

Next, the crowd marveled at twin, scantily clad

contortionist sisters. While balancing upside-down on one hand, each held a bow with one foot and drew a bowstring with the toes of the other foot, legs bent impossibly backwards. They released their arrows at one another. The crowd gasped. The blunted shots collided in mid-air and stuck together, then dropped to the floor as one. The audience went wild with applause.

Songs, dances and feats in the plenty were offered up to the crowd before the music subsided and an intermission was announced. The aroma of steamed shellfish filled the air as a new wave of vendors fought their way through the common stands to pawn beverages and niblets, no doubt for exorbitant prices. During that time, Bound Ones cleared the staging area.

The time had come for the main attraction.

CHAPTER XXXIV

Ritual of the brilliant

A slim, well-poised man stepped out onto the stage. He stopped and slowly swept his gaze over the crowd, smirking as he did so. A buzz of expectation electrified the air, building to a dull cheer. They knew him well. The man strolled casually to the central platform near the water's edge and stared through the arch to the Dim Sea beyond, his back to the bulk of his audience. He was not overly tall for these parts – the height of a normal old-worlder, well groomed and finely dressed, all in light blue save for his white, frilly shirt. His salt and pepper hair placed him at middle-age.

"Lord Marlin!" cried members of the crowd, sporadically.

"Lord Rhyale!" cried one vocal woman, high and clear above the rest. Whistles and cheers erupted. At that prompting, a handsome, tanned nobleman in the stands stood up and waved to all. A Tor Lord, no doubt, by the looks of him, so tall and proud, puffing out his chest. Grown women cried out his name in chorus and then giggled like teens when he waved them kisses, before reclaiming his seat.

All eyes soon returned to Lord Marlin, who displayed a talent for showmanship. By their lit-up expressions and contagious energy, the crowd clearly adored him, which might strike one as odd at first because he, in turn, seemed quite dismissive of them. It was his game and they knew it. They had to be louder to get his attention.

"marlin … Marlin … MARLIN … MARLIN!" they chanted, and continued to chant. There were no more "Lord Rhyale's" to be heard. "Ogres!" someone bellowed over the chants, and many smiled or chuckled at that.

When it seemed the cavern roof would collapse from the sheer volume of the noise, sudden flames sprung up along the edge of the stage, and then a ring of flames engulfed the central platform. Swaying, colored light filtered up from the bottom of the two small pools. Marlin, encircled by fire and still facing the sea, threw his arms up into the air, as though reaching to the sky beyond the stone. The chanting turned roar, and the longer he stood there soaking in the fame, the more deafening the roar of the crowd became.

Satisfied at last, he turned to face the masses and was met with shouts and wild screams. A faction began to chant his name again. The chorus grew louder and more rhythmic as it spread from end to end. At last, they were his and his alone. All eyes fell to Lord Marlin; all minds bent to his will.

The host raised one hand and waved it slowly around the room, then tilted his hand flat and gestured with a slight, downward push. His loyal onlookers gave him silence.

"Thank you," Marlin called out, tossing them one small morsel of the recognition hungered for. The lord's voice was strong and pleasant, and carried with it an air of refinement. "I want to thank you all for coming out tonight. Twice a year, Harrow comes here to pay tribute to the glorious Karna and

her magnificent vessel, and to honor our best and our brightest. Twice a year, you bear witness to the abandonment of flesh
as the mind ascends to become one with the divine. For this, I
thank you all."

The crowd shouted and whistled high praise, and then
dampened to a hush again.

"We have a spectacular evening planned for you." He
paused. "… and an absolutely *brilliant* line-up!"

The audience applauded. Marlin went on to introduce
himself as "Lord Marlin of Ogres," no less, and followed with
eloquent introductions for his noble kin.

"King Taeglin, Keeper of the Iron Tower and the Crown,"
Marlin started. Taeglin wore a purple robe, a newer version of the garment worn by his decaying predecessor seated
in the booth over, and he sipped red wine from a jeweled
goblet. Taeglin raised his cup in toast, to muted cheers.
Marlin continued.

"And his father of old, the founder of this brave city of
Harrow, I give you Taradin, Vicegerent of Harrow, and the
First King of Fortune Bay!" Taradin lifted a ringed, boney
finger in acknowledgement of the lord's introduction, but
remained mostly out of sight. He sat shrouded in the hood of
his purple robe, trimmed in gold, while tall and graceful host-
esses tended to his every need. The grim figure was flanked by
a pair of Red Maidens, on guard and holding firm their pole
arms. The crowd was even less than enthusiastic at the calling
of Taradin's name than that of his son of sons. Nonetheless,
the lich king drew many a stare.

Among them also sat a long list of Tor Lords, their Ladies,
and even their mistresses. There was Lady Gilirain of Limbo,
Ambassador Crulerion – a Gloom in naval attire, and of
course handsome Lord Rhyale of the Western Tor. Then there

were Ladies Barra and Ganadra, and Kimay. After Marlin uttered Kimay's name, he paused for a brief moment; just long enough to mouth the words of her less than flattering, non-official title. Nud had heard of her. "Kimay the Sea Bitch," many said. She was as haggard in appearance as her name implied, with long, knotted hair and greenish, wrinkled skin – reminiscent of a bog queen. The empty air seemed to resonate with her unspoken title.

Lastly, distinguished guests from Gan were recognized: "Lady Elise Faelin accompanied by Lord Sevalyr of the Crystal Grey." There were others among the nobles, ladies and gentlemen of various sorts, the likes of which he brushed over with a single statement of introduction: "… and the other fine Ladies and Gentlemen in attendance."

Some of the highborn afforded a weak wave to the crowd as though it were a chore; others raised a hand dismissively. Only Lord Rhyale stood high and mighty among them, one strong arm raised high and mighty in-and-of itself. His eyes scanned the audience for attractive young women, and he basked in the splendor of their suggestive remarks, exaggerated poses and crazed admiration. One overly excited girl flashed him some skin when he looked her way. Those in Rhyale's company smirked, or shook their heads, or whispered to one another. Rhyale raised an eyebrow, smiled and nodded to the girl.

Taradin remained subdued among his noble kin, withdrawn in the shadows of his private booth, away from prying eyes. Nud spotted one boney hand resting casually on his metal scepter.

Marlin called back the crowd's attention. "Let us begin with a glorious memory from the past." The charismatic lord exited his ring of fire. He strolled this way and that way on the greater stage and along the boardwalks as he spoke, pointing to individuals in the crowd and nodding his head.

"Some of you, yes you, and you, you too, may recall a small group of brilliant little Outlanders who graced our hall some years ago. They came upon us from a little-heard-of village in the marshes. You may also recall that Karna's great vessel was especially pleased with that year's harvest of fine minds. Although barely a morsel to the physical being of Karna's Vessel, the sweet nectar of their intellects was fit for the divine!"

The crowd cheered, and many chanted: "WE LIVE FOR GLORY!"

Watching the events unfold from his hidden place behind the seaward arch, a terrible thought crossed Nud's mind. His stomach dropped. He mouthed the words. "Who? When? ... Mother? Father?"

Marlin swatted a hand at the fiery edge of the stage, as though wafting out the flames there. The fires snuffed out; drawing focus to the ring around the central platform, still ablaze. He continued to inform his townsfolk.

"Today we have a special treat to refresh that knowledge and close the festival. Giants of the Tor, men and women of Harrow, Gropers of Dromeron Odoon, ... Kimay," the crowd laughed, "lend me your hands for the one and only..." He glanced down to a card held in the palm of his hand. "... Bobbin Numbit!"

From the back hall, a huge, muscular man pushed Bobbin out onto the walkway. The half-giant wore only a white loin-cloth with black and gold trim, together with a wide bead necklace – deep blue and white. The Pip was bound, gagged and frightened. He looked like a scared rabbit, and a well-fed one at that.

"Have you ever wondered what it would be like to be young again?" Marlin asked the crowd.

"FOREVER YOUNG!" came the reply.

Lord Marlin flipped the card in his hand to read the back. "Bobbin Numbit is an innkeep's son. He is twelve years old. He knows every rumor this side of the Outlands and every story that ever passed through the most popular lodgings and watering hole in the bog. Karna has a sudden interest in those quaggy waters. Let's hear it for Bobbin!"

The crowd applauded, blew whistles and rang bells. Some banged sticks together or thumped their feet. Bobbin was "led" to center stage.

Nud's gut felt rock hard. *There isn't much time.* He jerked his head around and scanned seaward for Gariff and Raven – it'd been hours since their departure. *Nothing.* Then he tilted his gaze to the sky-ceiling of the Dim Sea and to the high openings in the rock walls, hoping to catch a glimpse of a gliding cloaker. *Nothing again.* Nud needed to act soon, but not before seeing Holly, not unless absolutely necessary. He swung his gaze back to the stage.

Marlin adopted a reflective tone. "Before we move on to deliver our first gift, I'd like everyone to think back to the message that Karna's Vessel blessed us with at the Opening Ceremonies a few days ago. You all heard it, loud and clear."

The crowd didn't respond. Marlin made a disappointed face. "Oh, come on now!" he cried.

Taeglin rose from his plush chair amidst the nobles, swishing his goblet of wine and slurring his words as he shouted: "I will help them, Lord Maw-lin of Ogres." Taeglin beckoned the audience with open arms, then bellowed out. "Seek the stones with fire inside, the spark that never dies!"

"HE KNOWS THE WAY!" shouted the crowd.

"Take what is ours!" Taeglin cried, spilling his wine as he threw his arms up, showering the lady next to him.

"IT'S WHAT WE WANT!" shouted the crowd.

A servant refilled Taeglin's goblet, which he raised again to the audience. He drank deep, and nearly missed his seat when he sat down. In return, the stadium crowd, suddenly warming to the rightful heir and already under the spell of their own consumed spirits, cheered Taeglin on.

The announcer took over where Taeglin left off. "Harrowians, what do we want?"

"SPARKS!" cried the crowd.

"Why do we want them?" A long pause followed. No one knew what to say. "IT IS …" Marlin started. He led the audience on, rolling his hand at them in tight circles.

"Karna's … vessel … whim!" came the broken answer.

"One more time," said the lord, gesturing that they up the volume.

"KARNA'S WHIM!" the crowd shouted in reply, then awarded themselves a cheer.

Lord Marlin nodded in satisfaction. "Thank you," he said, waving to them. "Thank you all."

Nud was beside himself. *Unbelievable,* he thought. Apparently, a mere "whim" was enough to justify sacrificing his friends and family, and destroying the Pip's habitat. *Karna's Vessel tells them what they want, commands them to get it, and then calls it his "gift" to them. How wonderfully convenient.*

Lord Marlin reached into his vest pocket and pulled out a plain iron chain with a pendant – Holly's pendant. It sparked green fire as he held it up for all to see. The audience gasped in amazement.

"Behold! The first reward of Karna's Whim!"

The crowd cheered and whistled.

"Who leads the path to rejuvenation!"

"WE DO!" rang out a great many voices. The crowd roared, clapping their hands, ringing their bells, blowing their whistles and beating on their small drums.

Next, Marlin pointed to Bobbin. "That one is big on knowledge, but he makes a small, rather round morsel." Bobbin shook his head frantically. The crowd laughed.

"So, we are going to double up the roster for you tonight, folks!" He pulled a second card from his vest pocket and glanced at it. "Lend me your hands once again, this time for the lovely, wonderful, street smart and full-of-spunk, Holly Hopkins!"

Nud's heart sank as the crowd cheered on. A nauseous feeling swelled inside of him. Holly was shoved and dragged to the central platform in the same manner as Bobbin. They had her dressed in elegant white evening wear. It was ridiculous. Under the cover of Holly's own cloak, Nud crept in closer for a better look – nearer to the arch.

Marlin flipped the card, then put his arm around Holly's shoulder. He dangled her stone in front of her eyes and spoke in gentle tones. "Recognize this, my dear?"

Holly's angry response was muffled and restrained. She'd been bound and gagged just like Bobbin.

The host continued on. "Holly here works at the same inn as Bobbin and has the same perfect memory. That's right my countrymen. A perfect memory! Apparently, she's a *real* know-it-all."

A cheer began to build in the audience. He quelled it with a staying hand. "There's more," he told them, "she knows everybody's secrets – including where to find the sparking stones." Marlin shook his head slowly, and then he shook his finger at Holly. "Tsk Tsk. But she won't share her secrets with us, folks." The crowd grumbled and booed.

A terrible, hollow feeling washed over Nud. *I made this happen. I allowed her to get caught up in it all.* His stomach felt heavy. *Worse, I was about to leave her to face this angry mob alone.*

Marlin wasn't finished with her just yet.

"But guess what?" he went on. "She'll certainly share her secrets with Karna! Not only that, citizens of Harrow, Giants of Tor." Marlin paused to press his index finger to his lips. He let go of Holly and rushed to one side of the stadium, then whispered loudly to the group there. "She's never known a man." He rushed to the middle crowd, "Never once," then to the other side, "She doesn't know *everything* after all, does she?"

Marlin returned to center stage, gestured to Holly, and proclaimed loudly: "A perfectly pure sacrifice, fit for the divine! Let's hear it for Holly Hopkins!"

The crowd was ecstatic. They roared, and initiated a fateful chant.

"KAR-NA … KAR-NA … KAR-NA…"

The flames at center stage snuffed out. Seconds later, the seaward arch flared up. Nud jumped back and only barely escaped being set on fire. All eyes turned to the open water. Nud couldn't resist the temptation to do the same. And that's when he beheld the leviathan for the second time, gliding in alone from the edge of darkness: slow, steady and purposeful. The young diplomat glanced back to the two helpless Pips. Each struggled against a guard's hold at the top of the stairs that led into the water. The guard gripping Bobbin nudged him forward repeatedly, dipping the terrified soul's toes in and out of seawater. Bobbin's eyes grew as wide as the moon as he marked the advance of Karna's Vessel.

Holly also watched it coming towards the altar. And both knew what was at stake. One shove and a splash were all that separated them from certain death.

No one was coming to save them. Nud bit his lip hard. *It's now or never.*

The time for the Pip's distraction had come. He felt his pocket for Nekenezitter's sulphur sticks. *Still there.* Nud backed up one step, about to turn towards the dory, and bumped right into something … someone … big.

Nud planted his face into a thick, scratchy sweater, then slowly tilted his head up to the stunned gaze of the half-giant standing there. He was a huge dock worker by his grizzled beard, his wool sweater, and the mariner's cap he wore.

The man's view of Nud may have been blurred by the cloak, but he hauled Nud up just the same and stripped that cloak right off his back. The Pip yelped, legs flailing in the air.

The man growled. "What've we got 'ere?"

The mariner's actions didn't go unnoticed by the audience. People in the crowd began to exchange puzzled looks and point as Nud struggled to free himself. A chorus of hushed, gasping voices quickly rose out of the stands.

The dock worker had slipped in to watch the show, no doubt, and had decided to move right behind Nud for the same reasons the Pip was there – a good view and enough cover from the rocks to avoid attracting attention. The man stepped out into the open and, with one huge arm, held Nud up for all to see, like the catch of the day. The half-giant looked to Lord Marlin, who caught the shifting draw of the crowd and followed their eyes.

Marlin flinched when he beheld the pair of them. "Well now, what do we have here?" He tucked the cards for Holly and Bobbin into his vest pocket.

The mariner's voice boomed, "I caught yee another one of them bog children. Spyin', he was. And stole my boat. Dumped it full'o oil too."

The crowd murmured. The leviathan slowed its advance.

"Two's not enough," explained the mariner, "but three morsels make a nice bite for this lot, I'd say. And look!" The mariner held up the cloak, invisible side out, then spun it around in his hand so all could see the effect of the camouflage.

Taradin rose to his feet, waving his scepter. "Gan is spying on us!" came his gravelly yell. Then he coughed desperately.

Catcalls arose among booing and muttering. Harrowians shouted accusations of all kinds, and derogatory remarks about Pips, the Elderkin, and Stouts; even Glooms were not spared. A cantankerous old man shouted out, "Gan has broken the *Non-aggression Treaty*, so why shouldn't we?"

The two Elderkin nobles in the stands glanced to one another, and then to the exits. Food flung their way.

Lord Marlin raised a hand to stay the ruckus. An uneasy silence came over the stadium.

"What exactly do you think you're doing?" Nud asked Marlin directly. The dock worker answered.

"Let's help him figure it out," he gruffed.

The crowd screamed and shouted their agreement.

"Indeed," Marlin said, looking to his people for approval. A building cheer began to rise from the stands.

"This is illegal," Nud started to say, but his thin words were met with grumbles and groans from the audience, and people shouting insults. Even those voices were overtaken as the volume of cheering in the stadium soared to new heights; and higher still when the mariner hauled Nud to the platform, kicking and screaming. The young diplomat joined his friends there. Another guard rushed on stage to keep Nud from going anywhere, as big and burly as the ones holding Bobbin and Holly.

As the dock worker stepped aside, after receiving many thanks and a handshake from Marlin, a small minority of onlookers cried out in pity, including the doorman. "They're just children," cried the dwarf. Nud glanced his way and saw a look of pure empathy on his face. But most in the audience were content to mock the three Pips. And they went on to mock all Pips and anyone like them. Nud and his friends got to hear how good it was that they possessed perfect memories, because otherwise they'd be perfectly useless, and the Pips were reminded of just how small and weak and scrawny they were compared to Harrowians. Someone thought they should've remembered how *not* to get caught.

Holly shook her head in disbelief at this final turn of events, at how badly things had gone. Tears welled up in her eyes. Bobbin quivered beside her, cringing as though hoping to be overlooked. The fearlessness he'd shown against the bog queens had departed.

For a long moment, the banter between Marlin and the crowd faded to something far-off and hollow, and Nud's eyes locked with Holly's. Nothing had worked out for her – ever. Once again, high hopes drowned in tears.

As the White Whale drew near, an expectant hush came over the audience. Nud watched as it glided in. The creature was an awe-inspiring sight to behold. Majestic, really, with a presence that filled the stadium. Majestic yet terrible. And when the leviathan's graceful bulk loomed at the narrows of the inlet, Nud confirmed it to be the creature that he'd met. *That was the missing piece – Karna's Vessel is the leviathan, not Karna.* He wondered again how such a worldly and inquisitive creature could take part in the barbarism that was to follow. *Will it stop when it realizes who I am?* The leviathan had showed Nud kindness, once, going out of its way to expedite his return to the surface world. The Pip had thought the White Whale was an ally.

But now it's hungry, Nud thought. *Hungry for knowledge. And this is no joke.*

Grunting with the effort, Nud struggled with all his might against his captor. But the guard wouldn't budge and only redoubled his grip. Then, as punishment for the Pip's continued squirming, the man grabbed Nud's leg, whipped him up by his ankle, and dangled him out over the water's edge. To whistles and encouragements from the audience, the guard feigned twice to let him drop. The crowd laughed and jeered.

Marlin very publicly commented to the guard. "We should let him go; don't you think?" He shifted his gaze to Nud. "Look at him, he wants to be free." Then he squatted down to look straight into the Pip's eyes, and asked: "Do you want to be set free?"

"Toss him out to sea!" someone shouted over the crowd.

Nud did want to be free, and so he put aside his failures against the bog queens, the wraiths, and the undying king. He put them aside and focused on his most basic emotions and desires. After all, emotions and desires had been the triggers all along. Focused to a point, the young diplomat grasped the bog stone – still around his neck – and removed its leather sheath. And as he dangled over the water, Nud called to mind the lesson of the leviathan: thirst-hope-fulfillment-brightness.

Nud's thirst was the greatest it had ever been – his thirst for revenge.

Nud's hope was the greatest it had ever been – his hope for freedom, for himself and for his friends.

Towards fulfillment, he concentrated on his revenge.

Revenge against the First King, revenge against the White Whale. Nud felt a surge of energy at this juncture, as the elements looped in on themselves.

The stone around his neck brightened beyond compare. Gasps arose from the audience.

Taradin yelled out with a rasping voice, "Seize that pendant!"

The Pip clamped his fist tight around the gem as the guard's grasping hand tried to undo his grip.

I need more. Nud concentrated on the lesson of the dancing pool. He felt the energy rippling inside. For despair, he honed in on his helplessness and the coming fate of him and his friends. He drew upon the bitter fate of his parents and tied it all to his darkest thoughts about his enemies. A second jolt of energy coursed through his body; it opened a connection, like the one with the Hurlorns in the grove. Except this time, the connectedness he felt was between him and the water. But not just the water…

The Pip didn't fight the cascade of emotions that rushed over him from there, for he knew them to be true. He just let the feelings surge within, run their course, and break through to what lay beyond. Beyond was an inner tap. Like the deepest Hurlorn root, it tapped into a consciousness, but not just of the forest – a consciousness of all things material. He glimpsed the woven threads of the Orbweaver, of Karna, thin and ethereal.

With his free hand, Nud reached out and traced a circle in the water. He traced a circle and let the feelings swell. They swelled beyond compare. They swelled until his eyes rolled back in his head.

The cove water began to swirl. And as it swirled and rose to the level of the stage, a wide and shallow whirlpool formed.

The leviathan arched his thick body and held its place at the narrows, as though hesitant to enter the cove's swirling flow. Water spilled onto the stage. With wide-eyes and a bewildered expression, the guard responsible for Nud broke off his efforts to get the stone. He stepped back from the waterline and lowered the Pip to solid ground.

Calls from the stands claimed that a miracle of Karna was in the works. Stares of disbelief abounded. Lord Marlin backed away in wonder, then made a grand gesture at the phenomenon.

"Behold the glory of Karna!" he bellowed out.

With sudden enthusiasm, Marlin spun around to face the crowd. He rushed about the stage, addressing different sections as he spoke. "What do you think it means?" he said to one group. They didn't answer. He dashed to another. "It means she is here, with us today." The Tor Lord tilted his gaze to the high stands and shot them exaggerated, reassuring nods. "Right?" he called their way. Many heads nodded back in agreement. He shifted his gaze to the highborn section. "She has come to deliver her message to YOU, personally."

All the while Lord Marlin spoke, the whirlpool gained strength. All the while he went on and on about Karna, with subtle hand motions Nud retrained the sea.

Violently, a great swell of water heaved up in front of the stage and thrust out to sea, towards the leviathan. Then came another, and another, mimicking the pattern Nud discreetly traced into thin air.

Members of the crowd muttered all kinds of interpretations. Some praised Karna. Others showed their fear and called out "No, no." Concerned mothers hurried out of the stadium, children in tow.

The high waves smashed hard against the forebody of the

beast. The White Whale submerged a little more and made headway straight into the waves, rolling over them like a well-captained ship in a storm.

But the water dance was soon over. Having run its course, the whirlpool ceased and the leviathan pushed through the inlet and into the cove.

Lord Marlin had the crowd chanting in unison. "KAR-NA's WHIM … KAR-NA's WHIM." With an air of victory about him, he thrust his fist high above his head as he urged the crowd on. The crowd responded with fist-pumps of its own. The charismatic lord relished in the excitement and soaked in the escalating feedback. He and the crowd were of a single mind, rejoicing in the anticipation of just how dramatically three helpless Pips could be devoured.

The rage inside Nud pounded in his ears and elevated his pulse. An edgy, twitchy feeling came over him. *Blood for blood,* the young diplomat promised. Nud glared at the vile fiends responsible – the nobles, Lord Marlin, the guards – and then he glared at their mob of followers. *Just as guilty,* he decided.

Furious over all they'd done and what they were about to do, Nud rolled his thirst for revenge with one to be quenched by blood alone – their blood. He hoped a dark hope, far beyond wishing for the simple freedom of his friends. And he imagined the gratification, as though bearing a wolf's jaw. In willful coherence, the bog stone opened up to Nud and offered something more than the mere guiding light and the movement of water. She offered Nud poetic vengeance, and he accepted. Nud release his grip on the stone.

Suddenly, all hell broke loose.

A flash of scorching rays burst forth, striking down their captors. The guards let loose their grips, and instead grabbed at their smoldering eye sockets. Marlin's own eyes went wide and his mouth dropped open. The crystal pulsed as waves of energy passed between him and Nud, blackening the man's shielding arms until they smoldered. He fell to his knees in agony, convulsing. When the stone finally went dark, Lord Marlin of Ogre's charred body dropped. His blackened head dunked into the cold seawater.

Screams of horror erupted from the audience. People shielded their eyes or looked away in fright. Some ducked behind the stands. Blank faces stared in disbelief, unable to fully comprehend what'd just happened. The strike had been as precise as it was crippling. Only the half-giant guards and Marlin had been hit with the intense light.

Free at last, Bobbin yanked the gag out of his mouth, wriggled a hand loose of the rope around his wrists, and undid the bonds on his feet. A guard came charging at them from the back passage.

Bobbin shot up. With a grunt and a yell, the portly Pip charged the guard straight on. He barreled into the man with a leaping attack. His pudgy little hands gripped the guard by the neck and the two toppled into one of the pools, disappearing into its scintillating depths.

Nud cut the bonds on Holly's hands with the knife from the fishing hut. She pulled the gag out of her mouth and squatted to untie the rope binding her feet, then glanced up. "Lookout!" she said. "More guards!"

The Pip conjured up a host of dark thoughts in response – they came easy. He allowed the baneful shades to coalesce in his mind. The chamber began to flicker. And when the thoughts washed over Nud completely, the stadium went completely black.

Shouts and screams arose from the audience, and wild

speculations circulated among the commotion. "She's come for us all," some said, and "a demon is among us."

Nud reached for Holly. "Come with me."

"Wait," she replied, and scuttled off into the dark.

When she returned, Nud took her by the hand. It was wet.

"I had to get my stone," she said.

Nud led Holly to the boardwalk, drawing on his practiced skill of navigating in the dark. They made their way as far as the arch, then slammed square into someone blocking the way. The impact knocked the two Pips flat on their backs.

Nud lost his concentration. The darkness lifted. The fire of the arch flared up bright in front of them. As his eyes met the hateful gaze before him, terror gripped Nud's chest and squeezed the air right out of his lungs.

"Sweeet," called a wheezing voice.

Wraiths loomed over them like two black, crooked towers, claws raised to attack. Nud and Holly scrambled backwards and then sprang to their feet. But before they could retreat to the main stage, yet another wraith moved to block passage that way – the new slave master herself, wearing an eyepatch and carrying a scythe. The only way out was the inlet, where the White Whale lurked.

Over the mayhem, Bobbin's voice called out. He'd popped his head out of the pool. "Hey 'Bones,'" he said to the wraith leader. She jerked her one-eyed gaze to the pool. Bobbin waved his hands hysterically at her.

"Over here! Sorry I missed your funeral."

Nud and Holly used the distraction to edge their way along the boardwalk, back towards the main stage. When the two other wraiths came for them, Holly stopped them dead in their tracks. Her voice rang out, defiant.

"Dare me," she said, dangling the pendant above her head.

She stared down the advancing wraiths. Her stone flickered at its brightest.

Nud raised his own stone and stood at her side. The two gems pulsed as one.

The new slave master scoffed. "Get them!" she spat. "Take them now." She mocked the two Pips with her wicked grin.

"Sweeet," came the voice of that other wraith. Nud's skin crawled at the sound.

Without warning, a buzzing noise filtered into the stadium. Perplexed, the three wraiths stopped what they were doing and turned their gazes seaward.

Nud grabbed Holly by the hand. Their eyes met, and a kind of dare passed between them. Together, they stepped and took a wild leap over open water. It was a long jump, even by Pip standards. They soared through the air, cutting the corner from the boardwalk to the stage. Holly and Nud bypassed the slave master that'd blocked their way. The wretched woman glanced back at them over her shoulder. A mix of hate and bewilderment washed over her cadaverous face.

The buzzing grew to a deep, resonating drone that echoed throughout the chamber.

Screams arose from the remaining show-goers as they scrambled for the doors with a renewed sense of urgency, pushing and shoving and trampling over one another as they fought for position. The dwarf tried to calm people down, but was overrun. The leviathan, well into the cove, halted to raise its ghastly horns and orient them out to sea.

From across the dim waters, a dark cloud raced for the shore. The screeching mass swooped up at the mouth of the cove and poured through the arch – chaos on black wings.

Bobbin called again, "There's a way out at the bottom of the pool."

Nud heard a plop as the Pip dove underwater. Holly started towards Bobbin, but guards were in the way. The young diplomat grabbed her arm.

"Wait," he told her, and gestured to the incoming mass. "They're here to help us. There's no time to explain. Just trust me."

Young cloakers – the face suckers – swarmed the stadium like bats, so thick they blotched out the light. Showgoers already fleeing were sent into full hysteria, and even the wraiths were swarmed. A large cloaker swooped down out of the dark heights, hooked the wraith leader with its claws and flung her into the water. She flailed and thrashed furiously, screaming vile curses.

With barely a passing thought, Nud willed the cove's waters to swirl again, whisking the wraith away.

A dozen huge cloakers dropped out of the swarm. Mounted by Glooms, they swooped down this way and that way, escalating the panic and mayhem. The riders concentrated their efforts on the guards and the nobles, while clouds of smaller face suckers broke off and zoomed through the stands, latching onto bystanders.

The larger beasts clutched guards in their claws and carried them up, screaming, then dropped them to smash upon the stone floor of the stadium. Lord Rhyale drew his fine rapier to fend them off. With precision thrusts, he stabbed at his darting enemies. The Red Maidens and a handful of nobles mounted a coordinated defense. Cornered high in the stands near the arch, they clustered into a tight group to protect Taradin, poking at the cloakers with polearms and spears when the creatures drew near. Taeglin had already disappeared, but most of the high-born ducked down wherever they could or massed against the clogged exits with the Harrowian commoners. Some escaped the stadium through the flaming arch, only to find themselves blanketed by face suckers. With muffled screams, one after another they blindly tumbled into the water, grabbing and clawing at their smothered faces.

The acrobatic archers held up in a covered vendor booth, felling young cloakers with their deadly arrows as easily as swatting flies. Concentrating their fire, the two sisters brought a larger beast crashing down onto the central platform.

Nud and Holly darted across the main stage to the other side, dodging fleeing people and swooping cloakers along the way. They veered right towards the greater waters, then slowed to a stop when they reached the seaward arch. In the stands directly above them, the fight with the nobles raged on. Nud scanned the high reaches of the cavern.

"What are you looking for?" Holly asked.

"Gariff's up there somewhere," Nud replied. "Gariff and, well, Clickety-clack."

He spotted the two of them circling about together. Gariff spotted them in return, tagged the pilot, and the giant cloaker abruptly changed course and rushed their way.

Finally, he thought. But the leviathan had been pushing through the freshly-churning whirlpool. Waves pummeled its massive bulk, yet the beast stayed its course. Nud upped his focus on the water. The cycles grew larger and wilder.

As the White Whale struggled against the current, it began to glow from deep within and along its spiny ridges. The beast's horns unfurled like reptilian fans. They pivoted and angled this way and that way, and as they did so, cloakers plummeted to the ground. Show-goers still in the higher stands put their hands over their ears, shrieking, as juvenile face suckers fell in thick masses around them. Gariff and Clickety-clack splashed down into the cove, near the stage.

Their tortured mount writhed and twisted in agony beneath them. A scant few of the flying creatures evaded the assault – either the attack "missed" them or they were able to resist.

Gariff and Clickety-clack clambered up the alter stairs and out of the water, while other riders splashed about the cove along with their mounts, struggling to reach the shore against the rotating current. The White Whale swam in a wide circle against the flow and snapped at them all, thrashing its head when it trapped one in his great jaws. The swirling water ran red.

Holly called, urgency in her voice: "Leno!"

The White Whale broke from its course and throttled towards them. At the water's edge, it raised itself high until it loomed over Nud and Holly.

Nud drew *Shatters* from his pack and brandished it boldly. The beast's many eyes danced with pleasure, feasting on the promise of youthful flesh and secret knowledge. And from beneath its massive forebody, tentacles writhed out of the water. The two Pips were within its grasp. They both just stood there, paralyzed.

Still held up with the nobles, Taradin himself gurgled out a cry. "Many thanks, great vessel of the sea, for this superb intervention."

In Nud's head, a low and regretful rumble sounded, scrambling his thoughts. The water's motion ceased.

"HUUM ha ... Goodbye young Pip," the voice boomed – the voice of the leviathan. "I call you my friend. So sorry it ends this way. It is as it was meant to be." The beast inched forward. "Fear not. Huum ha ... All you have ever known will be preserved ... FOREVER!"

The last word resonated in Nud's mind as he stared at the brutal, bloody mess of flesh, blood and guts bobbing in the waters surrounding the beast. He squeezed his eyes shut and shook his head in denial, and in the process shook off the fear and wonderment of the leviathan's presence. *I've been misled. This vile creature devoured my parents, and now it wants us.*

The hard edge of betrayal cut into the young diplomat. It brought phantoms of fury and darkness to convergence. A strange vibration fed back into Nud from the rock beneath his feet and from *Shatters* in his hand. And the tingling presence of Holly's stone resonated with his. Something was happening, something different. Something BIG. The power of shaping flowed through him. Shaping and undoing.

A pulse of realization injected into his forebrain. *Betrayal is a command.* Nud shifted his gaze to Holly. Her bog stone pulsed bright green, in unison with his like two chambers of a single heart. The leviathan hesitated as the brightness shot up and the pulse quickened.

I need more power.

"Holly, hold tight," Nud said. He touched his gem to hers. Then he told her what she needed to hear. "It's over, Holly, I'm sorry. These simple lights will not do. Fyorn sent you here to your death. He sold you out to feed this hungry beast information. He sold us all out to get what he wants. I never should have introduced you to him."

"Whaa?" was all she said.

"It's true," Nud reaffirmed. "The Elderkin betrayed you." He saw in her eyes that she denied it, at first. Slowly, the young diplomat nodded. Holly's green eyes soon narrowed and her lips pursed, and Nud could see the realization spreading through her mind like a fast virus. She turned her burning gaze to the leviathan.

Kech exposed his gaping jaws.

Nud raised *Shatters* defiantly, but not to strike the beast

– no, that wouldn't do. Ready and willing to try something new, with his and Holly's minds saturated with betrayal, Nud smashed the platform at their feet.

A new command of matter unleashed. The strongest yet – a wave in the cold brittle stone. But unlike water, the stone didn't just 'bend' to his will so easily. A pulsing surge of energy set the vibration in motion. Nud felt it coursing through him, but he had no control over what happened next.

The stone platform shattered like a thin sheet of ice. Bodies scattered as it exploded outwards. Nud flew back against the stands, ears ringing. Holly was thrown into the air. The force tipped the leviathan off-balance and the beast came crashing down on the jagged rubble. The room flickered again, in and out of darkness.

Nud quickly regained his footing then looked to Holly. She'd landed nearby, scraped and bloodied but otherwise unharmed.

As a writhing tentacle lashed out at them, three arrows whirred past, pinning the tentacle to the beast's body and piercing one eye. Nud recognized the fletching – orange feathers. As the White Whale lurched in response, the air filled with arrows that plunged deep into its pale flesh.

Nud stumbled to Holly, gripped her hand, and met her gaze. She nodded as Nud raised *Shatters* a second time. He called on betrayal and bashed the stands next.

The two Pips leapt out through the arch and made a run for the seashore. Behind them, the stands snapped and cracked as they crumbled to the ground. Nud glanced over his shoulder to see Taradin himself come tumbling down, riding on huge blocks of stone. One Red Maiden quickly disappeared from his side, swallowed by the rubble. The other struggled to protect him from it. The vicegerent crashed at the base of the flaming arch, lost in the dust that billowed up everywhere. Shell-shocked, the last remaining crowd members stumbled around stupidly.

Nud caught a glimpse of Gariff and Clickity-clack. They'd made it to the other side of the inlet with many of the onlookers. With an ear-piercing stream of chirrups, the Glooms broke off their attack. A single wraith lay impaled in the water, twitching, and the leviathan struggled with a long sliver of stone wedged in its lower jaw, not to mention the many arrows. Those nobles who'd remained to fight in the stands now lay buried somewhere in rubble.

The Pip stopped when he came upon a wounded cloaker, of the small variety he'd first encountered, dragging itself along the rock floor by a single claw. Its other claw had been severed and a wing crushed. "There there," Nud said, as he quickly scooped up the poor thing by the tail and gently stuffed it in his pack. "I'll get you out of here." He continued towards the seashore.

The leviathan, jagged sliver and all, turned full about and made a break for the mouth of the cove. It got snagged.

Gariff's booming voice cut across the inlet. "LENO, THE ARCH!"

Of course! Nud dropped his pack, abandoned Holly and bounded back towards the stadium. *Gariff knows his structures.* He halted just inside the grand arch.

Taradin lay there, trapped under rubble. A Red Maiden lay crumpled beside him. The man's hood had come off and his body was broken, but no blood spilled forth. His scepter was nowhere to be seen. The First King beheld the young diplomat standing next to him. He looked up. "Councilor Lenokin," he gurgled, his voice failing.

Nud met his gaze.

The First King spoke again. "I once rolled dice to save all humankind, and won." Then he coughed dust and spat. The glob dribbled down from his lower lip.

Nud delivered to him the words of his uncle. "Yes, Taradin," Nud said. "You died a great hero long ago." Nud raised *Shatters* to him. "You should have stayed that way."

Taradin responded with a slow nod. At last, the First King laid his crowned head to rest on the stony surface. He looked tired to Nud. Tired of what his life had become, before the end. The young diplomat lowered his club, then brushed a hand over the resting corpse's eyelids to close them.

Nud took his crown – his heir didn't deserve it – and then looked away. It was madness. *This has to stop. Forever.*

The instant before the last cloaker was to retreat and moments before the struggling White Whale could make for open water, Nud raised the club one last time that day. He raised it high and smote the arch of the grand cavern.

And then he ran for his life.

The rock ceiling of the stadium came crashing down behind him with a thundering CLAP! And as Nud cleared the stadium, debris piled into the cove and a great wave spilled forth. Those on the shoreline took cover amidst the jagged rocks to shield themselves from the surge and the splintering fragments that rained down upon them. Dust billowed up to fill the cavern, and strong waves rolled in and out of the cove. When the air finally cleared and the waves dissipated, a heavy silence fell over the Dim Sea. Only the mutterings of survivors and the rush of distant falls dared to disturb the quiet.

CHAPTER XXXV

Karna's Whim

Along the shore of the Dim Sea, the Stout and three Pips gathered with a small band of misfits that would serve as crew. Together, they commandeered a vessel that went by the prophetic name of *Karna's Whim*. Fyorn took the tiller, the half-giants and Gariff had the oars, and the rest did what they could to bring her out to sea. Lord Sevalyr gave the orders – he had seafaring experience, while Lady Elise watched the shoreline disappear. Harrow would blame the lord and the lady for the catastrophe, no doubt.

Holly knew then that Nud had lied to her about the woodsman, and she knew why. Fyorn quickly explained that the Hurlorns had lied to Nud. The Pip had a pretty good idea why. He only hoped the Glooms would understand why he lied to them.

When they passed the rock wall, the faerie sky beyond luminesced a pale green and the calm waters glimmered in the twilight. A thin veil of folding sunlight broke through the darkness in the far-off distance. *Karna's Whim* caught a fair wind to carry them there. The rush of falls grew nearer.

Slip

The leviathan writhed and rolled beneath the watery surface of the cove to liberate himself of the splinter. After twisting it free from his jaw, he hoisted up both himself and the great rock set upon his back. Finally, he broke surface. The rock tumbled to one side. He paused to suck in a long breath, then wretched loose his pinned appendage. The other arrows he let be, for now.

Tentacles reaching between gaps in the rubble, Kech anchored his suckers on a fragment of the arch left behind, untouched. Through it, he tasted the cold stone. Then he wrapped another appendage around a broken column and others around the largest chunks of debris. Ignoring the intense pain in his jaw and the throbbing around his punctured eyes, the leviathan pulled itself onto dry land. He unfurled his horns until they fanned out and then emitted a low vibration.

The soundwaves reflected off the debris and revealed the location of the First King. The great beast stretched out its tentacles, gently grasped the broken slabs around the crushed body, and muscled them aside. At last, Kech drew Taradin's corpse towards his great maw, and then swallowed him whole.

Huum haa. Still fresh, he thought, as the body slid down his throat. Minding his wounds, the leviathan slowly dragged his bulk over the fragments of the stadium ceiling and in between the large chunks. He broke through a wall of rubble and dragged himself to the empty seashore.

Huum haa, fresh indeed. As the leviathan slipped into the open waters of the Dim Sea, his mind surged with new awareness. Kech cleansed his wounds in the pristine waters.

Intriguing! he thought, while the old-world knowledge poured in.

*It was the Orbweaver who created the universes for Her
own consumption,
but only after they produced Knowledge.
So, She infused a strand into every single thing
and She wove them altogether, like a Great Web,
to track the production of Knowledge.*

*One man learned the secret of the Orbweaver.
One man realized when it was time to reap what She
had sown.
And when She came for him, he rolled dice for
all humankind…
and won.*

*And this man devised a way to make peace with the
Orbweaver, or so he thought.
His people had to be disciplined though, and obedient,
giving,
and, most importantly, forever creators of new Knowledge.*

*But the man was wrong. The only way to beat Her was to
out-learn Her.
And the only way to out-learn Her was to become Her.*

- The Diviner, On the Folly of the First King